# DEAD HISTORY
## A ZOMBIE ANTHOLOGY

### EDITED BY
### ANTHONY GIANGREGORIO

# OTHER LIVING DEAD PRESS BOOKS
DEAD THINGS
JUST BEFORE NIGHT: A ZOMBIE ANTHOLOGY
THE WAR AGAINST THEM: A ZOMBIE NOVEL
BLOOD RAGE & DEAD RAGE (BOOK 1& 2 OF THE RAGE VIRUS SERIES)
DEAD MOURNING: A ZOMBIE HORROR STORY
BOOK OF THE DEAD: A ZOMBIE ANTHOLOGY
LOVE IS DEAD: A ZOMBIE ANTHOLOGY
BOOK OF THE DEAD 2: NOT DEAD YET
ETERNAL NIGHT: A VAMPIRE ANTHOLOGY
END OF DAYS: AN APOCALYPTIC ANTHOLOGY VOLUME 1 & 2
DEAD HOUSE: A ZOMBIE GHOST STORY
THE ZOMBIE IN THE BASEMENT (FOR ALL AGES)
THE LAZARUS CULTURE: A ZOMBIE NOVEL
DEAD WORLDS: UNDEAD STORIES VOLUMES 1, 2, 3, 4 & 5
FAMILY OF THE DEAD, REVOLUTION OF THE DEAD
RANDY AND WALTER: PORTRAIT OF TWO KILLERS
KINGDOM OF THE DEAD
THE MONSTER UNDER THE BED
DEAD TALES: SHORT STORIES TO DIE FOR
ROAD KILL: A ZOMBIE TALE
DEADFREEZE, DEADFALL, DARK PLACES
SOUL EATER, THE DARK, RISE OF THE DEAD
DEAD END: A ZOMBIE NOVEL, VISIONS OF THE DEAD
THE CHRONICLES OF JACK PRIMUS

**THE DEADWATER SERIES**
DEADWATER
DEADWATER: Expanded Edition
DEADRAIN, DEADCITY, DEADWAVE, DEAD HARVEST
DEAD UNION, DEAD VALLEY
DEAD TOWN, DEAD SALVATION
DEAD ARMY (coming soon)

## COMING SOON
BOOK OF THE DEAD 4: DEAD RISING
THE BOOK OF CANNIBALS VOLUME 1 & 2
END OF DAYS: AN APOCALYPTIC ANTHOLOGY VOLUME 3
CHILDREN OF THE VOID (FOR ALL AGES)
INSIDE THE PERIMETER by Alan Spencer

# DEAD HISTORY: A ZOMBIE ANTHOLOGY

Copyright © 2010 by Living Dead Press
ISBN   Softcover   ISBN 13: 978-1-935458-48-7   ISBN 10: 1-935458-48-5
All stories contained in this book have been published with permission from the authors.
All rights reserved. No part of this book may be reproduced or transmitted in any form or by any means, electronic or mechanical, including photocopying, recording, or by any information storage and retrieval system, without permission in writing from the copyright owner.
This is a work of fiction. Names, characters, places and incidents either are the product of the author's imagination or are used fictitiously, and any resemblance to any actual persons, living or dead, events, or locales is entirely coincidental. This book was printed in the United States of America. For more info on obtaining additional copies of this book, contact:

www.livingdeadpress.com

# Table of Contents

*THE EAGLE HAS REANIMATED* BY TONY SCHAAB ............... 1

*THE QUEEN'S PUNISHMENT* BY SPENCER WENDLETON 30

*THEM OTHERS* BY NICKOLAS COOK ...................................... 39

*EXTINCTION EVENT* BY MARK M. JOHNSON ..................... 53

*KHERFIN* BY T.W. BROWN .................................................... 66

*KRAMER'S FOLLY* BY ANTHONY GIANGREGORIO ............... 78

*SAMURAI ZOMBIE KILLER* BY DAVID BERNSTEIN ............ 94

*THE COURIER* BY ERIC S. BROWN ..................................... 103

*WILD WITH HUNGER* BY LEE CLARK ZUMPE ................... 109

*LEGACY OF DEATH* BY MARK RIVETT ................................ 122

*THE CASE OF THE SPITTALFIELDS* BY G.R. MOSCA ......... 146

*ONLY THE DEAD WILL STAND* BY KEVIN J. BREAUX ....... 161

*STALAG 44* BY JOSE ALFREDO VAZQUEZ .......................... 178

*ABOUT THE WRITERS* ........................................................ 190

# THE EAGLE HAS REANIMATED

## TONY SCHAAB

The three men walked out of the launching pad and onto the tarmac, blinking in the bright Florida sun. Two of the men began to walk towards the shuttle stop, but one remained behind and addressed the other two.

"Oh, come on, you guys, it's a beautiful summer day, and we don't have any meetings until later this afternoon...let's walk it!"

The two men stopped, looked at each other, then turned around, as the taller one spoke first. "Neil, why do you always feel the incessant need to walk everywhere you go? The Control Center is *three* miles away...let's just take the shuttle?"

Neil rolled his eyes and spread his arms wide. "Come on, Mike, what's the rush? Buzz, help me out here, huh?"

Before Buzz could respond, Mike spoke, with more than a hint of annoyance in his voice. "How many times have I asked you not to call me Mike? It's Michael. Michael Collins. I'm very proud of my full name, and would appreciate it if you would address me as such."

"*Fine, Michael*, I apologize, I really do," Neil said. "But that's all the more reason to go for a stroll, the three of us...so we can get to know each other better. After all, in a few short weeks we're going to be spending a lot of time together in a very small amount of space, and if we aren't chummy before then, it's going to be a *long* ride." Neil once again addressed the third man, who had yet to say a word after leaving the hangar. "Buzz? Thoughts?"

Buzz looked from Neil to Michael and shrugged his shoulders. "I'm up for the walk. We do know each other pretty well as professionals, but this could be a good opportunity for us to chat, just as guys, about non-mission stuff, y'know?" Buzz winked, stuck out an elbow and lightly nudged Michael on his side. "I don't have to order you to walk with us, do I, Lieutenant Colonel Collins?"

Michael smiled and sighed as he and Buzz moved back down the tarmac to join Neil. "No, sir, Colonel Aldrin, no order neces-

# DEAD HISTORY

sary. Besides, if we start slinging military talk around, we might make the 'civvy' here feel left out."

"Hey," Neil said, feigning impunity, "of the three of us I may be the only civilian, but last time I checked, I'm still the Mission Commander."

All three men shared a laugh as they began their trek down the paved road. Buzz stuck his hands in his pockets and squinted up at the sky. "Titles and ranks aside, I do think it's great that all of us have had actual spaceflights before this mission. I know it sure makes me feel a hell of a lot more comfortable knowing that we've all had practical experience with this before…I don't think many other crews can say that, right?"

Michael was quick to chime in. "Only two, actually; we'll be just the third crew in the entire history of NASA to all have previous spaceflights before embarking on this mission."

"Thank you, Mr. Walking Trivia Book!" Neil said with a laugh. "In any case, I thought the conversation on this little stroll was supposed to be non-work-related, am I right? Michael, how's the back feeling?"

Michael reflexively straightened up a bit and flexed his torso from side to side. "It's a hundred percent good to go. It feels great, and I have no residual aches, pains, anything." He took in a deep breath as his mind flitted over everything he'd been through medically in the last year. "Hard to believe it was just this time last year I was having cervical disc surgery…stupid back kept me out of the Apollo 8 mission."

"True…but," Buzz said while wagging a finger in Michael's direction, "you obviously didn't want to go up there hurt, now did you? Plus, by missing the '8' mission, now you get to join us on '11,' which I can guarantee you is going to be a whole lot more exciting!"

"I'm all for that," Michael said with a smile. "All I know is that my back feels great, and I don't anticipate having any problems with it for a long time. I hope Lovell enjoyed piloting '8' in my place, because I'm gonna go up there next month and run space tracks around the moon-orbital patterns he did!"

Buzz and Michael both enjoyed a laugh at the half-barb aimed at James Lovell. Lovell had indeed been lucky enough to pilot

# DEAD HISTORY

Apollo 8 when Michael had to step down due to his medical concerns, but Michael's quick recovery had allowed him to join the current Apollo mission. Lovell was definitely a man they both admired, and he was actually the backup Mission Commander for the current mission, should anything go wrong with Neil, who both Buzz and Michael now noticed had fallen strangely quiet and was looking absently off to the north.

Buzz and Michael looked at each other, and Buzz spoke first. "Neil? You okay?"

Hearing his name called, Neil snapped back to reality. Shaking his head slightly as if to brush off mental cobwebs, he turned his head back to the other two men, smiled and said, "Yeah, I'm good, thanks. Just a little concerned about what's been going on at home."

The other two men knew exactly what Neil was talking about. Over the last few weeks, there had been a lot of strange news stories coming out of the northeast and Midwest. While the specific details of the accounts were sometimes confusing or vague, they all had common themes. Stories about seemingly random acts of violence where people attacked other people without provocation or motive. Stories about an outbreak of a new kind of sickness, possibly a virus, where people could become so seriously ill to the point where they almost didn't feel any pain. The tales seemed to start coming out of the northeast, but reports had slowly been spreading across the South and Midwest, including several recent disturbing accounts from Neil's hometown in Ohio.

Buzz was quick to speak up and try to fill the awkward silence that had settled over the men. "Yeah, I've been hearing the stories on the newscasts and in the papers, but I'm sure it's just kids trying to fit in with some new fad or a weird string of coincidences or something? Have you had a chance to actually talk to your kids or parents yet?"

"Yeah, after our simulation runs yesterday I talked to Eric for about an hour," Neil said, referring to his phone conversation with his oldest son. He aimlessly kicked some loose gravel on the side of the road as he walked. "I really shouldn't worry too much about random stuff like this, but...I don't know, Wapakoneta is a small town, and these kind of weird things just don't happen there every day. Earlier this week, a kid comes to the elementary school sick, and before lunchtime a teacher had to be taken to the hospital and they sent all the students home; after doing a full medical examination on each kid, of course. Eric said that Mark still won't talk about what he saw happen at the school that day. They still haven't re-opened the school, and nobody really knows what was wrong with the sick kid to begin with. It's just...scary to think that something dangerous might be going on there, and I'm here, getting ready to rocket off into space, powerless to help them."

Neil gave a shrug and forced a smile as he faced the other two men. "Okay, that stinks but let's focus on the good, shall we? Mainly, like I just said," Neil stopped walking and assumed a dramatic stance with one hand reaching up into the sky, "in less than a month, on July 13, 1969, we're going to be flying off into space and, in a few short weeks, be making history as the first men on the moon! *Wa-hoo*!"

Neil let out a whoop and a cheer, and Buzz quickly joined him in the celebration. Michael took a quick look around to make sure the men were alone on the crawlerway, and then joined the other two in an impromptu celebration as they continued on their walk towards the massive NASA Control Center.

* * *

It was a particularly humid night, and the air seemed to hang low and damp. A lonely beacon in the darkness, the harsh yellow light of the street lamp washed down over the small guard's building at Post 12. Stationed on the northern side of Merritt Island where Kennedy Space Center ended and the wildlife preserve began, Post 12 was a little over five miles away from both the new launching pad facilities and the Control Center, making it the most remote guard station of the entire facility. Private Albert Rose knew this when he was first assigned to overnight guard duty at Post 12 six months ago, and, quite frankly, he couldn't have been happier about it.

He stifled a yawn as he sat in the small booth with his feet propped against the wall and flipped lazily through the latest issue of *Life*. He looked up from the magazine just in time to see the desktop clock's digits flip from 11:59 p.m. to 12:00 a.m., and the date indicator flip to July 14.

*It's officially Monday morning*, he thought. "Another rip-roaring weekend of excitement come and gone," he said out loud to no one in particular.

Albert didn't consider himself a 'loner' by any stretch of the imagination. He wasn't necessarily opposed to spending time with people, as he had a good amount of friends and family, and often found himself out at parties or other gatherings. He simply enjoyed his alone time and didn't really think there was such a thing as *too much* of it. Especially in the Army. Sharing a living space with a squad of twenty-three other men in tightly-packed barracks in the hot American South usually meant *very* little time spent alone, whether you wanted it or not. So, Albert was grateful for his eight hours of overnight solitude.

He was especially happy for the time away from the barracks after the weekend he'd had. One of the squad's newest members, Jay Harper, had really been getting on Albert's nerves lately, and it didn't help that Jay occupied the bunk directly above his. Jay had spent the entire weekend obsessing over the recent wave of news stories about the violence that seemed to be slowly sweeping the eastern part of the nation. He rolled his eyes at the mere thought of Jay bouncing around the barracks, showing people all the newspaper clippings of the strange stories, telling anyone who would listen all about his theories and half-asking questions that he would simply go on to answer himself before anyone else could get a word in edgewise.

Albert had gotten the worst of it, of course; Jay had just assumed, since *fate* had put the two of them together in such close proximity, that Albert wanted to hear—no, *needed* to hear—every minuscule point of every odd tale he had heard over the past weeks.

"It just ain't right, Al!" As he thought back, Albert could almost hear Jay saying the words as the man hung his head over his bunk on Saturday evening, looking down at Albert and shaking his head as he talked. "People acting silly, bumbling around like they're all coked up, or worse yet, the ones that attack other people without reason...heck, there's this story here," Jay had pulled himself back up on his bunk to rummage through the newspaper clippings to find the right one to wave in Albert's face, "this one here is from Warner Robins, Georgia, and it says that at their 4th of July Festival a few weeks back, the police had to come and arrest one of the guys at the rib-eating contest...apparently he wasn't part of the contest, just some random guy who showed up with ribs in his hand and sauce all over his face. Here's the kicker, though," Jay continued as he looked down and began to quote the newspaper, "'witnesses say that, in addition to the man acting disoriented and insatiably hungry, it appeared the man was eating from a rack of ribs significantly larger than the pig ribs provided by the festival.'"

He dangled the article in front of Albert's face, but he shooed it away and tried to return his focus to the book he was reading. But Jay wasn't done yet. "The article goes on to say that the crap covering the guy's face wasn't exactly barbecue sauce, either. It was blood, guts, viscera, all that nasty stuff. This fella had been eating somethin' raw and been eating it all savage-like!" The look of awe mixed with wonderment on Jay's face was permanently etched into Albert's memory. "You know what's going on, right? People acting funny, walkin' around all stiff, eating flesh and drinking blood...the government and news-types are trying to cover it up, but you can't deny the truth, that our country is slowly being overrun...by vampires!"

Albert laughed out loud at the memory, his short, repetitious laughter filling the small guard station. *Vampires*, he thought to himself. *That idiot has seen one too many horror flicks if he thinks any movie monster like that could ever be real.* He put down the magazine, stood up, stretched his arms out in front of him, and rolled his head around his shoulders to get some of the kinks out of his neck. He sighed and began to sit back down when he heard a low moaning sound coming from outside the booth.

He quickly stood back up, the mental haze of being awake in the middle of the night suddenly replaced by his training taking over and telling him what to do. He turned and looked through the windows of the tiny station to the north, where the sound had emanated from. Beyond the halo of the streetlight hanging directly over the guard station, all was dark and seemingly calm. Albert picked up his flashlight, instinctively patted his gun holster on his right side to ensure the firearm was still there, and stepped out onto the road. He walked a few steps to the edge of a lighted circle, clicked on his flashlight, and swung the beam around in the darkness.

"Hello?" he called out authoritatively, using his army training to keep his voice calm and his nerves steeled. "Is there anyone out here?" Traditionally, Post 12 was a very quiet duty, but occasionally there would be a larger animal that would try to wander out of the wildlife reserve and onto the Space Center property. Sometimes a civilian car would wander down the unmarked Avenue J and wind up, miles later, at Post 12's crossbar and barbed-wire fence that separated the wildlife reserve from the government base and research center. But those instances were usually few and far between, and rarely happened in the middle of the night on a Monday morning, so Albert had to make sure he thoroughly checked out any strange situations.

After piercing the darkness with his flashlight for a few minutes, directing the beam up the roughly-paved street and off onto the sides of the road where the underbrush wasn't so thick, Albert was just about to give up and head back into the guard station when he heard the noise again. A groan, a noise a person or animal might make if hurt or in pain. He saw movement slightly up the road, and as the figure drew closer, he could see it was a human—a woman.

She looked like she was badly hurt. She was walking with a severe limp, and had what appeared to be blood splattered on her pants and most of her shirt. Albert looked more closely, and he could actually see one of the woman's leg bones jutting out through her skin at a gruesome angle. She looked up at him with vacant eyes and groaned.

"Oh my God, miss! Are you all right? What happened?" The woman just groaned again and continued to stumble towards him. Albert's first—and only—thought was that the woman had been attacked by one of the larger animals living in the wildlife reserve, and had been stumbling around aimlessly for God-knows-how-long looking for help. She was obviously going into shock; that would explain the vacant stare and the lack of verbal communication.

Leaving the light of the streetlamp, he ran up to her and put one arm around her shoulders, attempting to help support her weight so he could assist her into the guard station and radio for help. "How long have you been out here? Where did you..."

His sentence was cut short when, upon his approaching her, the woman turned her face into Albert's body—what he initially thought was a subconscious move for protection on her part—but she abruptly and fiercely bit into his neck, Albert's blood spewing all over her face. He tried to scream, but only a gurgling sound came out.

Albert pushed the woman away roughly. She still had her teeth sunk into his neck, so she fell away from him and onto the pavement of the road with a large chunk of his muscle and skin in her mouth. His hands instinctively clamped around the wound, and he could feel the warmth of the blood quickly and steadily gushing out of him. His mind was spinning, reeling with thoughts of what he was supposed to do or feel at this point, when he looked down at the woman and watched her *swallow his flesh*. Then she slowly rose to her feet and started limping towards him again.

Albert's body felt numb. He wanted to run for the guard station, but his limbs didn't respond to his mental commands. Fighting through the haze and confusion of injury and massive blood loss, his training was still able to win out and guide his actions. He managed to mentally pry his right hand away from the wound on his throat and reach down to his gun. He drew the weapon, aimed, and fired.

His first shot rang out in the night and struck the woman in her shoulder; she staggered backwards slightly, then re-oriented herself and kept coming at him, unfazed, as if the gunshot wound was simply an inconvenient bug bite.

Albert's world started to spin as the amount of blood rapidly exiting his body continued to take its toll on his rapidly fading consciousness. He swayed in the night air, and for a brief moment, the world went quiet to him, and he was strangely calm. He snapped back into reality as the woman, right in front of him and reaching out to grab him, moaned again. As he fell backwards, he fired one final shot at her, striking her on the left temple. They fell, side by side, into the long grass on the side of the road.

She was silent and unmoving, he, nearly the same, except for his shallow breathing and his head twitching slightly. When he fell, his arms had landed at his sides; he'd given up on applying pressure to his wound, and Albert knew he was dying; he could literally feel his life force leaving his body. But he still had enough mental acuity to be upset that his last thought ever was, *Dammit... Jay was actually on to something.*

His eyes closed for the last time as a living being.

A few moments later, they snapped open again.

\* \* \*

The three men walked off the tarmac and up to the launching pad, and slowly looked up at the towering structure in front of them. They shared a moment of awed silence before Neil spoke.

"That...is one big-ass rocket."

Michael rolled his eyes as he spoke. "The Saturn V rocket is the biggest payload ever successfully launched. With the Apollo spacecraft sitting on top and fully fueled up, it's 363 feet tall, 33 feet wide, and weighs over 6.5 million pounds."

"Thank you, Professor Know-it-all!" he laughed as he turned to look towards the other two men. "Did either of you see the rocket come out of the Vehicle Assembly Building and onto the crawlerway Monday morning? I heard it only cleared the top of the VAB's doors by about five feet! How embarrassing would that have been for NASA if we couldn't even get the spaceship out of the assembly building?"

Buzz, who had been staring up at the Apollo module on top of the rocket, looked from Neil to Michael as he spoke soberly. "About as embarrassing as it would be if word gets out that some of our maintenance men and army troops have gone AWOL over the last few days. Let's not forget to stay focused when we do our final press conference this morning. We're not commenting on any questions related to strange attacks or sickness in the area, and as far as we know, everything on the base has been in tip-top shape and the mission prep has gone exactly according to plan. Are we good with that?"

# DEAD HISTORY

Michael nodded quietly; Neil did the same as the men started to walk around the side of the launch pad and towards the press site auditorium.

As he watched the numbers on the giant launch-countdown clock tick to just under five hours, he spoke up. "Obviously we're not going to speak about the missing men to the press, but between the three of us...what do you guys make of it? Do you think they're just deserters, or..."

"Stop right there," Buzz said sharply. "If you're going to speculate that they were attacked or got sick in relation to what's been going on lately, just save it. Without any evidence, there's no point in thinking that, and it'll just be running through your brain during the press conference, which will make you all the more prone to talking about it by accident. Just let it go."

Neil bobbed his head, slightly embarrassed. "You're absolutely right. It's time to get into full-on professional mode, gentlemen." He adjusted his flight suit as he straightened his back. "In less than five hours, we'll be blasting out of Earth's atmosphere..."

Michael smirked as he completed Neil's sentence for him: "...in that big-ass rocket!" He laughed in his typical high-pitched manner, and Neil and Buzz couldn't help but join in once they heard Michael's laughter. The three men had really gotten to know each other fairly intimately over the last three weeks of mission preparation, and after all the stress of training and instruction, it felt good to let loose and relax, even if it was only for a few brief moments.

The men composed themselves as they approached the rear door of the press auditorium. Neil put one hand on the door handle, took a deep breath, and turned to face the other two. "All right, guys...let's go make nicey-nice before we go make history."

They entered the auditorium's side foyer, where they were greeted by an attractive NASA Media Relations Specialist. After a few short moments of receiving yet another round of instructions, *suggested speaking material*, as the Media Relations Specialist put it, she led the three men into the press auditorium, to a barrage of flashing bulbs and noisy murmuring.

The trio posed for some official press pictures, then sat behind the lone table on the elevated stage. The press conference went surprisingly well; this was clearly not the Media Relations Specialist's first time running a press conference, and she was able to deftly sidestep the majority of *non-mission-centric* questions before the questions were even posed directly to any of the three astronauts. The event ended relatively quickly, and the astronauts thanked the Media Relations Specialist as she walked them out of the building.

"I must say, you were quite masterful with all those journalists," Buzz remarked admirably. "You have a very commanding presence, Miss...um..." he stopped, realizing he had either never gotten her name or simply couldn't remember it.

"Barrett," she answered quickly. "Majel Barrett. And thank you for the compliment, sir. I've always enjoyed talking in front of people, commanding an audience, if you will... I've always had a special affinity for outer space, and I grew up in the area, so coming to work here for NASA in Media Relations just made sense. It was either this, or go to Hollywood and become an actress!"

The three men laughed along with her.

"Well, Miss Barrett," Neil said. "I think NASA is where you were meant to be. You might have done well in Hollywood, but I don't think you'd find nearly as much 'outer space work' there as you have here!"

The trio thanked her again and made their way to the launching pad. They spent the next few hours working with the NASA technicians to complete their final pre-flight checks, finally strapping in and preparing for the actual launch. Over the past few weeks, everyone had worked diligently to ensure that all the various stages of the rocket, the lunar module, and the command module were flight-ready. Through testing and re-testing, performing lengthy visual and physical inspections, the rocket had finally been transported to the launching pad, where it had sat, untouched, for the last twelve hours in anticipation of lift-off, which was now less than three minutes away.

\* \* \*

"*Eagle*, this is *Columbia*. I've completed final visual inspection and have been given the green light by Houston. You are free and clear, I repeat: you are free and clear. You're looking good, gentlemen."

Michael looked down to check his instruments, and seeing that everything was as it should be, he looked back out of the Command Module's main window. The Lunar Module was slowly moving away, having just successfully completed its separation maneuver. "You are green for lunar descent at your discretion. Have fun, boys."

Michael smiled wistfully as he waited for the radio response from the Lunar Module. The launch had been flawless and the last few days in transit to the moon had all gone according to plan, but he was still a little pensive. While he understood that, as the mission pilot, he had to stay behind and remain in control of the Command Module, a very large part of him wished he could go with Buzz and Neil to actually perform the moonwalk. But, this was his duty, and Michael was nothing if not a dutiful soldier.

"*Roger, Columbia,*" came Buzz's distorted voice over the radio. "*Eagle* is running hot and free. Beginning our lunar descent now. We'll try to remember to bring you back a souvenir or two."

Inside the cramped lunar module, Buzz turned awkwardly in his space suit to look across the cabin at Neil, who was situated in front of the automated flight controls, intently peering at the data being presented to him on the control readouts. "Everything looking okay over there, Neil? Are we ready to do this?"

Neil looked up and smiled, his helmet's faceplate catching the soft light of the cabin and giving his face a momentary ethereal glow. "Yeah, we're good. One of the internal systems was reading *Eagle* at about a hundred pounds heavier than normal when we undocked from *Columbia*, but I'm sure it was just a blip…it's not a significant enough discrepancy to worry about. Anyhow, we've been on *Columbia* for the last three days during our approach and initial moon orbits, and I'm ready for action…let's get in contact with Houston and make history already, shall we?"

Buzz rolled his eyes as he turned back to his control panel. "I wish you would stop over-using that phrase. We're about to be the first people in the history of mankind to walk on the moon…of course we're going to 'make history'!"

# DEAD HISTORY

The two men laughed as Buzz worked the radio to connect with NASA Headquarters back on Earth. "Houston, this is *Eagle,* do you copy?"

"*Eagle,* this is Houston, we read you loud and clear," came the reply, laced with the light static of a transmission just having traveled millions of miles. "Your telemetry is good and all boards indicate green. You boys ready to make some history up there?"

Buzz let out a sharp sigh as Neil smiled to himself and tried not to giggle. Buzz muttered to himself before he clicked the radio back on. "Roger, Houston. Dukey, you're lucky I'm so far away from you right now, otherwise I might have to slap you."

Charles Duke, the voice coming from NASA Headquarters as the CAPCOM Commander for the mission, chuckled lightly but chose not to get into a verbal sparring match, even a light-hearted one, in the middle of a critical United States Army mission. Buzz continued, "We're go for lunar descent. Beginning continuous *all-way* radio broadcast...now."

Buzz flipped the switch that allowed permanent radio conversation between the Lunar Module, the Command Module, and the control center in Houston.

"Beginning initial descent," Neil announced as he flipped the necessary switches to make the autopilot begin the journey to the moon's surface. With a slight hiss of the altitude thrusters, the craft deftly changed its pitch and began maneuvering towards its targeting landing site.

They traveled in mostly silence, with Buzz calling out basic telemetry information at routine intervals. After a few minutes, he looked up from his readouts and called out, "Neil...take a look at these numbers and tell me what you see."

Neil took his eyes off the landing controls to glance over at the telemetry numbers coming across his readouts. He frowned slightly as he responded to Buzz. "Yeah, I see what you're talking about...we seem to be passing our marks about...four seconds early."

"Not good," Buzz said through taut lips, Realizing he was still in constant communication with Headquarters, he addressed them directly. "Uh, Houston, we appear to be long...please review current telemetry readings and confirm, over."

"Roger that, *Eagle,*" came Duke's reply. "Our boys down here have already seen this discrepancy, and that is confirmed, you're currently running long. If you stay on your current trajectory, you're going to land miles away from your target landing site. We advise letting the computer auto-adjust to choose a new landing site for you, over."

"Roger, Houston," Neil called out quickly. "That'll be our plan, over."

Buzz was about to interject when he stopped and thought better of it.

*After all,* Buzz thought to himself, *Neil is the Mission Commander, and landing a little ways away from where we had originally planned really isn't that big of a problem, especially when you stop and think about all the different things that could possibly...*

A shrill buzzing noise interrupted Buzz's train of thought. He turned quickly to the guidance computer, the source of the alarm, and tried to keep any sound of panic out of his voice as he reported, "Guidance computer is sounding a '1202' alarm!"

Neil looked up sharply as another piece of equipment starting sounding another noise alarm. "Now the Navigation console is giving us a '1201' alarm..." He looked away from the computer to lock eyes with Buzz for a moment, who simply shook his head quickly and slightly shrugged his shoulders. "Houston, we're unfamiliar with these alarm codes. Please advise, over."

"Checking now, *Eagle.* Hold tight for just a second up there, guys, we'll get you an answer ASAP."

Having nothing else to say, Buzz and Neil sat in an uncomfortable silence for the next thirty seconds until the radio crackled to life again. "Okay, *Eagle,* I've been given assurances by Garman and Bales down here that your computer systems are having simple processing errors and you're clear to continue with descent and landing. I'll save you all the technical mumbo-jumbo they gave me, but we're confident you can proceed unimpeded, over."

Both men in the lunar lander let out audible sighs of relief. If Jack Garman and Steve Bales, two of the brightest computer officers on the NASA team, gave them the green-light to carry on without worrying about the alarms, then that was good enough for them. As the two men started to settle back into the routine for landing, which was now less than a minute away, Neil looked out of the lunar module's main window,

Caught off guard by what he saw, he yelled, "Holy crap!"

Buzz, surprised by the uncharacteristically-unprofessional outburst, jerked his head around quickly to look at Neil. "What is it, what's wrong?"

"We're not going to be able to land where the computer wants us to," Neil said quickly. "It's targeted landing site is right on the lip of that sizeable crater right in front of us, with a lot of huge boulders strewn about the area. I'm going to have to take manual control and set us down myself." He hit a few buttons and repositioned himself in front of the flight control console. He stole a quick glance over at Buzz. "We're going to be just fine, I did this plenty in our simulations. Did you copy that, Houston?"

"Roger, *Eagle*. We trust you to do what you have to do." Duke was wisely keeping his radio chatter with the two men at a minimum, as he realized that trying to control the situation from Earth was just going to complicate an already complicated situation in the Lunar Module.

"Count me down," Neil called out to Buzz, his eyes darting between the console and the main window.

Buzz nodded as he started to relay navigation data out loud to Neil. "Seventy-four feet from lunar contact...altitude thrusters are firing normally...sixty feet from contact..."

Buzz was interrupted as another computer alarm sounded. He muttered under his breath, "Oh, come on...what now?" His heart leapt up into his throat as he relayed the news to Neil. "Low fuel warning! According to the computer, we have less than thirty seconds of fuel remaining!"

"We'll make it!" Neil retorted, trying to keep his ever-raising voice from yelling. "Just keep giving me the numbers!"

"Forty feet from contact!" Buzz could feel the beads of sweat forming on his forehead as he worked to keep the panic out of his voice. "Thirty feet...twenty-five..." He glanced furtively at the fuel gauge, which now read that they had less than twenty seconds of fuel remaining.

# DEAD HISTORY

"Here she comes...I've got this..." Neil was talking more to himself than anyone else, trying to keep himself focused as he slowed the *Eagle* down to prepare for contact with the moon's surface.

"Ten feet!" Buzz yelped. "Seven...six..." A light on Buzz's console lit up, indicating that the sixty-seven-inch probes dangling from the bottom of the Lunar Module's footpads had made contact with the surface. "Contact light!" He immediately looked at the fuel indicator, which was counting down the seconds of fuel they had remaining: six...five...four...

He felt the light jostle of the spacecraft settling on the moon as Neil called out, "Shutdown!"

Buzz immediately flipped the necessary switches to shut the engines off as he replied. "Okay, engine stop. ACA–out of detent." He breathed a sigh of relief and a silent thank you prayer. He turned to Neil, and the two men shared a smile and a quick congratulatory handshake. Neil patted Buzz on the back as he turned back to his workstation.

"Out of detent." Neil echoed as he flipped switches and turned dials at his console. "Auto," he said as he put the ship back on automatic pilot, even though they had landed already.

Buzz continued calling out post-landing checkouts. "Mode control, both auto. Descent engine command override off. Engine arm is off, 413 is in."

Duke, who had been silent on the radio during the landing crisis, now spoke up with a short interjection. "We copy you down, *Eagle*."

Neil finished up the landing checklist before responding to the radio transmission. "Engine arm is off. Houston, Tranquility Base here," Neil said, referencing the unofficial name given by NASA Mission Control for the base site where the Lunar Module was to touch down. "The *Eagle* has landed."

After a momentary delay, the response came through the radio. "Roger, Tranquility, we read you on the ground," Duke sounded a little confused by Neil's reference using the alternate lingo. "You got a bunch of guys about to turn blue. We're breathing again. Thanks a lot!"

Neil looked at Buzz, who nodded slightly. "Copy that, Houston. Hey, Dukey," Neil said confidently, "Buzz and I were talking during

16

orbit, and neither of us think that we're going to be able to get any sleep during this six-hour down period we have scheduled before doing our EVA on the surface. We respectfully request to immediately begin preparations for the moonwalk, over."

The two men waited in breathless anticipation while their request was being considered by the team back home. After what seemed like an eternity, the reply from Duke finally came.

"*Eagle*, Houston here. I know you boys have been awake for a while and really should get some sleep...but hell, I'm sure none of us here would be able to sleep either, if we were in your position. You're clear to begin EVA prep immediately."

"Roger that, Houston!" Neil exclaimed with glee. He and Buzz immediately set about preparing for their lunar excursion, checking and testing various systems and pieces of equipment. After a short while, they were fully prepared; after depressurizing the cabin, they opened the external hatch, gazing out at the lunar surface in awe. They'd been looking at it through the *Eagle's* windows for the last few hours, but there was something different about seeing it in front of them, unimpeded with the exception of their helmet visors.

Neil backed out of the hatch, stopping on the ladder to look up at Buzz. "Okay, here we go. All the drama of the landing is over...it's smooth sailing from here."

"Good luck," Buzz said with a smile. "Be safe down there. I'll see you soon."

Neil took a few cautious steps down the rungs of the ladder leading to the surface. His spacesuit was so big and bulky he couldn't see his feet, so he moved slowly and carefully towards the surface. "Houston, do you copy?" he called into his radio.

"We read you loud and clear," came the reply from Duke. "Go slow and steady there, Neil, and watch that last step. The last thing you want is to have traveled this far and trip up at the end."

Neil laughed slightly as he replied. "Roger that, Houston. I'm pulling the D-ring to release the MESA now." Neil reached to his left and pulled the ring-shaped lever that released the Modular Equipment Storage Assembly. A compartment on the bottom of the *Eagle* opened near the base of the steps to reveal additional equipment to be used on the lunar surface, as well as the American flag the men would be ceremoniously planting later.

Neil continued down the ladder, until he was standing on the bottom rung. "I'm going to step off the LEM now," he said into his radio. He took a deep breath and calmed himself. As he turned on the ladder and moved his left foot to step down to the surface of the moon, he could finally see his boot peeking out from under the bulk of the spacesuit. He smiled as he said, "That's one small step for man, one giant leap…"

A hand shot out and grabbed his ankle. Neil screamed.

Confused, scared, and caught off guard, Neil's feet gave way and he tumbled off the ladder, landing with a soft thud on the fine grainy surface of the moon. He craned his neck up to look down at his feet through the cloud of powder his abrupt fall had kicked up. What he saw was so incomprehensible that it took his brain a few seconds to process it correctly.

A hand had indeed grabbed his space suit at the ankle. The hand was gray and mottled, and was connected to a man; a better description might be, what *used* to be a man, wearing army fatigues and staring up at him with vacant eyes.

Much like his hand, all of the man's skin was a dull gray color, and since he was in the vacuum of space without protection, the skin had expanded, giving the man a brutish, muscular appearance. For the briefest of moments, Neil's mind flashed back to what he had learned on one of his very first days working with NASA.

*Human bodies don't freeze or explode in a vacuum like you might see in movies,* a scientist once told him, *our skin is airtight, so it inflates like a balloon, but you'll pass out from lack of oxygen after about fifteen seconds.*

Then he snapped back to reality as the man tightened his grip and pulled himself out from underneath the Lunar Module. The man had a sizeable gash on his neck where it appeared his skin and muscle tissue had been ripped away, and the wound was now caked with dried, brown blood. The man's uniform had a name patch over the left breast. Neil read the name, **Rose**.

And the man's body was gone from the waist down!

# DEAD HISTORY

Amazingly, this wasn't the part that scared Neil the most. What chilled him to the bone was what he now noticed in the man's semi-translucent, glossed-over eyes.

It was the look of pure hunger.

The man opened his mouth as if to say something. Neil, still absolutely stunned and frozen in time, could do nothing but watch. He saw the man's tongue floating in his mouth, succumbed to weightlessness, seemingly the only thing about the man that appeared to be obeying any of the known laws of physics or nature. Instead of speaking, the man clamped his open mouth down on the space suit just above where he was grabbing Neil's ankle.

As if awoken from a dream, Neil sprang to life. He rolled over onto his stomach, hastily pushing himself up off the moon's surface. The half-man was still attached to his leg, trying desperately to bite through Neil's space suit. Fortunately, NASA made the suits strong and thick enough to withstand even nature's harshest element, the vacuum of space. But Neil knew that the thing grasping onto his leg was definitely *not* natural, and didn't want to take any chances. He grasped the sides of the ladder and started to pull himself back up towards the hatch, the grotesque freak in tow.

"Buzz!" he called out frantically through his headset. "Help!"

Inside the *Eagle*, Buzz heard Neil's cries through his radio and made his way to the exterior hatch. Looking down, his eyes grew wide with incredulous confusion that quickly turned to horror. His mind seemed to slow down, and the inside of his head started to swim. He heard voices coming through the radio, garbled and sounding like they were coming through a tube half-filled with water. It was Duke and Michael calling to him on multiple frequencies, asking what was going on.

Buzz shook his head, trying to bring himself back to reality. As Neil awkwardly climbed the stairs towards him, Buzz pressed the button to activate the radio.

"Uh, Houston, we have a problem. Please stand by." He clicked the frequency off without waiting for a reply.

Neil got to the top of the ladder, and Buzz grabbed him under the armpits and hauled him into the hatch. Neil twisted his body to look down at the half-man, still furiously gnawing and scratching on his suit's leg.

# DEAD HISTORY

The suit leg had begun to show signs of distress, growing thin under the constant wear of the man's teeth. Neil twisted his free right leg around, hitched his knee up to his waist, and kicked the man square in the face as hard as he could.

The man didn't even flinch. He didn't so much as look up, just continued frantically trying to rip through Neil's suit.

Neil felt the panic growing slowly inside of him. He thought it would be so easy to get this *thing* off of him once he was back inside the lander with Buzz, but now, sitting on the edge of the hatch, frantically kicking away at the thing attached to his leg with Buzz watching helplessly from behind, he was becoming increasingly concerned that the man would get to his leg before Neil could dislodge him.

His panic turning to anger, Neil repeatedly kicked the man in the face. His free leg working as fast and furiously as possible, Neil kicked down on the man's head again and again. After what seemed like an eternity, one of Neil's well-placed kicks was successful, extricating his leg from the ravenous mouth. As the man's body jerked backwards under the force of Neil's strike, the mottled and rotting hands grasped on to the spot of the space suit that had worn down.

His cracked, decaying fingernails finished the job that his sneering, rapacious maw had started. With a muffled rip, Neil's spacesuit tore open from mid-shin down to the top of his boot. He instantly felt the stinging chill of the vacuum on his skin, instantly emanating from his left ankle to shoot up and down his entire body.

Then he felt the bite.

The *thing* had held on to the cloth, saving itself from flying off into space and frantically scrabbling to hang on to Neil's leg, zeroing in on the exposed flesh in front of it. Hungrily, it grabbed onto Neil's leg, craned its neck forward, and chomped down on the prize.

Neil yelled out in pain, making Buzz wince as the loud scream momentarily overloaded the radio speakers.

Buzz felt amazingly helpless through the entire experience, as the small hatchway of the Lunar Module only afforded enough space for one person through at a time, and he could barely see around Neil to know what was going on, let alone try to help him fight off the attack. He finally managed to half-sit, half-crouch behind Neil and stick both his legs through a small opening between Neil's body and the side of the spacecraft door. He kicked as hard as he could with both legs at the same time, connecting full-on with the dead man's face. The head snapped backward, its mouth taking a chunk of Neil's leg with it.

The minor gravity of the moon wasn't enough to bring the body down to the surface. Having lost its grasp with both of its hands and mouth, the man-thing actually seemed to have a brief look of surprise and confusion on its face as it slowly spiraled, head-over-torso, off into the blackness of space.

As he watched the man float away, Buzz turned his attention back to Neil, whom he suddenly realized was still exposed to the void of space from the rip in his space suit. He staggered back to his feet, pulling Neil the rest of the way into the Lunar Module. He quickly shut the hatch and pressed the button to begin the re-pressurization of the cabin. "Neil, can you hear me? What the hell was that thing?"

Neil grimaced, both of his hands grasping the piece of space suit cloth the thing had tried to tear away; holding it as tight as possible around the exposed section of his leg, he replied in a low, strained voice. "I have no idea. It must have been on the bottom of the LEM, but I'll be damned if I know how it got there or how it survived the trip without adequate protection."

Buzz glanced up at the interior pressure gauge, watching the cabin slowly gain the balance of oxygen and pressure needed for him to remove his and Neil's helmets and assess the injury in the correct environment. He slowly became aware of Michael's voice ringing in his ears through the radio. "Guys? What's going on down there? Are you two okay? Please talk to me, I am freaking out up here!"

\* \* \*

In orbit above the moon, Michael had been sitting hunched over the communications console of the *Columbia* for the last fifteen minutes, staring intently at the controls as if he could will

# DEAD HISTORY

his compatriots on the surface to respond. After what seemed like an eternity, he finally received a radio response from Buzz.

"*Columbia, Eagle* here. Neil was attacked by some...thing. His space suit's protection was compromised and he was...bitten." Even through the static of the radio, Michael could tell that Buzz was trying to remain as professional as possible, but the confusion and madness of the situation was evident in his voice. "I'm currently in the process of re-pressurizing the cabin so I can properly assess the extent of Neil's injuries. After that, we'll work with Houston to assess the feasibility of continuing the mission."

During Buzz's transmission, Michael was so focused on intently listening to the details of what had transpired on the surface that he failed to notice the hatch leading from the Command Module to the cargo area swinging open. It was only when he heard a low moaning sound behind him that he looked up from the console, whipping his head around quickly.

What he saw made his breath catch in his throat.

A man in a tattered orange NASA maintenance suit was standing behind Michael, staring at him intently with clouded-over eyes. Before Michael's brain had time to fully process the question of how the man came to be on the spacecraft after having traveled millions of miles from Earth unbeknownst to anyone and with no protective gear, his senses were immediately drawn to the man's physical condition.

His skin and muscle were hanging off him in chunks, with large pieces seemingly missing entirely. His extremities looked like they had been through a meat grinder, bending at impossible angles and showing large stretches of exposed, cracked bones. His stomach had split vertically right down the middle, and many feet of intestines and unidentifiable entrails, wafted out of the man, hanging in the weightlessness of space like some slow-motion explosion.

Michael was absolutely mesmerized in terror. He could do nothing but sit and watch as the man limped forward. One of the man's legs was broken in so many places it was entirely useless and being dragged behind him. Only when the man was within a few feet of Michael, and he could smell the putrid stench of death in his nostrils, did he snap out of his trance.

# DEAD HISTORY

Michael blinked and twitched his head violently. He had to get away from this thing as quickly as possible! He braced his arms against the side of his chair and sprang forward.

He forgot he was still strapped in by his safety harness.

He bounced back into the chair, realizing his mistake. He began to fumble with the harness, but somehow he already knew it was far too late. The man was upon him; he grabbed the back of Michael's head, pushed it forward, leaned down, and sunk his rotting teeth into the top of Michael's back.

Michael screamed out in pain as he felt the man's teeth clamp on to his thoracic vertebrae. Twisting his head forcefully, the man used his teeth to begin to pull Michael's spine away from his body. With a sickly *snap*, Michael knew the man had accomplished his mission: his spine had broken in two.

Michael's world started to go dark as he succumbed to unconsciousness. His last thought was a simple one: *Dammit...more back problems.*

\* \* \*

As Buzz continued to watch the pressure gauge inside the Lunar Module continue to rise towards full pressurization, he wondered why he hadn't received a response from Michael to his last radio transmission. He quickly decided that he had more important things to worry about as Neil, who was still lying on the floor in pain, had fallen silent. Suddenly, Neil's body started to spasm wildly.

Buzz's concern quickly turned to confusion as he called out to his suddenly non-responsive partner. "Neil? Neil? Can you hear me?" How could such a minor leg injury cause this severe of a reaction? Granted, Neil's leg had been exposed to the vacuum of space for close to half a minute, but their space suits were designed to seal off their limbs from their torso and head, so Neil's important bodily systems shouldn't have been too badly compromised by the lack of pressurized environment.

Abruptly, Neil's body fell still, his eyes closed. "*Neil!*" Buzz shouted through his helmet, glancing up at the pressure gauge helplessly. It was almost in the green; just a few more seconds, and

# DEAD HISTORY

the cabin's pressure would be enough that he could take off Neil's helmet to better assess and assist his friend. The gauge's needle finally moved into the green, and he quickly moved to disconnect Neil's helmet.

As he did so, Neil's eyes snapped back open. Buzz, startled as he finished unhooking the helmet, breathed a sigh of relief when he lifted the helmet away from Neil's head and said, "Oh, thank God you're awake. I thought…well, I don't know what I thought, to be honest. How do you feel? Do you have any pain, or is…"

Buzz was cut off in mid-sentence when Neil sat up and swung his arms to grasp Buzz's spacesuit on his chest. Quickly drawing Buzz's face close to his, Neil opened his mouth wide and quickly moved to bite Buzz's face.

His mouth slapped hard against the visor of Buzz's helmet, but in his hurry to remove Neil's helmet, Buzz hadn't gotten around to taking off his own.

Buzz, more confused than ever, pushed his hands under him as he moved to stand up from the floor of the Lunar Module. "Neil? What the hell are you doing? Are you…feeling okay?"

Neil, awkward and struggling, moved to stand up as well. It was only now that Buzz noticed the glazed-over look in Neil's eyes.

*The same look as that half-man-thing had when he attacked Neil,* Buzz thought to himself. His logical mind reeling, he tried to bring himself to the realization that he didn't want to face; somehow, Neil had become a monster just like that other thing, and was now trying to attack him. If he wanted to avoid the same fate that had apparently now befallen Neil, he would have to act quickly and decisively.

Buzz backed away from Neil, who was now staggering slowly his way. Buzz's back connected with the exterior hatch, and suddenly Buzz had a plan. "Neil," he said with an air of confidence and authority that he honestly had no idea where it was coming from. "If you can understand me, stay back. I don't want to hurt you and I don't want you to hurt me. If you come any closer, I'll be forced to do what I have to do to protect myself."

Neil seemed to be oblivious to Buzz's words. He took another slow step across the cramped cabin towards him, now almost within arm's reach. Buzz nodded grimly. With his right hand, he grabbed on to the handrail attached to the *Eagle's* wall next to the escape hatch, and with his left hand he grabbed the large red lever labeled **ESCAPE HATCH EMERGENCY RELEASE** and yanked it downward as the hatch flew open. Buzz was glad to see that, on a day when the laws of science and reason seemed to have been thrown out the window, the law of physics governing the interaction of a pressurized environment and a vacuum still held true. Anything that wasn't bolted down or being held inside the Lunar Module was violently sucked out of the hatch, including the strange creature that had once been Neil.

As the force of depressurization gripped Neil's body and pulled him through the hatch, Buzz's mind flashed back to when he had kicked the half-man- thing off Neil and how it went floating away into space. Even though the event had only been a few minutes prior, it seemed like the entire surreal occurrence had actually happened lifetimes ago.

He felt a quick pang of remorse that the same fate was seemingly about to befall Neil, and he wondered if he had acted too soon; was there something still inside of Neil that could be saved; something that could of brought his friend back, if only Buzz would have had more time to interact with him?

As if in response to Buzz's thoughts, as Neil was sucked through the hatch, his shoulders came into contact with the top of the hatchway, altering his trajectory out of the *Eagle* and downwards towards the moon's surface. Tumbling erratically, Neil hit the ground with a soft thud, bounced up about ten feet in the air, and came back down to the surface, rolling end-over-end to a final stop about thirty feet away from the LEM, where he remained, motionless, a cloud of moon dust slowly settling over him.

The equalization of pressure between the cabin and outer space now complete, Buzz felt the familiar lightness of weightlessness replace the tugging physics trying to pry him free of the handrail. Keeping his right hand firmly attached to the rail for safety, he used his left hand to activate the radio.

"*Columbia,* come in, do you read?" His call was answered only by static. Frustration with the entire surreal situation finally began to creep into his voice. "*Columbia*, do you copy? Dammit, Michael, what's going on up there?" A feeling of helplessness started to

# DEAD HISTORY

creep over him as he switched frequencies. "Houston, this is *Eagle*, do you copy?"

The radio immediately sprang to life with the concerned voice of Charles Duke on the other end. "*Eagle*, this is Houston here. Buzz, you've got us all scared shitless down here...what the hell is going on up there?"

Buzz took a moment to take a deep breath before he responded. "Things have gone absolutely crazy here, Dukey. There's some *thing* resembling a man that attacked Neil as he was climbing down to the moon's surface. The man tore through Neil's EVA suit, exposed him to the vacuum, and then bit him on the leg. We dispatched him, but Neil continued to suffer effects of the attack and now seems to have...gone crazy or something. I had to eject him from the LEM via depressurization. He's on the surface, about thirty feet away, and I want to go down to check on him. Please advise, over."

"Hold right there, Colonel," came Duke's quick reply. "Do not move a muscle. Stand by." Buzz could hear Duke step back from the radio and speak to someone in the room at Mission Control with him. "Global transmission for the actual moon landing is obviously a no-go," the new voice said. "Tell them to get the actors and the soundstage set ready. And get Captain Rhodes or Doctor Logan on the horn. Tell them that one of those...things somehow managed to get on board the Apollo."

Not understanding everything he had heard but not liking the sound of it, Buzz addressed Duke as he looked out at Neil's still-motionless body. "Sir? With all due respect, what the hell is going on?"

It was a long moment before Duke came back with his reply. "Colonel, from what you've told us, it seems clear that Mr. Armstrong has been infected with a very new and very dangerous virus that was recently discovered. I'm sorry to have to inform you that, despite whatever appearances to the contrary you may think you see; Neil is dead. Your orders are to leave Armstrong's body on the moon, secure yourself in the LEM, and launch immediately from the moon to dock with *Columbia*. Is that understood?"

Buzz, more dejected and confused than he had ever been in his entire life, let his military training take over. "Orders received and understood, Houston. I'll be..."

He stopped in mid-sentence as he caught a glance of motion out of the corner of his eye. Incredulously, Neil was pushing at the moon's surface with his arms, trying to stand up! His head and neck, showing out of the top of his space suit, had ballooned to about twice their size, consistent with the effects of exposed flesh to a vacuum.

*But he's been out there for well over three minutes*, Buzz's brain chimed in. *There's no way he could still be alive...just like Duke said.*

But Buzz's military training had also taught him never to leave a man down. His decision made, he spoke into the radio. "Houston," he said through a dry mouth and hoarse lips, "Somehow...Neil is up and moving. I'm going to the surface to see if I can assist him."

"Don't you dare!" Duke's quick and clipped reply dispensed with all the formalities of call signs and rankings. "Aldrin, whatever it is you think you see up there, rest assured that it's *not* Neil Armstrong. You'll be in immediate and serious danger if you don't isolate yourself from him immediately!"

"Look, dammit," Buzz hissed through gritted teeth into the radio. "I clearly have no clue what's going on anymore. The only thing I do know is that the only other human being on this Godforsaken rock with me is out there, possibly in trouble, and I can't consider myself a real man, or a real Christian, if I just leave him there without going and seeing for myself if I can help him first!"

Buzz snapped off the radio before he heard the reply. He turned around and started slowly down the ladder. Reaching the bottom rung, he hesitated for just a moment. Almost absentmindedly, he mumbled to himself, "Here's another small step for man..." He stepped down onto the moon's surface, turned around to face Neil, and immediately knew he made the wrong decision.

Neil had already covered half the distance between where he had landed and the base of the *Eagle*. Thanks to the lighter gravity, his awkward, shambling gait had turned into a disjointed, bouncing half-run that allowed him to move much quicker than Buzz had expected. Even through his swollen cheeks and eyelids, Buzz could make out the intensity of Neil's eyes.

*It's hunger*, Buzz thought to himself. *He's not going to stop until he takes a bite out of me, kills me...unless I stop him first.*

With Neil less than ten feet away, Buzz turned back to the bottom of the *Eagle* and glanced around desperately for something, anything, he could use as a weapon. His gaze fell upon the MESA compartment that Neil had opened on his first trip down the ladder, and he grasped the first thing he could, pulling it out of the compartment.

Buzz turned back to face Neil and found himself practically face-to-face with the grotesque thing that had once been his friend. Letting out a primal roar he didn't even know existed inside of him, Buzz reared back and put all of his energy into the attack. He thrust his weapon forward, spearing Neil right through the heart with the American flag's pole. The pole went right through Neil's chest, emerging out of his back. For the briefest of moments, all was still and quiet, as Neil's gaze fell downward to the flag and pole with a blank stare.

All Buzz could do was stand still, drained of all emotion and rational thought, as he watch Neil's face lift back up, the two men's eyes meeting in the semi-darkness of the *Eagle's* shadow.

Both men sprang into action at the same time. Buzz turned back towards the ladder, hoping to somehow escape Neil's grasp and make it back into the LEM cabin. Neil, working through the awkwardness of having a flag planted in his chest, took a step forward while reaching out and trying to grasp onto Buzz. He clumsily got his hands on Buzz's shoulders as Buzz was turning away. Neil tripped over the tangle of the two men's feet; slamming himself into Buzz's back, and both men began to fall forward.

As if in slow-motion, Buzz saw himself falling face-first towards the rungs of the ladder. With Neil on his back and powerless to stop his fall, he closed his eyes and felt an odd sense of serenity fall over him. A moment later, his helmet visor made abrupt contact with the ladder, smashing the visor and exposing him to the freezing vacuum of space.

Before he could scream, his lungs constricted, feeling as if they were filled with ice. Not knowing what else to do with his last few seconds of consciousness, he flopped onto his back. Neil was there, waiting for him.

In one swift move, Neil, shoved his face into the space where Buzz's visor used to be and bit down on his nose. After a few seconds of prying, the nose came away in Neil's mouth. Because Neil's face and throat were so swollen, it took him longer than usual to chew and swallow, working the skin, flesh, and bone down his throat and into his stomach.

After a few minutes, he went back for another bite, only to find that his meal was no longer fresh meat. His prize had been replaced by another of his kind.

With a vacant stare and a head devoid of human thoughts, Buzz sat up as Neil stood and looked around for another source of food.

Overhead, *Columbia* completed another silent orbit, its two undead inhabitants staring out the main view window, waiting for the ship to turn so they could get another view of Earth.

Below on the moon's surface, the two reanimated astronauts, one with an American flag impaling his chest, stood motionlessly and looked up into the star-filled sky. All four of them seemed to somehow know that, even though there was no food to be had anywhere in their immediate vicinity, the source of the food was the large blue-green orb that they were all gazing at so intently.

They stood there, staring at the Earth.

And they waited.

# THE QUEEN'S PUNISHMENT

## SPENCER WENDLETON

Henry Fulke anticipated spikes, fire, or decapitation while shackled to the trough. He had been ushered into the Tower of London's bottommost chambers upon Queen Elizabeth's instruction hours ago. Henry was promised an execution outside of public spectacle; what he didn't know was that the Queen's plan extended beyond the agonies of the living.

Cries resounded throughout the mysterious chambers, and among criminals guilty and innocent alike, Henry awaited his fate blindfolded and clueless to what may come next. Last night, he captured a wagon of flour and yeast—enough bread to feed the entire peasant class for a month—and sent his wife and two girls from London with the goods. The wagon also contained special items beyond consumables. Henry was awestruck by the collection of the finest fur coats worn by the Queen herself, Venetian pearls, and Rhenish wines. The Queen was especially infuriated at the loss of a special item: a gold crested box filled with personal belongings owned by the departed Anne Boleyn, Elizabeth's mother. The Queen vowed to retrieve what was taken.

He was now presently unguarded, but again, not alone. The concentrated stench of death was thick as chamber pot sludge flowing down the cobbles of London. His lungs sucking in the offal to the point his eyes watered. Whatever the Queen had created, the infernal chamber threatened to bleed the truth from the most determined criminal. He vowed to keep silent in the name of his family.

The stretch of rope and clink of chains resounded further down within the belly of the pit: "Is someone there? Speak you!"

Murmurs like stray winds called to him, though no breeze vented through the chambers. "Who is there? I demand an answer. Who is in this chamber with me?"

A rotten fluid from on-high pelted him. Frigid cold, thicker than water, oozing down his face, coating his flesh, quickly drying and itching, Henry wiggled in his restraints to avoid the bizarre rain, but he couldn't dodge the torrent. Soon, a thicker object landed into his mouth in a solid mass. "Phaaaah! Let me loose. Jailor. Executioner. Queen Elizabeth! Forgive me, your majesty! Release me. I demand a trial. Please, my Queen, *forgive me!*"

Steps resounded from the stairway, a steep spiral of a staircase. The voice of his jailor said, "Where are the goods, Fulke? The Queen demands your confession. You must confess everything you know. Where is your family? It's your life for the truth, Fulke. Spare yourself her tortures. The Queen is merciless."

"Let me free," he begged, ignoring the jailor's words. "What is covering me? It's putrid. If you're going to execute me, then be on with it. This isn't torture, it's madness."

"The Queen insists that your family be detained," the jailor repeated. "Where is your family hiding? There's so much more we can do to you, Fulke. We would have criminals ruling England if we simply released you. Our people must fear our mother, Queen Elizabeth. She is everything to this country. It's filth like you, the peasant trash, which ruins England's glory. Let the words spill from your mouth, Fulke, or so face the Queen's punishment."

"Not a word to any of you!"

Henry clamped his mouth shut. The Queen couldn't harm his family. They would prosper from her goods.

"We will see how long it takes for you to speak," he laughed "You are one of *them* now."

The cloth over Henry's eyes was removed. The horrible sight nearly caused his body to suffer an involuntary spasm of truth. The words threatened to come undone from his body. The ceiling suddenly rained sheets and sheets of blood again. He couldn't see through the flood, albeit short-lived. Eight bodies hung upside down tied by their ankles. Slit from their necks and bellies, their innards slowly uncurled and flopped upon his body. Henry was wading in human organs. He couldn't unleash the horror pent up in his throat, so he lost his gorge.

The Tower of London was notorious for being a bloody stockade, but Henry didn't expect this reprehensible dungeon. Fifty bodies were shackled to the walls. Pikes of corpses were impaled from the anus to the mouth. More peasants hung from gallows by the dozens. A pit of fire burned farther down the corridor, the bodies shackled and in wire cages as their flesh were smoked, flecks of ashes spreading across the room like Hell's snowflakes. Iron maidens slammed open and closed with the vicious squeal of metal, the victims mashed to strings and pulp. Whips cracked bare backs; the leather parted skin and rendered blood.

More shocking, the punished were already dead. Henry checked his sanity and closed his eyes to ensure his vision. Fetid corpses, black and green fleshed, maggot ridden—fat grimy bastards—and drying carcasses haunted the chambers. The bodies above him continued to twitch hours after their throats had been cut. Heaps of bones, organs, and the shells of bodies were stacked chest high in corners. The torturers shoveled the entrails into wheelbarrows and carted them into other sections of the chamber for disposal. The executioners wore brown cloth sacks over their heads to stifle the smell.

Then, two jailors escorted a lady of elegant dress down the stairs. Aside from the cloth headpiece, she was fancifully adorned in a needle lace dress bejeweled in ornamental bands. The mask's slits over her head were thin, but her eyes were content on watching Henry sink in the corpses' juices.

"Have you spoken of the stolen goods, Fulke? My wine was on that wagon. My beautiful coats." Under her breath, "*My mother's belongings*. They are irreplaceable. I always believed what belonged in the family should forever belong in the family. You have ruined that sacred tradition, Fulke, with your peasant treachery. Speak what you know, Fulke. Spare yourself my chamber of torments. I will have my way regardless of your choice."

Henry shouted, releasing the pent up hatred and fear and reproach of such a terrible place. "My wife and children were starving. I lost my tile-shop in a fire—a fire one of your men started, I can safely believe. You hate to see the peasants prosper. It was either stealing or perish, my Queen. Now, I have secured my family's future. To hell with your belongings! To hell with you, your majesty!"

"Then let the bastard rot if he refuses to acquiesce," the Queen announced. "I will let you become like the others. I shall interrogate you forever, living or dead."

# DEAD HISTORY

The Queen was escorted up the stairway. Henry was lifted from the trough dripping and oozing blood. He was heaved into a cell. Four others were chained to the floor by their ankles, and soon, he matched their confinement. The iron door closed. Henry studied the men in the shadows. Their skin was busied with flies and writhing maggots, their feasting audible, the constant squishing grating to Henry's ears.

"You will be like us, peasant," one of the dead spoke. "Welcome to Hell."

"Hundreds have suffered in this fashion," another spoke and almost lost his mandible in the process. The corpse forced it back into place. His eyes had long-since popped and degraded. The man dug his phalange-bare fingers into his chest and pried out his heart and dashed it across the wall. "We are dead, you can see, my fellow prisoner. Our executioners wheel barrows upon barrows of our entrails and dump them throughout the dungeon. A disease has festered from this heap of death. This is the Queen's creation, an accident on her part, but still, something she has proudly crafted and inflicted upon us. When swallowing this festered blood, it has turned us into living dead men. Now that you have ingested the blood, our blood, you will become one of us."

A torso of melted skin and tangled bones bellowed: "The Queen will rend the secrets from you! Her lust for blood and death is unending! It is worse than Bloody Mary's."

Henry asked: "Why has she let this happen?"

The torso returned, "I learned her motives when I courted her in secret of the public. That's when I discovered these chambers. She uses her power to collect suspected criminals without the Parliament or the Privy Council's knowledge. The death of Mary, her sister, at Fotheringhay Castle has turned her into a lunatic. She detested her sister who challenged her birth-rite to the throne; Elizabeth smiled when it took three swings of the axe to remove her head. She cheered and clapped, and in private chambers, she bathed in Mary's blood. After that day, bloodlust has filled her mind. Death pleasures her so much she let these bodies pile and rot, and now, this place teems with the disease...*it teems with the dead.*"

Henry couldn't sleep once they went silent. Exhausted and beyond understanding the dead men who shared council with him, he stared at the iron door waiting for it to open. The Queen would have her way, but he had to resist her power. He imagined his family living without the threat of starvation and escaping the scrutiny of the Queen's taxes and the daily harassment delivered from the Queen's men. The idea was enough to coax him into an uneasy rest.

The next morning, the iron door finally opened. As the light poured in, Henry noticed his flesh had changed pigment. Sheet white, white as the wax the Parkers used to dip their candles in; not an ounce of blood flowed through his veins.

He was a living corpse.

The dead men were frightened, staying still to avoid notice. They wanted Henry and Henry only. The jailors dragged him from the cell and strapped him into a water chair. He was dunked into the frigid water for minutes on end. His lungs were about to burst when they finally lifted him back up to suck in lungfuls of air. Elizabeth observed him through the eyeholes of the cloth sack. "Where is Joan? Where are your children, Fulke? You know the location of my belongings. My mother's ceremonial wedding dress was in that box among her jewelry and personal diary. I must have them. *I must.*"

His lungs produced a gasp, "My family will be the ones prospering instead of you. Your throne has made you a coward. A bloodthirsty, evil bitch!"

"Let us see what you believe when I'm finished with you," the Queen smiled lasciviously. "You are dead, but you still feel pain—*my agonies will follow you into Hell!*"

Next, the Queen helmed the whip as she administered twenty lashings on the platform. By then, his flesh was loose under the shackles. Blood randomly leaked from his mouth, nostrils, and ears in clotting lines. After being clamped down in the iron maiden, his midsection bloody strings, the truth sank in without mercy. Indeed, he was a dead man. A living corpse. Joan would be captured without a trial and tortured if she was located. His children—like other children of criminals—would become orphans, and worse yet, executed. The people of London would witness the debauchery including his friends and family, and they would be forced to enjoy it. He'd been a participant of such activities and now begged forgiveness from the lord and his fellow peasants.

Elizabeth trapped him in a wire chamber above a pit smoldering with fire. She would smoke him to death. "Where is your family, Fulke?"

"Never." The habitual response lost its vigor. He watched the skin of his feet evaporate. The bones blackened. The fire crawled up his legs. Ashes of flesh blew in the air, spreading until the particles dissolved.

"I demand an answer, Fulke!"

Henry didn't bother to reply. The food and gold would last Joan a lifetime. She wouldn't work another day as a chandler. The children wouldn't starve. They were safe.

His legs boiled and dripped. Gangrene infection soiled the air, and it was excruciating. "*END THIS TORTURE IN THE NAME OF GOD! IN THE NAME OF THE QUEEN*!" he screamed.

The last sentence inspired a merry rise from Queen Elizabeth. "Where is your wife, you wretched fool? Shall I continue your agony forevermore?"

Arcs of flame grazed his torso. "NO!"

The cage was lowered. The Queen's jailors tossed buckets of salt upon his wounds. Henry buckled to the agony. Queen Elizabeth kicked a skull across the chamber. "Let him sulk in his pain. Maybe then he will confess. I am not through with you, Fulke. Not ever."

Henry was returned to his cell. He couldn't take anymore. The salts bred horrid and unimaginable pain. The memory of the fire upon his skin recycled to no end. He missed Joan and the children, but they were in danger if he satisfied the Queen.

He was returned to the chamber to fester and a limbless torso asked with gargles and pops, "How much longer before you submit, Fulke?"

It begrudged him to consider tomorrow's endeavor. He wept, though there were no tears, only grief. Henry held fast to the memories of his wife and children before the tile-shop burned down.

"Those executed in public have it easy. Look at me, my flesh is melting, I have no insides, my heart no longer beats, and my legs are roasted! I will not last. I can't confess. You can understand that, can't you?"

"Despair all you want," a voice in the shadows advised. "There is no way to defeat the Queen. All of us have tried to no success. Nobody owns a threshold great enough to outlast Elizabeth's scorn. You will reveal all your secrets to her. It's inevitable. Then, she'll keep punishing you out of scorn. Anybody who trespasses against her, may the good Lord be with you."

Henry growled, "My threshold has outlasted many of you vile bastards, and I won't submit! You gave up too easy. If she's going to punish me until I'm dust, then she can forget her confession. She'll never know my secret."

Henry stretched an earthworm from his eye socket and crushed it with his fist. "My family will surely die a detestable death," he growled. The urge to cry arrived, though his tear ducts were singed closed. "I cannot be the cause, but I must. *I must!* You're right. Her punishments are intolerable."

He crumbled to the floor. Henry pictured Joan on the scaffold and his children beheaded by a dull axe. Henry stared at his prison mates. Skeleton showed through islands of melted waxberry skin threads. They were unraveling abominations. Henry couldn't show himself to his family; even the most loving of people couldn't work past his deterioration. He'd be reduced to walking bones by the time the Queen awarded an unlikely reprieve to him or his family. The only gift he could offer his family was silence to the Queen's interrogation, and that gift was impossible to give.

He wept. The silence of the chambers overwhelmed him. There was no solution to his problem, only defeat.

"You will live with it," a voice groaned. "You have no choice, Fulke. Your heart is in the right place, but you, my friend, are in the wrong place for emotions."

"There is nothing more for us out there."
"It will never be how it used to be."
"Our families are better off thinking we are dead and gone."
Henry groveled, "*DAMN THE QUEEN!*"
Blood gushed into his mouth.
"He is losing his body like the rest of us."
"The disease has him."

"This is only after one day of torture, Fulke, imagine days, or weeks, or months of the Queen's ways?"

"You are indeed damned."

"Rest your body; you'll be facing more tortures tomorrow and the days thereafter."

"I'm sorry for your family; you're an upstanding man, Henry."

"We were all good men once, and it doesn't matter. We're still dead."

Advice and condolences from the dead men sent Henry into a fury. He couldn't fight the Queen. His family would forever be without him. He went without trial, his tile shop had been burned down, and now he was a living magpie.

"She won't take my confession!" Henry shouted

The corpses laughed, tickled by his useless rage.

"Oh, Henry, you must stop this."

"You're embarrassing yourself."

"Die with dignity, Fulke."

"Give yourself peace."

Blood continued to flood his mouth from yelling so loud: "*I WON'T DIE THIS WAY!*"

Henry, aggravated, reached into his mouth and tugged. Fibers ripped and stretched, and with a great force, he wrenched off his tongue, tossing it into the center of the chamber. Before realizing what he'd done, his audience cheered.

"My God, look at that."

"Hurrah for Fulke!"

"That will teach the dreadful woman!"

"Damn the Queen! Damn the Queen! Damn the Queen!"

The uprising spread throughout the chamber and the ones beyond. Soon, the jailors arrived, and then Elizabeth when the rejoicing failed to conclude. She discovered his discarded tongue, the purple black muscle. She clutched it in her hand and squeezed the blood from the hunk of meat.

"What is this? So you cannot speak. You think you have outsmarted me, huh?" she yelled, enraged.

Henry eyed the woman. She was helpless for the first time. He nodded his corpse head and smiled with blood dripping lips.

Insulted beyond her honor, the Queen shrilled, "Then out with you, Fulke! May you fester in hell—*FESTER IN HELL FOREVER!*"

That wasn't the end to the Queen's insult. The rest in the chamber shredded and clawed their tongues in retribution as Henry watched in astonishment. The living corpses throughout the dungeon followed their cue. Hundreds of tongues were forced out of decaying mouths and walloped the Queen's body. She was covered in black blood and green bile.

The scene compelled Elizabeth to her knees, nearly fainting. "This...this insult will cost you your lives! You are as good as truly dead."

Within the next hour, Henry was delivered in shackles at dusk into the Thames River, marching alongside his dead brethren. One by one, they treaded into the rushing water. The current dismembered them.

The waters changed into a brilliant crimson and bile hue. Henry dissolved into the sediments of the river bottom, knowing Joan and the children would prosper from the Queen's riches after all.

# THEM OTHERS

## NICKOLAS COOK

Boss led the long line of shambling slaves by the red glow of dawn. To the other slaves working the South field, the hunched shapes looked only vaguely human. And the way Boss dragged and kicked and screamed at them made them all the more wretched looking and mysterious.

"Why they still keep 'em chained, Mama?" Henry asked.

She shoved the cotton bag at him and shook her head. "Ain't no reason why we need to know anything 'bout them. Just keep your mind on your work. We gots a lot of land to cover this morning, 'fore we can start on the beans."

But Henry continued to watch the moaning silhouettes.

"You hear what I say, boy?" she asked. "The only reason you gets to stay by my side is 'cause you work hard. Now don't get lazy on me, or Boss is sure to tell them up to the house you ain't workin' right. They'll take you away and make you a house nigger for sure. I won't never gets to see you exceptin' holidays and when I'm layin' cold in my grave. You want that, boy?"

Henry pulled the empty cotton bag to his chest as if to protect against such a dire happening. "No, ma'am."

It killed her to see tears glitter in his soft brown eyes. "Then get to it," she said. But as her son walked away, barely holding in his terrified tears, to the adjoining row of dew-dappled white burst, she snuck a peek at the moaning ones, them others that smelled so bad when the wind blew their scent down to the others. They stunk like rotted meat in the sun.

There had been talk. Talk of voodoo. Talk of some kind of sickness from way cross the sea. Every slave had his or her own tale of what they were. No one but old Catfish had been allowed to see them up close and the old man wasn't talking about what he'd seen. When pressed during the evening fireside conversations held before the slave quarters, he'd only roll his yellow tinted eyes and shake his head. But she could see the unspoken fear in those

# DEAD HISTORY

moments. Old Catfish knew something wasn't right about them others.

"Elsie," a quiet woman's voice came from the row opposite hers. "You see them?"

She turned to her friend Jube with a guilty smirk. "Rather see 'em than smell 'em." Boss kept tugging them further and further away, until the line of them was nothing more than dim stick shapes in the dawn light. Elsie was about to add more, but Jube nodded towards the dirt road, where a thin white man was riding up on a brown mule, a coiled whip bouncing on his hip.

"Here come Rattler," Elsie said and her eyes narrowed with spite. The white man was always looking for a reason to use that whip to lash a shoulder or two. Man, woman, or child- didn't matter to Rattler. And she sure didn't like the way he kept looking at her when he thought she couldn't see him.

"Better not let him hear you call him that, Elsie," warned Jube. Then the old woman gave a groan and bent to her work so the overseer wouldn't pester her. Elsie also turned her attention to the job at hand. The less attention she got from Rattler, the better for her and her boy.

As the sun poured its heat up past the spike wall forest of pine and oak, Rattler sat upon his bent-backed mule, watching them pick cotton. Elsie could feel his eyes on her backside. She ignored him, edged closer to her son, who was lagging behind.

"Boy, you gots to work faster. Rattler's watching," she whispered.

Henry dragged the cotton bag along, his hands already bleeding from the sharp spikes of the bushes. Time and time again, she'd told him the best way to pick. But the boy was hard-headed, kept right on doing it the wrong way, the way that was sure to hurt his hands so he couldn't pick the cotton fast enough.

Elsie stopped her own picking, fought back the urge to look over her shoulder at Rattler, and knelt next to Henry. Looking the boy in the eye, she tried not to sound angry and frightened. "Boy, you don't listen. How many times I tell you not to snatch at the bush? Now your hands is all bloody. That gets all over the cotton, the Boss gonna lay his whip on us both."

# DEAD HISTORY

But the boy flinched at her repressed tone and his voice hitched as he tried to hold back a sniffle. "S...sorry, Mama."

"Don't be sorry, boy. Just do whats I tell you to do."

She tore a couple of sweat-soaked strips from her ragged cotton work dress and twisted them into makeshift bandages for Henry's hands. Several small pokes along his palm oozed blood and he had a gash down the left thumb. They'd heal, but she knew from experience his hands would swell to near uselessness by tomorrow morning.

"Girl, what's the goddamn hold up over here?"

She turned to find Rattler had snuck up on them. He held the whip by his side, idly thumping the savage length of creaking leather against his leg. The nasty grin on his face reminded her of the bloody smile of a chicken-eating dog who's cornered a couple of slow hens.

"Nothin', mister," she said, pushing Henry back to his cotton bag–a bag she noticed looked too empty for having gone so far down the row. "Just makin' sure my boy's workin' hard."

Rattler chuckled, eyeing the boy's back. He raised the whip. "I got the one thing that makes every nigger work harder."

Elsie's heart thumped hard with panic.

"He work harder, mister! Honest he will!"

Henry, for once, did exactly the right thing, and ignored Rattler and began to pull at the cotton with bandaged hands.

Rattler's smile faded into a leer, and he stared at Elsie. "I ain't a hard man, girl," he said, his voice all syrupy rich now. "I just want to see ya'll do right by your masters. And ya'll know ya'll got some special privileges gettin' to keep your boy with you. Most boys got to go to the house to work with the kitchen niggers."

"Yes, sir, mister," she said, keeping her eyes on the ground.

Rattler edged closer. She could smell his stink, a heady mix of body odor and sour whiskey that made her want to gag. His crooked fingers rubbed her shoulder and she quivered in disgust. "I can be a good man to know," he said. "Yes, sir, a good man. Ya'll be good to me and I'll be good to you. You understand, girl?"

Elsie could barely control her revulsion. She fought against it with all her might.

# DEAD HISTORY

"Hey! Mister!" Jube called from down the field. "I sees me a snake down here's a way. A big 'un, mister!"

Rattler gave the distant Jube an aggravated wave, hesitated for a moment, then sighed in resignation. Elsie sent a silent thanks to her friend. It was a well-known fact that Rattler loved to kill snakes, and this was the time of the year the snakes came out of their dens to sun in the open rows. Before he started back to his mule, the shotgun nestled in the saddle holster, he turned to Elsie once more. "Think bout what I say, girl. They's lots of good things I can do for you, if'n you let me."

Elsie never looked up, not wanting him to see the hate in her eyes. And the fear.

Near twilight, as she and Henry were making their weary way back home, she saw the Boss leading his shambling, stinking charges across the fields towards the wooded part of the property. She wondered where they slept. Weren't no shacks back there as far as she knew. If there were, someone would've had to build them, and that would've been slave work, which meant someone in the slave quarters would've talked about it. And to add to the mystery, she knew for a fact that no one was cooking any extra vittles for them. Kitchen niggers would've been the first to talk, 'cause it made them feel important to know something the field niggers didn't.

There was one more sight that sent a cold chill up her spine; Rattler dragging a butchered heifer behind his mule in the direction of the Boss and them others.

All that evening, as she sat with the other slaves around the fire in the circle of shacks they called home, she looked for a cooking fire in the distance. But she saw none, and soon she forgot to care as she sang for Henry, teaching him the songs her mother had taught her when she was a little girl.

During a pause in the songs, while the other slaves talked about homes they'd never see again, or lost family, Henry asked about his father again. "You think he's rich by now, Mama?"

She nodded. "Could be. He been gone a long time."

# DEAD HISTORY

"Maybe…" but the boy stopped in mid-sentence, stared into the fire, and frowned.

"Maybe what, child?" she asked. "Maybe he come back for us? Buy us from the master? Then we'll all go North and lives free?"

Henry nodded, unwilling to look at her.

Elsie gave a sigh and gathered the boy against her chest. She rubbed his hair, whispered into his ear. "Your daddy was a smart man. He know all kinds of things. He sure to make it North. He probably busy workin' right now to get money enough so's he can come back and get us. So you keep holdin' onto that hope, son. Pray to God every day for it. I knows I do."

"But how could he?" Henry asked. "Catfish say he couldn't ever come back again. The old uns say the Boss sure to shoot him dead if'n he ever sees him again."

"Don't listen to them old uns, boy. Especially old Catfish. He don't know everythin'. They don't know your daddy like I do. He wasn't never scared of no man, gun or not. If'n he can, he'll come back for us both, Henry."

Later that night, long after the fire had burned down to a glowing mound of embers, and they had retired to their cramped beds of hay and stained sheets, Elsie awoke to the sound of something crying in the distance. She shifted in the bed she shared with Henry, held her breath, and listened. It was an inhuman sound, but not like any animal she'd ever heard.

Jube's voice from across the room startled her. "It one of them," the old woman whispered.

"Don't know that," said Elsie. "Could be a hurt animal out in the woods."

"But it ain't," Jube said.

Elsie almost woke one of the men to go check the woods around the shacks, but she knew by doing so she would be giving in to her fear of the unknown. The sound didn't repeat, but as Elsie was about to fall back to sleep, Jube spoke again. "My grandmamma told me long time ago about them that's alive but not living. Said they's come back 'cause Hell is full and they can walk the earth again."

"You believe that voodoo, Jube?"

# DEAD HISTORY

Jube was silent for a moment, as if thinking it over. "Don't know. But I do know they's ain't right. The smell is enough to tell me that. I gets a strange fear in my belly when I sees them crossing the fields. Them others is evil juju, Elsie. Mark my words on that." The room was quiet for another few seconds, then, "Elsie, you ought to be careful what you tell that boy. Chillin believe anythin'."

Elsie frowned in the dark and hugged her sleeping son closer. "I know, Jube. But he need hope, don't he?"

The next morning, Elsie and Henry worked the cotton fields again; trudging down row after row of the thin brown bushes, picking the seed riddled white clumps, feeding handfuls at a time into the long cotton bags. Mind on her work, it wasn't until mid-morning that Elsie caught sight of them others again. Boss had dragged the line of them down near the mudflats where the pigs usually laid up during the humid afternoons. Boss was a huge white man. Like Rattler, he always carried a shotgun and a whip, and he wasn't afraid to use either. Since she'd come to live here on the plantation, she'd seen him shoot two men, and lash at least a dozen slaves until their backs were like glistening sides of raw beef. He was a hard, cruel man and they all feared him. It was said he could hear your thoughts, know when you were thinking about running. She didn't think any slave had ever made it off the plantation alive.

As she watched the moaning shapes tugging listlessly at muddy boulders and rotting tree stumps, with Boss yelling and flailing their backs with his whip to encourage them, she thought about Jube's words from the night before, and that terrible sound they'd heard in the deep midnight wood.

"Can you smell 'em?"

Elsie turned so suddenly she dropped her cotton bag. Wadded bunches of cotton balls flew across the dusty ground. Rattler's shadow fell across her as she bent to pick them up. "I can smell them," he said. "Hell, I can smell them stinkin' sonsabitches in my sleep."

She wiped sweat from her eyes, tried to keep from looking up at Rattler or them others down the hill.

"I saw them up close," he said. Unable to stifle her curiosity, she looked up into his shadow-painted face. "They's all messed up. Some of 'em ain't got no ears. One ain't even got a lower jaw bone," he said. "Can you believe that? Don't even know how he eat."

Elsie looked over her shoulder. The shambling shapes were too far away to know if Rattler was telling the truth or not. But then a sudden shift in the air brought the combined stench of pig shit, mud, and their decayed stink up the hill. She barely contained a gag.

Rattler's mouth split into a greasy smile. "You think bout what I says yesterday, girl?"

Her face burning with disgust, Elsie turned her attention back to the cotton on the ground. It was dusty, but not too dirty that Boss would get angry. "No, sir. I been workin' too hard to think 'bout much but this here cotton."

Rattler gave a nasty chuckle. "Shoot, girl, I know you tryin' to play stupid, but I know better. You whip smart, ain't you? A fine nigger woman, too." He rubbed his chin, looking her body up and down with an open lasciviousness. "All I wants to do is get to know you better, girl. That's all." He moved closer. "I'm gonna give you something to change your mind."

Then he was over her and his body blocked out the sun, the world, his hands reaching out. Elsie panicked and threw the bag at him. The cotton bounced off his chest and he kicked it aside, still grabbing for her. She was trapped. She knew all he had to do was shove her down behind the rows and no one would be able to see them from a distance. He was going to take her whether she wanted it or not. Feeling a sense of numb calmness, she prepared to rip out his eyes with her thumbs, praying to God that someone would watch over Henry when she was dead.

Then a scream ripped through the air.

And for a moment, Elsie was convinced it was hers.

But the sound continued; a woman's high scream of terror.

Rattler jumped up, looking for the raucous. She heard his half-muttered, "Oh, shit," and then he was running across the field. Elsie pushed herself up from the dirt in time to see Rattler leaping the rows, shotgun in hand.

Where was Henry?

# DEAD HISTORY

Elsie ran after Rattler, the fear lashing at her soul.

Rattler came to a stop, yelled in rage, and shot at something near his feet. The sound echoed through the humid still air. The cicadas and birds went silent in its aftermath.

Some of the other slaves had stopped working and rushed to see what happened. Elsie sobbed in terror. Their bodies blocked her view. She shoved past the sweaty mass, until she stood beside Rattler. The white man was shaking his head at the sight on the ground.

Jube was curled up into a fetal ball of agony. Next to her a diamondback rattler twitched out the last moments of its life. Henry was squatting next to Jube. He had his hand in hers. The woman's fingers spasmed and clenched; viscous white spit flew from her gasping mouth, as the wide white of her eyes rolled around the circle of onlookers in terror.

"Mama!" Henry cried, but he didn't let go of Jube's hand. He stayed next to the old woman. "Mama!"

Elsie pushed the overseer out of the way, who continued to watch the old black woman die, picking at his rotting teeth with a piece of bark in contemplation. Elsie gathered Jube into her arms. Tears of rage and frustration rolled down her cheeks. "Can't we stop it, Mama?" Henry begged past his own tears.

Catfish reached down to pull the boy away. "Ain't nothin' we can do for her now, boy. Gawd done put his finger on her. She ain't gonna make it more than a minute or so more. She too old to hold out against the poison. And old snakes that big carry lots of poison, son."

Jube clenched Elsie close. She gasped something unintelligible to her friend. Her body gave one last great heave and then she died.

"Bad luck," Rattler said.

Elsie felt the rage rise; she couldn't hold it in any longer. "Wasn't no damn bad luck, you bastard," she said. "You been doin' your job, this would've never happened to Jube."

Rattler looked stunned for a second, an unbelieving smile playing across his lips. The slaves glared at him with open contempt.

"You jus' best watch your mouth, girl," he warned. "Snakes all over the place this time of year. You know that. Jus' happen to be her time to go. You heard old Catfish here. She jus' too old is all. Her heart couldn't take the poison."

Elsie let her friend's dead body slip to the ground and leaped up, the fury burning hotter by the second. "You hadn't been tryin' to force your skinny, ugly ass on me, she wouldn't be dead."

Rattler felt the gaze of furious eyes all around. He took a step backwards, as if a deeper part of him recognized his danger. The shotgun rose, leveled at everyone and no one all at once. "I don't know what the hell you're goin' on 'bout, you nigger bitch. Best shut your mouth right now. I ain't gonna stand here and take no more of your sass."

Elsie started forward; but suddenly the shotgun was pointed directly in her face.

Henry cried out in horror. The old man held the boy close in a strong grip as he struggled to run to his mother.

Elsie's steps faltered. The twin black barrels stared back, daring her to take another step. The fear-filled eyes at the other end of the gun told her how close she was to being blown away in front of her son. She clenched her fists, squeezed her eyes closed, mewled out a half-scream, and sank to her knees. "Oh, God! I'd kill you if'n I could, you stinking pig. I swear I'd tear your filthy heart out."

"Quiet, Elsie," someone said in the crowd.

She looked up with a sad smile. But she never got the chance to find out who had spoken. Rattler stepped up and snapped the barrel down across her temple. The pain was sudden and blinding, and then the world went black.

She woke to the familiar stink of pig shit and the cool of night. Her head felt too large and wobbly on her neck and her arms were numb, thrust above her head. She opened her eyes and found herself down the hill from the cotton fields, past the pigsty, and in the Yard. It was where she had seen bloody punishment doled out many times. Slaves tied up, beaten within an inch of their lives, and then cut down to wallow in the dirt until someone was allowed to come and gather their bleeding, bruised bodies, and to apply the healing salves.

# DEAD HISTORY

She turned around as far as she could. The distant light of the evening bonfire in the middle of the slave quarters glowed a roseate orange above the trees, and seemed like a hundred country miles away to her at the moment. God, she was so thirsty.

She couldn't ever remember being this thirsty in her life. Not since the first day her Mama had brought her into the fields to help pick the cotton for the master. The Boss had been around even then; she could remember his judgmental eyes burning down upon her as he spoke to Mama and the others; Mama's ragged dress, blue and yellow faded flowers, that gapped tooth smile, the boy with the thick hair and the soft brown eyes.

Oh, why had he left her? Elsie snapped awake again. How long had she been out this time?

The distant firelight looked dimmer than before.

The thirst still raged hotter than ever through her. It was like a fire had caught in her throat.

"Mama," a voice called from the dark of the trees.

She whimpered a reply, although she wasn't sure if the boy heard her.

Henry stepped out of the tree gloom at the edge of the Yard, his eyes wide with fear.

"Go on home, boy. They whip you for sure if they sees you here with me."

"I ain't gonna, Mama," he said, a sort of quivering defiance in his tone. "I come to help you."

"Ain't no help for me, Henry. They's gonna whip me and that's all there is to it."

Henry moved closer, his shadow long and tall and proud in the moonlight. "I come to get you out so's you can run away. So's you can go North like Daddy. You can find him and come back for me."

Elsie laughed, but the sobs broke through. "Boy, you don't know what you talkin' bout. Go back home now, for they's find you here."

But Henry ignored her and moved to her chains. He began to tug and pulled at the locking mechanism. "I thought 'bout it, Mama," he said. "I can make it here by myself, as long as I know you come back for me."

Something gave in the lock, one of her arms fell by her side, weak and useless. Then the cold creeps gave way to hot knitting needles being shoved through her veins. "Henry, stop," she said weakly. "Don't do this."

His fingers were sure and soon her other arm fell; she collapsed to the cold muddy ground. He stooped to help her up, grunting in his efforts.

"Get up, Mama. Go. Run. Get away from here."

Elsie sobbed again. "I can't go, Henry."

"Yes, you can. Don't worry 'bout me. Find Daddy."

"I can't, son. I don't even know who your daddy is."

Henry dropped her, stepped back as if he had been hit. "You say he went North. He run away, Mama. Don't you remember?"

"I knows what I said, boy. But it ain't the truth." She slumped forward, wincing at the pain in her arms and head. "I told you them things so's you wouldn't give up hope."

Henry's eyes glistened with tears; his mouth wrenched into a silent cry. Then like a wounded deer, he turned and loped back into the woods, leaving her free but in agony.

Elsie lay for a time, letting the heavy sobs wrack her weakened frame, feeling as if part of her was already dead. But, finally, the undeniable thirst drove her onto her feet. She couldn't stand the hot, dry pain in her throat any longer. She stumbled away from the Yard, past the trees, and down a footpath to the pigsty. There was a water gutter for the pigs, but one look at its moonlit surface, with accompanying leaves and pig detritus and she decided to seek a healthier source. A little way down the path, she knew there was a water well that the field hands sometimes used when they were clearing the woods for more field space.

Into the woods again, deeper into the still darkness. The night birds called to one another. An owl flew low overhead, fluttering and whistling its indignation that she wasn't food. She found the well with no problem. The moon played along, its molded rim in shades of green and gray. She could almost smell the water emanating from its lichen-riddled surface as she leaned to grope for the dangling algae-covered rope. Deep echoes sounded back from its bottom and the sound of cool water almost made her cry with delight.

# DEAD HISTORY

Finally the bucket was in her shaking hands and she was gulping it down, killing the monstrous thirst inside her, clearing her head. Afterwards, when she could think straight again, she patted her face and head with the chill well water until she gave a heavy sigh of contentment.

Elsie was about to drop the bucket back into the well for another taste, when she heard the sound of hooves on the old beaten dirt path behind her. A light grew brighter by the second, someone carrying a torch.

She slowly lowered the bucket down without a sound and scrambled for the concealment of a copse of trees near the well.

A few moments later, the Boss and Rattler came out of the arch of tree limbs. They were hauling something behind a mule, something tied in a long cotton bag that thumped like a deer carcass across the bumpy ground. She ducked behind the tree and waited. Both men remained silent as they trudged by her hiding place. Elsie remembered the heifer from the day before, and knew where this cargo was headed. This was her chance to see what exactly them others was like. She allowed the men to move forward a few more yards, and then she followed on silent cat feet, curious and scared.

The pathway curved left, into a natural cul-de-sac. She waited behind a large oak, hugging its rough bark to her chill flesh. Boss and Rattler had stopped. The mule snorted anxiously.

By the light of the moon, and the flickering torch that Boss held aloft, she finally saw them others and she almost fell backwards in horror.

Jube had been right. These were things from Hell.

There were eight of them, chained and tied together. Their faces, once black, were now the uniform color of gray decay, rotting fruit in the bottom of a pond. Pasty eyes stared at nothing, as open mouths dribbled and moaned. Some, she could see, were missing parts. An arm, half a leg, bloodless and black with corruption. One had a nest of maggots writhing in one empty eye socket. Its black tongue sought the falling grubs, licked at them hungrily. Elsie wanted to look away, but her eyes were drawn to their slack, dead faces. This close, the stink was almost unbearable. She coughed down a gag of revulsion.

# DEAD HISTORY

The two white men had rags tied around the lower part of their faces as they approached. Rattler made some noise of disgust, then lifted his rag so he could vomit at his feet. "Holy Christ, Boss! I don't know how you stand it day after day workin' with these hellish things," he said, wiping the vomit dripping from his chin. "They's make my stomach turn over somethin' fierce."

Boss gave his co-worker a sidelong look of contempt. "Boy, you got some things to learn about making a plantation work. This here's the best money Mr. Thomas spent this year. These 'hellish things', as you call them, are going to make our old niggers obsolete in a year's time. A few dozen more and we could keep this here place running in the black for many a year to come. You ain't got to tend them. Don't need to doctor them."

"Yeah," said Rattler, pushing the rag back over his face, "but you do got to feed them, and we's runnin' out of cows, Boss."

Boss chuckled. "That's the best part. We ain't gonna need the cows much longer. Long as we can use them." He pointed at the sack.

With a snicker, Rattler moved to open the glistening bag. "Want me to throw it to them?"

Boss nodded and hefted his shotgun. "I'll keep them under control."

Rattler dug into the bag and drew out a hefty black arm. It had been severed cleanly with some large cutting tool.

"Here, chicky, chicky, chickies."

Rattler moved with caution, leaning forward, but always ready to dart away. At the sight of the dripping arm, the undead things went crazy. No longer indolent, they pulled at their chains and each other to get to the meat first. The low moans became high groans of tortured lust. In disgust, Rattler tossed the meat into their midst. They fell upon it with ravenous hunger, and it was soon nothing more than strips of muscle and shiny white knobs of bone.

"Give them some more," Boss said, eyeing the feeding frenzy with amusement.

Rattler reached deep into the bag, winced at something he touched, and then pulled forth Jube's severed head by a curly scrub of hair. He held the dripping trophy aloft and giggled.

# DEAD HISTORY

Elsie felt as if the air had been punched from her body, as if someone had taken the world out from under her feet. She saw spots before her eyes and almost fainted at the sight of her friend's head staring back at her.

"You got to get closer this time," Boss said.

"The hell you say," Rattler replied.

"You wanted to feed them, didn't you? You got to get closer, boy."

Rattler gave the big man an uncertain smile and then edged closer to the groaning flesh eaters. He made to toss the head into the fray...

A blast exploded in the night air.

A ragged hole appeared in Rattler's chest and parts of his body splashed the undead and Boss. A fountain of bloody froth gurgled from Rattler's gasping mouth. Then he fell face first to the ground. Jube's head bounced out of his grip and rolled to a stop at Boss' feet. The big man turned to see what had happened, surprise etched across his seamed features.

The mule gave a grunt of terror and bolted off into the woods.

"Holy hell, girl," he said. "Do you know what you done?"

Elsie pulled the second trigger on Rattler's shotgun. The man had been foolish to set it down and leave it unattended.

Boss' left side turned to shredded raw meat. The sound echoed and died.

His shotgun thumped to the ground, sliding from limp fingers, followed by the torch, with a sizzling clunk, the flames leaping in a crazy dance.

Boss staggered back, still staring at Elsie in disbelief. With his good hand, he tugged the rag from his face, gasping for air, trying to speak. He tried to move back on uncertain legs, but his feet tangled up, and he fell back into the waiting arms of the flesh eaters. They pulled at his bloody skin, tore at the muscle beneath, gnawed like starving babies at his intestines, and slurped at viscous body fluids.

Feeling numb inside, Elsie watched them feast for a time. Then she found the end of their chains and gathered them up in her shaking hands. She picked up Boss' shotgun, too, and began to drag them down the moonlit path to the big house.

# EXTINCTION EVENT

## MARK M. JOHNSON

Fleeing into the blinding white curtain of driving snow, the burrower ran for her little life and the flesh hunter followed. The numbing cold habitat of the small, fur-covered mammalian quadruped would have killed the flesh hunter long ago, if she had not been dead already.

She was from the warm lands, and far from what had once been her natural habitat. Her frost-covered, rough leathery skin would have sparkled in the sunlight, but in the storm, the sun's warmth couldn't reach her. Unlike her current prey, she walked upright with her long powerful tail suspended behind her for balance. From her snout to the end of her tail, she measured almost twelve feet. The fearsome, highly intelligent pack hunter was now only a walking dead eating machine.

Perhaps in her frozen undead brain, something remained of her extensive hunting experience. Five days ago, when she scented the pod of burrowers, she stalked in from downwind in the cold, dead air and surprised them.

After being flushed out of their old warren by the invasion of the living dead, the small pod of mammals had fled north, and was digging a new den when she fell upon them. Out of the family of six little fur-covered mammals, only the mother escaped the snapping jaws of the undead hunter. The survivor fled deeper into the northern territories, and she pursued, tracking the lone burrower deeper into the cold lands.

She was the only one of her kind in this part of the world. The cold that would have killed her had she still breathed now stilled the decay of her undead body. Only her constant relentless motion prevented her decomposing flesh from freezing solid. The bloody festering bite wounds on her tail and back had long since frosted over from the frigid winds of the blizzard.

Back in the warm lands, the newly risen dead never lasted more than twelve to fifteen suns. In the oppressing heat and humidity, their dead flesh began to fall away from their bones after five to seven sun cycles. Here in the cold lands however, she could last indefinitely or until her body froze solid from the rapidly dropping temperature, despite her ever-constant movement.

It was close now; she could smell its warm living flesh and the scent drove her stiffening legs onward into the whiteness. She longed for the warm life in the little creature's body, the warmth taken from the creature's dead pod, was now as chilled as the rest of her body.

Gradually, the driving storm began to dissipate. She stopped abruptly, almost walking into a wall that materialized out of the blustering snow. She found herself at the base of a towering wall of solid ice, hundreds of feet high along the foot of a mountain. To her left, she spotted a massive crack in the wall, which went up and out of sight along the mountainside. The burrower's tracks led into the dark crevice, and she followed without hesitation.

* * *

Almost an entire cycle had passed since the fire rocks fell from the clear blue sky. The pack was already moving north for the warm cycle hunt. Although they watched the fire streak across the sky with surprised interest, the pack had been to far away to see or hear them make landfall. Where the fire rocks landed, great fiery explosions killed every living thing for miles. Hours later, the dead felled by the fire rocks fury began to rise and attack the living animals around them.

It didn't matter whether the risen animals were green eaters, or meat eaters; they were all eaters of the flesh now. The fire rocks fell across nearly half of the entire surface of the bountiful green and blue planet. The plague they brought burned through the planet's abundant inhabitants like a wind driven wild fire.

For the current warm cycle, she'd brought her pack farther north than usual, deeper into the cold lands and away from the crowded hunting grounds to which they were accustomed. In the past two warm cycles, more flesh hunters had invaded this territory of the cold lands and prey was getting scarce. Moving this far north was a risk, if they went too far and could not escape the cold cycle, they would all die in the cold lands.

She was the alpha female however, and the pack followed her lead without question. The risk paid off when the pack came across a large group of shoreline dwelling swimmers on the edge of the great water. The swimmers, gathered on the land's end looked to be there for mating rituals and the laying of their eggs.

While in their home element of the great water, the blue and gray-skinned swimmers were no doubt fast and agile. On land however, the large and cumbersome swimmers were at the mercy of the pack. With no other flesh hunters seen or scented in this area, the pack had it all for themselves. At her command, the pack separated, moving up and down the coastline, laying down their scent markers and claiming this territory for the pack.

\* \* \*

The hunting migration for this warm cycle was a great success, the pack fed well and three newborns hatched healthy and were coming along well. With the two female and one male hatchlings, the pack numbered nine, she and her life mate, one almost a full grown male who would be pushed out of the pack soon, and three females.

The time had come to leave, and she signaled the pack that it was time to head back to the warm lands for the cold cycle. Fourteen suns into the return trip to the warm lands, they encountered the first of the fire-rock plague victims.

The pack was down wind, and picked up the scent of death long before they saw the walking dead green eater. Her life mate scented the green eater first, and called the pack to the hunt.

They were all well fed, and there was no real need for food. However, the pack could not pass up an easy meal, and it would be a good learning hunt for the hatchlings. As always, her life mate and the male would charge the prey head on, while she and the females split up and attacked from the sides. The hatchlings would stay out of site for this hunt; it would be only a visual learning experience for them.

# DEAD HISTORY

The scent of death grew strong in the air, and then they heard it coming. The death reeking green eater was a thunder foot, and the ground trembled before the giant. It was then, just before the thunder foot broke the tree line, that she noticed something wrong in the death scent.

The scent was wrong somehow, and she stopped to consider it. Then it came to her in a rush, it was a sickness scent. Unlike anything she had ever scented before, the odor was confusing but filled with sickness nonetheless. She called out warning to the rest of the pack but the attack had already begun. The attack however, was not her pack hunting the thunder foot, the massive green eater was hunting them.

The walking dead giant caught the male and her life mate in a small clearing as it exploded out of the tree line. On the beast's flank, legs, and neck wounds from many savage and obviously fatal attacks dripped putrid congealed pus. The wounds were old and alive with maggot infestation, this thing looked many suns dead yet still it walked.

It roared and lumbered forward unsteadily, acting as if it were the dying animal they thought it to be. Her life mate called out to the young male in warning, but he stopped charging far too late to avoid the massive jaws of the staggering monster.

The undead behemoth caught the male in mid-leap, chomping down on the hunter's back. It lifted the screaming male high into the air and shook him viciously. Bloody, twitching pieces of the male fell around the thunder foot's feet as her life mate leaped onto the things shoulder, clambering up onto the spinning monster's back, furiously biting and clawing all the way.

Her life mate clawed his way up the thing's towering neck, searching for a killing bite in the monster's soft gray flesh. He never saw the titan's swinging tail coming for him, she cried out warning but in the chaos, he never heard the call. He shrieked in pain when the immense tail slammed into him, sending him sailing through the air and into the trees.

She cried out in despair and charged into the trees to where her life mate had fallen. The three females moved aggressively into the clearing, circling and distracting the attacking green eater away from their injured alpha male.

She leaped into the dense foliage, searching franticly, and after a few yards, she found him silent and crumpled against the exposed roots of a large tree. She cried out in grief as she approached his still form. Crouching over him, she called out, softly nudging his broken body. Whimpering, she thumped her tail against the ground. A tear fell from her reptilian eye as she gazed uneasily at the bones protruding from his side, his precious life fluid leaking from him.

His body groaned and shifted over slowly, and she leaned in warbling hopefully. His pain shrouded eyes opened and gradually focused on her face. He hissed in agony, struggling to hide his weakness from her as he tried to stand and failed.

She knew he was dying and mourned for him. He had been her only life mate for many cycles and losing him hurt terribly. She licked his snout affectionately, and weakly he returned the warm gesture while still struggling to hide his pain. She looked deeply into his pale blue eyes, holding his gaze. He looked back longingly and for just a moment time stood still for them. He gasped faintly and his eyelids fluttered over sorrowful eyes. He looked up, his eyes cleared one last time, and then the light in them faded away and went out forever.

She lifted her head high and screamed her anguish into the uncaring sky, the cry of pain shifting into a howl of rage. Her broken heart cried out for bloody vengeance. She would kill the crazed giant green eater with her own claws. She would rip the beast's heart out, and return it to lay with her life mate's body in tribute.

Drawn in by the sound of her cry, the three, five-week-old hatchlings gathered around her and her mate's body, chirping in confused excitement. For a moment, she was lost in a fog of pain, anger, and sorrow, but seeing her hatchlings brought her crashing back into the real world. Just a short distance away from her and the hatchlings, the sounds of the battle between the remainder of her pack and the thunder foot raged.

The sickness scent!

She remembered it now and realized they were all in danger from it. Running, with the hatchlings at her heels toward the clearing where her pack still fought the giant sick green eater, she called out for them to break off and retreat. A thunderous ground-shaking thump, and the tortured scream of her youngest daughter, told her that she was too late.

Stopping at the edge of the tree line, she took in the scene of battle. Her youngest was pinned beneath the massive tail of the thunder foot. The young female flesh hunter shrieked in suddenly excruciating pain as the monster caught her exposed hindquarters in its jaws and tore her in half.

Shrieking in frenzy, the two remaining sisters darted between the giant green eater's legs, slashing and rending at the already ravaged limbs. It paid them no mind as it bent low and snatched the rest of the freshly killed victim off the bloody ground. The rage-blinded sisters came around the thunder foot's rear and turned to attack again. She keened loudly at them and they stopped suddenly, looking around in confusion. They could barely hear anything over the roaring groans of the walking dead thunder foot, but their mother's call cut through the din and reached their sensitive ears.

As the behemoth turned looking for them, the two sisters sprinted between its massive tree-limb sized legs, and leaped into the dense foliage at the tree line, disappearing from view. The beast let out a frustrated guttural groan as it plunged into the forest, snapping the trees into pieces as it pursued them. Unseen behind it, the two sisters burst out into the clearing. Pausing for a second to make sure the insane green eater hadn't seen them; they again dove into the trees, this time at their mother's side.

Behind them, groaning and staggering into the clearing, more animals began to emerge from the southern tree line. They were drawn to the area by the sounds of a fight, the motley crew of beasts filling the clearing in a matter of seconds. Like a flash flood of death, the wave of undead beasts consumed every living creature in their path.

The large herd was comprised of several species of green eater large and small, accompanied by many mid-sized flesh hunters, small scavengers, and a big hunter. All of them reeked of the sickness death scent and many looked like walking, rotting carrion. It was time to get her pack away from this madness. Signaling for them to follow, the alpha female led what was left of her pack northeast, away from the more populated coastline and into the highlands.

Eating on the run and sleeping for only short intervals, the pack outran and escaped the plague of sickness death. However, the reprise was only temporary. Though they had escaped the ravenous infected animals, the pack could not outrun the sickness itself.

Her two remaining females unwittingly carried the sickness death with them into the mountains. After falling ill, they both died and reanimated within hours of passing.

She fought and killed both of her offspring with a heavy heart, finally stopping one and then the other, by tearing off their heads. Shortly thereafter, she became sick herself. She knew what was coming and tried in vain to persuade her hatchlings to flee from her side. When she rose from death the following day, three tender morsels of vibrant young living flesh presented their bodies to her as if in sacrifice, she didn't hesitate to accept.

\* \* \*

She possessed no memory of the loss of her pack, or the killing of her own young when she awakened from death. They were only living flesh to be consumed, nothing more. Weeks later, she continued on her single-minded mission, pursuing the living flesh she coveted into the colossal ice crevice in the glacier.

The narrow fissure barley admitted her, but a few yards in, it widened into a cavernous expanse of glittering ice. She now treaded on bare rock, where there had only moments ago been solid ice. Taking no notice of this change, she continued in her unyielding quest for living flesh. After following the mammal's scent through the ice cavern for hours, she came to a dark, yawning hole in the rock floor where the glacier had sheared away the side of the long extinct volcano.

The scent led her into the dark chasm. She clawed her way through the stalactites of ice covering the opening and leaped in without hesitation. She found herself in the twelve-foot wide circular tunnel of an extinct lava tube. Unsure as to the direction of the living flesh scent, she turned around in the darkness several times in confusion. Hearing a soft chattering sound, she looked up and realized her mistake. Far above her on the wall of ice over the opening to the lava tube, the tiny mammal looked down and hissed venomously at the killer of her family.

Many days had passed since she last looked upon the little mammal, and seeing the living animal drove her into a frenzy. She growled loudly and franticly clawed her way up and out of the dark chasm. But her body wasn't built for climbing. Nonetheless, she clambered up the wall of ice, slowly but surely. The little mammal waited for her to get close to the ice shelf she was perched on, and then skittered out of reach further up the ice wall.

The undead flesh hunter reached the ice shelf after a few minutes of struggle, and pulled herself up onto it. With the living flesh still out of reach several yards above, she began to climb again, unmindful of the crackling sound beneath her hind feet.

Unnoticed by the undead hunter, the ice shelf she now stood on was unstable due to an extensive amount of clawing and digging. With a loud crackling snap, the shelf gave way from beneath the hunter. She scrambled in a futile attempt to hold onto the ice wall, and then tumbled back down into the darkness of the lava tube. She went down howling in an avalanche of rock and broken ice, landing with a thunderous crash on the floor of the chasm.

Pinned and helpless beneath several tons of rock and ice, the undead hunter groaned in frustration. The borrower scrambled down onto the mound of avalanched debris and hissed at her pursuer in triumph. The living dead monster had climbed right into the vengeful mammal's trap, and now the chase was over.

In the struggle for survival, the undead hunter had been outsmarted by the next dominant species of the earth. The little furry mammal looked down through the ice, glared at the trapped undead dinosaur a moment longer, and then ran off into the ice crevice, leaving the monster trapped forever in a cold and icy grave.

* * *

After nearly seventy million years of absolute silent darkness, a light flashed through the gloom across the glittering ice walls of the cavern. A single dancing beam of light reflected through the ice, shimmering as if a hundred thousand diamonds were imbedded in the walls. A second beam of light appeared, and in the echoing sounds of crunching footsteps, two wonderstruck voices joined the light.

"My God, Robert, it's beautiful," a soft female voice uttered in awe.

"I know. I just knew you'd love it," a young deep male voice replied. "It's only been exposed by the ice melt for about a week or two, I'm estimating."

"Is it dangerous?" the young woman asked with a slight tremor in her spellbound voice.

"No, I don't think so," Robert replied confidently. "The ice walls are stable, and there's solid rock just a few feet under the surface."

The two came around a bend in the nine-foot high circular tunnel, both dressed in cold weather mountain climbing gear. As they hiked deeper into the ice cavern, their numerous tools and climbing equipment clinked and jingled on their belts, echoing throughout the cave's expanse. The well-built athletic man stood six feet two inches tall. He still wore his climbing helmet but his glasses were missing, showing his wide expressive blue eyes. His handsome, well-bred face showed just a hint of blond stubble. His companion had removed her glasses as well, her long brown hair stuck out from beneath her climbing helmet. She stood almost a full head shorter than her partner did, and her smiling, attractive, hazel-eyed face looked ruddy and flushed from the cold air.

"How did the tunnel get so perfectly round, is it from the way the ice is melting?" the young woman asked, panning her flashlight across the sidewalls. Her light flashed down to the two-foot wide, and one-inch deep, steady flow of melt water running across the bare rock floor beneath her spike-soled climbing boots.

"No, I think this is actually a volcanic lava tube," Robert said, and stepped closer to the right wall, brushing his gloved hand across it.

"I think you're right," she replied. "But if it is, it has to have been long extinct and inundated with glacier ice for a very long time."

Robert nodded in agreement, "Millions of years, maybe. Just think Shannon, this lava tube has been iced up all this time, and we're the first living things to see it for God only knows how long!"

"Yeah, God only knows," Shannon, whispered reverently. "Look, I think it ends up there." Shannon directed her light up and deeper into the cavern where it sloped slightly upwards, to end in a series of tightly spaced ice pillars and stalactites.

"Yep, this looks like the end of the line," Robert said in disappointment, angling his light upward and following the ice pillars to the ceiling. "Hey look at that!"

"What?" she asked, following his flashlight beam and adding her own to it.

"There, in the ceiling, it looks like a pretty large fissure in the upper part of the lava tube's wall."

Their lights revealed a six-foot wide, ten foot long, ice-filled opening in the rock of the cavern's ceiling. The ice coming through the fissure resembled a waterfall frozen in time, and glistening moisture created an illusion of movement.

"Turn off your light for a second," Robert whispered.

"What?" she asked; reluctantly looking away from the frozen walls of the cavern.

"Your flashlight," he repeated. "Turn it off for a second."

"Oh, okay," she answered as she complied. Robert turned off his light a second after her light extinguished, and for a moment, the cavern was plunged into darkness.

"What are we looking for?" she whispered in an almost conspiratorial tone.

"Look at the frozen waterfall, Shannon," he whispered back, unseen in the darkness. She turned back towards where she thought the waterfall would be, and saw it. While the rest of the lava tube cavern remained in absolute darkness, the icefall glittered with a faint soft glow. The glow came from within the ice itself, and as they watched and their eyes became adjusted to the darkness, the light seemed to grow ever brighter.

"How?" Shannon whispered in wonderment. Stepping forward slowly, she reached out and touched the glowing ice. The glow faintly illuminated the entire area around the icefalls in dancing,

# DEAD HISTORY

shimmering shadows. The ice seemed to move as thin streams of melt water cascaded down the outer surface.

"The light's coming from outside, I think; through the body of the glacier. It's shining through the fissure in the rock and into the lava tube," Robert answered as, he too, stepped over to the icefall. Pulling off his glove, he ran his bare fingers across the freezing water on the surface.

"It's like magic," Shannon said, laughing softly.

"This is what did it!" Robert stated confidently. "The melt water coming through the fissure cleared out this entire section of the lava tube."

"I'll bet you're right, and the way that water's coming through, it's not going to look like this for much longer," Shannon said almost sadly.

He nodded silently. "I wish we had the right equipment to photograph it, we could get a natural formation like this into National Geographic or something."

Following the formation's shimmering surface towards the bottom near the floor of the cavern, Robert noticed a dark shape in the ice. Dropping down to one knee, he switched on his light, and directed the beam into the ice near the floor. Induced by the shimmering glow of the ice, Shannon's almost trance-like state was broken abruptly by Robert's light.

"Hey, what?" she asked, in slight annoyance.

Robert was silent at first, eyes wide and mouth agape as he leaned in closer to the dark shape in the ice.

"Holy shit!" he gasped in shocked amazement.

"What is it?" Shannon asked, kneeling down and adding her light to his.

Beneath the radiance of their lights, almost two feet deep into the ice, a cloudy yellow-green eye looked back at them.

"An, animal?" she murmured, looking closer as a long row of gleaming white teeth came into view just below the dead eye of the frozen creature.

"Jesus Christ, I think it's a dinosaur! But it can't be," Robert blurted out excitedly, brushing his free hand across the surface of the ice.

"My God, Robert, it really looks like one. Look, you can see the snout!" She moved her light closer, trying to clear up the blurry view through the melting ice. The animal's eye, snout, and both lower and upper sets of teeth were visible through the blurred ice, albeit only just barely.

"It's just not possible, Shannon. It must have been frozen in the ice for millions of years. Like sixty or something," he said skeptically, still shifting his view from left to right.

"Well, you said this cavern might have been sealed up in the ice for a long time," Shannon said, standing up and stepping back to see the whole creature frozen in the ice. Now that she knew it was there, she could make it out a little better, but it was still like looking through bathroom glass.

"Yeah," Robert replied, "But I didn't exactly have sixty million years in mind when I said that."

"It has to be at least eight feet long," Shannon said as she panned her light from one end of the animal to the other. "Maybe more." As her flashlight beam moved over to where the creature's tail might be, her light stopped abruptly. "Robert look!" she shouted loudly, her voice reverberating back through the cave, the echoing two words repeating to slowly fade away.

"What?" he shouted back excitedly. Standing up and following the direction of her flashlight, he saw what she was shouting about and fell silent. "Oh my God," he huffed in disbelief.

Down to the left of the frozen animal, part of one foot stuck out from the melting ice. One long toe ending in a sharp, hooked claw extended out from the surface of the ice. Stepping forward, Shannon reached out to touch it.

"Stop!" Robert shouted, grabbing her by the shoulder and pulling her back.

"Hey, what's wrong?" she asked angrily.

"If that is what we think it is," he answered intensely. "And it's been frozen in there all this time. It may start to decompose very quickly once it's exposed to the air. Touching it might contaminate it somehow."

"Yeah, you're right." She looked away from him, gazing at the shape in the ice over her shoulder.

# DEAD HISTORY

Robert gently led her out of reach of the icefalls. "I think we need to head back to camp and make some calls on the radio."

Shannon agreed, nodding her head in the gloom. Unseen in the darkness behind them, the exposed claw twitched and curled as the frozen dinosaur again tested the ice prison's hold.

"Shannon," Robert asked with a little breathless excitement in his voice, he reached out and took her hand in his.

"What?" she answered, laughing playfully.

"We're going to be fucking famous!"

"I know," she said in elation. "That just might be the find of the century in there."

"The century? Shannon, that might be the single greatest discovery in the history of modern man!"

"I know. Just think... if that is a real honest-to-God dinosaur, and the skin and internal organs are still intact... Well, you saw the eye. It looked pretty good for being frozen for millions of years didn't it?"

"Hell, yes, it looks good," he said. "That thing could answer so many questions about the past! All that stuff the scientists could only theorize about; the whole world is gonna freak out when they see this!" He was almost jumping for joy. "So," he looked back at the dark shape in the ice. "At the rate the ice is melting, how much longer do you think it'll be before it becomes completely exposed?"

Shannon looked high up at the top of the ice formation, slowly following the flowing water down to the dark shape of what might be a perfectly preserved, sixty million year old dinosaur.

"A few weeks, month at the most," she answered, sounding surprised.

"Then we'd better get moving, c'mon," Robert said. Letting go of her hand, he turned and motioned for her to follow.

"Right," Shannon said, turned, and then followed him out towards the entrance of the cavern. The two of them continued to talk excitedly as their lights faded, returning the cave to darkness.

Behind them, tracking their every move, a pale-clouded yellow green eye watched patiently in the icy darkness, burning with a sixty-five million year old hunger insatiable enough to consume the entire world.

# KHERFIN

## T.W. BROWN

"My Lord, the Hebrews have gone," Haran-ka prostrated himself at the Pharaoh's back.

The Pharaoh said nothing. He stood before the enormous statues of Osiris and Isis. The gleaming white marble reflected the blazing Egyptian sun onto the tiny figure nestled atop the joined arms of the silent gods.

The Pharaoh's son was dead. The screams of last night's horrors still echoed in the ears of all those who had survived. Haran-ka felt his eyes well with bitter tears. Only, he did not weep for the son of the Pharaoh. Instead, his tears were for his oldest brother, Isto-Ra, who, at this very moment, lay on the death altar in his parents' home.

Throughout the land, families mourned. The death of the first born had come in the night just as the Hebrew promised. These past weeks had been one nightmare after another. The heads of all the royal magicians still adorned the staffs that had once been symbols of their office.

Well…all heads but one.

"Ready the men. Prepare my forces. We march within the hour. I will see this Moses on the end of my spear," Pharaoh rose slowly, head still bowed over the lifeless body of his son. "And tell Neraphatte to come at once. He will be given the same chance his nine brethren were given." The venom of anger displaced the sorrow in his voice.

Haran-ka could feel the Pharaoh's eyes bore in the back of his head.

Neraphatte gripped his staff so that his knees would not buckle. Why could he not have been called to rid the waters of blood or banish the frogs?

# DEAD HISTORY

"You will undo what Moses has done or your head shall join the others, and your body shall be cast into the endless sands for the scorpions and serpents." Pharaoh stood in his full battle dress, his spear leveled at Neraphatte's chest.

"By Isis and Osiris, I shall do as my Pharaoh demands." Neraphatte's eyes dared not drift up from the point on the floor he fixed them to the moment Pharaoh entered the chamber.

"When I return, my son shall greet me," Pharaoh gripped Neraphatte's chin, tilting his head up. He locked eyes with his court magician and his gaze turned ever colder. "Otherwise, your head shall rest on the staff your fist clenches so tightly."

With that, the pharaoh and his men left. The sounds of an army thirsty for vengeance filled the morning air. Eventually the roar faded as the might of Egypt raced after those responsible for the smell of death filling the city.

Neraphatte's quarters were dark and cluttered. Scrolls lay on tables, benches, and the floor. Still curled up in a corner, was the lifeless body of his favorite assistant, Kherfin. Like so many others, his face was locked in that visage of pure terror. Perhaps he had seen this Angel of Death sent by the God of Moses just as he took his last breath.

"I know it is here." He snatched up one scroll after another. Scanned its contents, and discarded it. How long would it take Pharaoh's men to deal with the Hebrew slaves? Perhaps two days at best.

"A-ha!"

Wading through the mess, he had added to in his urgency, Neraphatte rushed to the doorway. A thought came as the sour smell of death tickled the back of his throat. He had no idea if this ritual was worth the papyrus it was written on.

If he did some elaborate ritual on the Pharaoh's son in the palace and it failed…

He laid Kherfin on the long wooden table, brushing everything to the floor with no regard for the mini scrolls he spilled the day old pitcher of wine on. If this failed, none of his belongings would be joining him in the afterlife. He would be killed and never granted the Rites of Death that would allow his life to be weighed before the gods.

Hastily he scrambled about the chamber. Neraphatte rummaged through bins and ransacked his shelves as he gathered all of the oils and other associated items needed for the ceremony. Satisfied that everything was in order, he began to pour fine white sand in the forms of the symbols called for. With oil, he traced more symbols on the cold, stiff body stretched out before him. He only became aware of how profusely he began to sweat when stinging drops trickled into his eyes.

Calling out to Osiris, and singing the words on the scroll, Neraphatte began to feel a coldness fill the room. It was like the chill on a night where no clouds masked moon or stars; where each star blazed, and skin bunched up as the air kissed it. His eyes followed the markings as he sang each line. He watched the ink fade into the scroll and vanish! Something tugged deep inside. For a moment, it felt as if the spirit was too large for his mortal body. With tremendous effort, he spoke the final word. He stared perplexed at the scroll; all that remained in his hands was a blank sheet of age-browned papyrus.

A moment of uncertainty mixed with fear struck him like an invisible fist that sent him staggering back from the table. Then...relief. The words remained in his head! Neraphatte had no doubt that he could recall them at will. Every symbol traced on the body seemed to vibrate at the ends of his finger tips. His arms felt strangely limber, and could easily repeat the intricate patterns they wove with shaky effort just moments before, when they had spilled the fine white sand around the prone and rigid figure on the table.

But, was there any reason to repeat the ritual?

So far, Kherfin lay still. Cold. Dead.


The sun had just vanished behind distant hills, leaving the sky tinged in reddish hues. Several hours passed in agonizing slowness and still nothing changed in the condition of his acolyte. Neraphatte paced back and fourth. His mind was cluttered and full of unsettling images. He was haunted now by the smiling, laughing severed heads of his fellow court magicians. In his visions, they laughed and called him "Fool!" How could he think to wield the power of a god? How could he expect to defeat Death?

A low moan filled the room.

Neraphatte froze. His eyes locked on the body stretched out on the table as one hand clenched slowly into a fist. Moving closer, he felt a rush of triumph as he witnessed Kherfin's eyelids fluttering open.

Success!

Not wanting to waste another moment, Neraphatte scooped the small urns and jars he would need into his arms and rushed to the door. The Pharaoh would have his son, and he, Neraphatte, the last of Pharaoh's court magicians, would keep his head right where it belonged...firmly atop his shoulders.

"Meet me at the palace as soon as you're able," he yelled over his shoulder, not waiting for his acolyte to gain his feet. He dashed through the door and down the street.

Kherfin rose.

In a slow, awkward series of movements, feet swung off the edge of the table and landed heavily on the floor. Vacant eyes sought out something.

Only one need filled the being that was...but was not...Kherfin.

Hunger.


Queen Meraseti sat on the floor, cradling the body of her dead son in her arms. The magician had pleaded that she not disturb the body until the magic took hold and returned him to life. The moment his hand had flinched, she had shoved the frail, sickly looking excuse for a man aside and grabbed her son.

The young prince's body convulsed violently against her once and stopped. Then, in fits and starts, she felt him move against her. His hands flexed and closed on her arms. She felt his head shift slightly and nuzzle into her. Memories of how she, Queen Meraseti, had nursed her son flooded her mind. She had refused to allow a slave the privilege of tending to the needs of the beautiful boy who had broken free from her womb. Now, it was as if this *re-birth* brought with it the desire to nurse. She knew there would be no milk, but she could not stop what was happening for fear that just as suddenly as life returned, it would vanish again.

Cold lips touched the bare skin at the curve of her left breast. With a defiant gaze, she looked up to see the magician staring with mouth and eyes wide. She dared him to speak a word in protest. For giving her back her son she would not kill him, simply remove his tongue. That would prevent him from spreading any sort of gossip.

A sudden jolt of pain caused Queen Meraseti to cry out. She looked down in time to see her beloved son pull away with a mouthful of her breast. Blood gushed from the jagged and ugly wound, turning her white dress crimson. She looked into blank, white-filmed eyes that displayed no emotion or recognition as her precious son's blood-soaked face came forward...mouth opening wide. Teeth closed on the tender flesh of her throat and tore.

Queen Meraseti wanted to scream, but nothing came forth except a froth of hot blood. She watched in frozen terror as a thin stream of it shot several feet, splattering the sandals of the magician who still continued to stare...unable to turn away. Darkness began to narrow her vision. Before total blackness fell, she saw her husband's final remaining royal magician turn and flee like the coward she knew him to be. She thought she heard him whimper something just before he left. Had she lived but a moment longer, she would have heard him shout a name that would echo throughout the empty palace corridors.

"Kherfin!"


Down the dark street Kherfin wandered. A sudden noise made him turn his head. Something was coming closer. The hunger rose and the painful coldness that suffused the thing that had once been Kherfin sought the warmth filling this source nearby.


Ulina sat in the doorway, sniffling. Her parents were still praying over the shrouded body of her big brother, Nepara. All the food prepared for today's feast sat untouched. Nobody wanted to celebrate her eleventh year when so many had died in just one night. Knees pulled up under her chin, she watched the stars reveal themselves in the total blackness above.

A sound caused her to jump just a bit. Somebody stood at the end of the path leading up to her family's house. None of the lanterns that were lit would allow a visitor to see clearly up to the door. It also kept Ulina from seeing exactly who stood waiting to be invited up.

Perhaps it was somebody who remembered that today was her special day! She unfolded her coltish legs and stood. A glance over her shoulder revealed nobody moving inside the house. She considered calling out, but did not want to disturb her parents. Besides, they might send whoever it was away, saying it was a bad time for visitors.

First walking fast, then breaking into a run, Ulina rushed to greet the visitor. Just as she got within arms' reach, she noticed something that made her halt with a slide in the still warm sand of the walkway. This person smelled like her brother. It was definitely a man, and he had that same sourness odor that made her stomach churn and had caused her to be out on the steps in the first place.

She thought she recognized something about the man. He worked a couple houses away at the home of one of the Pharaoh's magicians!

"Acolyte Kherfin?"

Without warning, hands lunged forward, grabbing her shoulders and jerking her off her feet. She thought to scream, but before any sound left her mouth, something clamped down on her tiny throat. White-hot pain seized her, and in a total state of shock, her body coped with the fright and sudden pain the only way it knew how...she fainted.

The warmth filled him. Tearing into his prize, Kherfin immersed himself in the heat that rose like a fountain, pouring forth from the figure in his clutches, and seeping into his coldest places.

For just a moment, the warmth sent a flicker in a part of the mind that had been the living Kherfin. In the horror, during this brief flash of conscientiousness, he dropped the body. Then, just as quickly, the coldness returned in a rush, tightening its grip. The tiny spark was gone forever.

He looked down at the body sprawled near his feet. Much of the warmth he craved was gone, but deep inside he could sense something pulsing faintly. Each pulsation sent a ripple of that much desired heat throughout the tiny figure.

Once again, Kherfin tore into the unmoving form. Finally, he found the prize he sought. Burying his face in the waning warmth remaining, he fed until the coldness completely suffused the body.

A moment later, he stumbled down the narrow street in search of new warmth. There was another source nearby, and Kherfin was once again so very, very cold.

Neraphatte burst through the wide open doorway and raced to the room he first performed the ceremony on the cold, dead body of his assistant.

Empty! No sign of Kherfin anywhere. Fearing it was useless, he still dashed from room to room. Equally useless. He stepped out onto the balcony. "Kherfin!" he cried out to a strangely quiet city.

The warm night breeze wrapped around him. The stench of death was growing stronger. Looking out into the darkness, past the city, he thought he could spy a faint glow on the horizon. Not the sort you would expect from a large encampment. Instead, this glow seemed to reach up to the heavens. On any other night he would think to investigate…but not now. Now he must find Kherfin.

Side-by-side, but oblivious to one another, Queen Meraseti and her son Prince Haru-Tanis moved haltingly along the smoothly polished stone floor. The wide passage allowed them to be several feet apart. Yet, they felt drawn close to one another even though neither had any idea why.

Through a gauzy curtain, warmth awaited. A large, open sleeping area for the servants who tended to Prince Haru-Tanis directly sat at the end of this long corridor. A few lanterns burned along the way, casting a soft glow over everything.

## DEAD HISTORY

Together they stumbled into the curtains; neither slowing nor bothering to push them aside with their hands. Queen and Prince staggered into the circular room. Some of the servants awoke, looking up from their beds at the two dark shadows standing outlined in the entryway.

Moments later, there was screaming. Trained since birth to endure whatever royal punishment was given, all thirty-two of the servants died at the hands and mouths of their master and his mother.

Making unsteady progress down the stairs, the gore-soaked girl paused on the path that led to the street. Stepping out onto the small landing from the darkness of the house to join her were a man and a woman. Dressed in black gowns of mourning, it was impossible to see the bloody holes torn in them in the darkness of the night.

The woman moved first to join her daughter. The husband tried to follow, but toppled from the small rise and landed with a splatter. Slowly climbing to his feet, he set off down the path after the other two figures. A long, ropy strand uncoiled from his stomach to lie on the ground like a nest of serpents. He continued to walk away oblivious, only pausing slightly as something tugged just for a moment before tearing away.

Animals of all sorts crawled from the shadows to investigate. None of them fed on the vile strand. Not even the rats.

Neraphatte reached the palace for the second time that night. He heard screams of anguish and fear as he climbed the many stairs leading to the Grand Entry.

He had searched frantically, but found no sign of Kherfin near the house. He could be any place in the city by now. He must see to the prince.

The main door remained ajar, just as he had left it when he had run from the Queen and her son. The child had been like an animal, tearing into the flesh of his mother. So much blood. He must have done something wrong.

# DEAD HISTORY

He stood in the middle of the hall, thinking. This had been where Pharaoh had given his edict. Well...he had obeyed. Hadn't he? The son of Pharaoh was...alive?

Now that was the predicament. Neraphatte had not stayed once the boy tore into his mother's throat. Perhaps it had been some instinctive reaction, like how the body shudders when exposed to cold air after being submerged into a tub of hot water.

He must find the boy. That was all he could do. Of course, the screams he heard as he approached the palace cast doubts. Deep down, the feeling he was only fooling himself did a poor job of hiding.

His gaze paused on the nine stakes with the impaled heads of his fellow court magicians. Each face seemed caught in between an expression of pain and peace.

Perhaps death was not such a terrible thing.


The trio had grown. All down the street, there were more stumbling out of doorways. Somewhere, there would be warmth. They could sense it as they passed darkened houses. Each time they would enter in search of it. Yet, when they left, they were once again unsatisfied and cold. Each instance they found the opportunity to bathe in that warmth, the satisfaction from it was more brief.

In ones...twos...packs...they converged on random houses. There seemed no reason or pattern as the blood-soaked horde added to the woes of an already demoralized Egypt. Numb from the previous night's terror, people ignored the screams and wails of their neighbors until it was too late. Those that did answer did so alone and fell easy prey.


Kherfin turned. Nothing of his former self remained. Yet, he was driven to seek out that one source. It called to him. With no control of his actions, he walked on. It was closer now. He did not understand the flickering signals in the small part in his brain still remaining. He simply allowed them to lead him.

# DEAD HISTORY

As the sun began to crest the distant hills of sand, he arrived. His feet stopped, and for just a moment, Kherfin stood unmoving. The head turned first, then the body followed. Step by grueling step he climbed. The coldness in his body seemed to reach out for that warmth.

Behind him, the streets were dotted with more just like him. Some walked, some crawled having lost one, both, or parts of their legs. A low moan had begun. First it was like a buzz heard when a swarm of locusts would arrive. Many of the living who remained were hiding in their houses fearing, perhaps, their return. Any who saw the true source of the horrible noise cowered in terror.

As the moaning had grown, so too, did their numbers swell, as the dead converged on the living.

Many began to pray; some even to the mysterious God of Moses.


Neraphatte opened his eyes. He found the pale and drawn face of Queen Meraseti only inches from him. The stench of death poured from her, filling his nostrils with a smell so thick it was as if he were breathing through sand.

The gaping hole in her throat still oozed dark fluid gurgled slightly as she opened her mouth. A cold hand brushed his face and many others clutched at his clothing, but none of them did anything more. They all stood...waiting.

He had run down empty palace corridors in search of the Pharaoh's wife and son. When he found them, it was as if his mind refused to accept what it saw.

Neraphatte fainted.

When he awoke, and that alone had been a surprise after the bloody carnage he had walked into, he found a sea of legs on all sides. Looking up, he saw the queen, the prince, and several of the royal servants. Each was torn, mutilated and covered with blood and gore. There were smells worse than death.

Yet, he was whole.

He climbed slowly to his feet, knowing that at any moment they would fall on him and tear him open in the manner done to them.

His heart thundered as all who surrounded him turned almost in unison toward him.

At first, none of them moved.

Neraphatte held his breath. Partially to avoid breathing in what could only be the most pure essence of what was death. But also, because he was so frightened that he momentarily forgot how. Finally, he gasped and sucked in a lungful of sour air. This made him gag. A shuffling sound of several feet moving caused him to close his eyes in preparation for the violent death sure to come.

Nothing.

So he had opened his eyes. They crowded in, but none attacked. There were no teeth ripping into his flesh, no hands tearing him open to feast on his innards as had clearly happened to some who stood close by.

Blood, sticky and cool, smeared his face, arms, and robe as more and more they seemed to push at one another in an effort to be close to him…to touch him. For several moments, Neraphatte stood in the center of the room. Finally, he had to move. Either they would fall on him and kill him or they would not. No matter what, he could no longer stand still.

He waded through the bodies. Their hands continued to reach out and grasp, but then, as he continued to walk, they let go.

They began to follow him.


Kherfin reached the top stair. Below him, a hundred or more just like him were climbing up. As a whole, they could sense that what they sought was very near. Their moans seemed to grow louder. Throughout the city, the smell of fear began to mask the stench of death.


Neraphatte glanced at the severed heads of those he had once called brothers. Only he remained of the Pharaoh's magicians. He had done what each of them had failed to do.

He, Neraphatte, had overcome the final and most devastating plague of the God of Moses. The Pharaoh would have no choice but to acknowledge his power. Perhaps he would be granted his own temple, or even better, a city.

He reached the large double doors that led out of the palace. Behind him, the queen, the prince, and all those servants, still followed. Pulling the doors open, the golden light of the sun flooded in. Light and warmth rushed to meet his face.

And Kherfin.

Standing before him was his favorite assistant.

Blank eyes stared out of a face empty of any sort of recognition. For a moment, Neraphatte once again feared for his life as cold hands reached out and grasped his arms. Looking past Kherfin, he saw hundreds more on the stairs and in the main street leading to the palace.

A low moan grew for just a moment, then faded in a sigh from the throng seeking him. Neraphatte smiled. Yes, the Pharaoh would indeed be grateful.

Or else.


The dust cloud grew nearer. It seemed very small if it were indeed Pharaoh and his army. Neraphatte stood at the gates the Pharaoh would enter, now victorious after destroying the rebel Moses and his Hebrews.

Finally, the individual chariots could be made out. Something was very peculiar indeed. There were so few. Perhaps things had not gone as smoothly as expected. Perhaps this Moses and his God had more tricks at the ready.

Oh, well, at least he, Neraphatte, royal magician, had succeeded. At his side, the small figure seemed to grow restless. The prince began to pull away. As the Pharaoh's chariots drew to a halt in a cloud of dust, Neraphatte let go his hold on the young prince's shoulders.

Over the din of the pounding on the gates at his back, Neraphatte announced, "I present your son, my Pharaoh!"

# KRAMER'S FOLLY

## ANTHONY GIANGREGORIO

Kramer slapped the bugs away from his face as he made his way through the dense underbrush of the African coast and back to his hired ship. Sweat beaded on his skin, making his entire body feel like a slick eel. His thighs chaffed and he had more bug bites on his skin than he could count.

For the hundredth time since setting sail from Charleston, he was regretting his decision to come to Africa.

But then he thought about the money he was saving by finding and capturing his own slaves and his pains went away.

The slave trade was one of many mouths, all wanting to be fed. By the time a slave was captured in Africa and transported back home, it had exchanged so many hands that the price was quadrupled, if not worse.

So Kramer, being the thrifty soul he was, had decided to hire a ship and set sail for Africa himself, planning on taking his own slaves to bring back to Charleston to work on his cotton plantation. And he knew in the economy of 1854, every penny saved was a penny earned.

And though he was miserable beyond miserable, his plan had worked flawlessly.

Behind him, led by two Spaniards helpers, he led an even score of slaves, each manacled to the last so that if one tried to escape, the other nineteen would stop the escapee fast.

Kramer had swooped into their village just before sunrise, and after killing five of the village men who tried to attack and stop him, the rest had fallen in line, fearing for their lives. There had been so many before they had escaped into the surrounding forest and it killed him to let them go, but he had filled his quota nicely.

Kramer smiled as he eyed the ten dark men and ten women, admiring the exposed breasts of the women. Well, all except one that is. Nine of the women were young and healthy, but the Spaniard hadn't followed his orders to the letter and had taken an old woman for the tenth. She was weak and could barely keep up the pace he set.

As Kramer turned to look at the old crone, she fell yet again, her fellow slaves picking her up again.

Kramer motioned to one of the Spaniards as he gestured to the old, woman.

"Why in blazes did you pick her, José, she can barely walk as it is. She'll never make it back to the ship."

José nodded respectfully and moved closer to Kramer.

"I am sorry, señor Kramer. When I took the other women the old woman insisted on coming, too." His accent was heavy but Kramer could understand him. The other Spaniard didn't speak a lick of English, but that was fine as long as one of his helpers could.

"Are you serious? That is madness. When they see slavers coming, the black bastards run for the hills, they don't demand to be thrown into irons."

"Si, si, señor, but she did. I had no choice. It was either that or kill her."

"Hmmph, should have killed the old maid." He pulled his revolver and prepared to do just that when the Spaniard stepped in front of him.

"No, wait, señor. I know a little of the language and the old woman is holy to them. If you kill her the others will be trouble."

"So what? I will just kill one or two to keep the rest in line."

"Si, si, but won't that cut into your profit, señor. *Our* profit?"

Kramer halted then, realizing the Spaniard was correct. He had promised to pay a cut of the sales of the slaves to José in payment, and if he went ahead and began killing them, then his gross earnings would suffer. That would be foolish. No, he would only kill a slave if he had no choice.

"Very well, José, I have to agree with you. But the old woman better not slow us down. We need to get to the ship by nightfall so we can sail out with the morning tide."

"Si, si, we will, señor." He turned and barked a few words in the native tongue of the slaves and they seemed to stand taller, though the hatred in their eyes never waned. The old woman was helped to her feet and they set off again, all the while Kramer thinking of the money he would make once he returned to Charleston. For he only

# DEAD HISTORY

needed fifteen slaves to work his plantation, the rest he would sell on the open market. Those would pay for the entire trip, leaving him with what basically came down to slaves taken for nothing, and a profit to boot. He only wished he could have taken more than twenty, but they were enough of a handful with only himself and his two helpers to keep in line. As he trudged through the underbrush, he was already making plans to return with a larger crew next month. And then he would take back triple the number!

Why, it was like minting coins himself, this doing it yourself. Cut out the middle man. He was just glad more people didn't think of it.

Less than a mile from where the ship was moored, the old woman faltered once more, stopping the other slaves in their tracks. As Kramer turned to investigate, the slaves surrounded the old woman, wanting to protect her.

Kramer shoved the barrel of his pistol under a tall, male black's chin, his eyes cold as he stared at the slave.

"Best you move out of my way, blackie, or I'll make an example out of ya."

José moved to Kramer's side, touching his shoulder slightly. "No, señor, wait, please. Let me see if I can get them moving again."

"Fair enough, but my temper wanes with the night," he told his helper as he lowered the pistol. José called to the other Spaniard in his native language and the two moved into the crowd of slaves. Kramer stood a few feet away, wary of any of the slaves trying anything. Kramer knew it would be foolhardy on their account to try, but he had heard stories from other traders when at the market for purchasing new help.

They told tales of how faced with a life of servitude under the white man, slaves were known to do desperate acts, even if it meant losing their lives.

Kramer could hear José talking to some of the slaves, the banter going back and forth for almost two minutes before he called José to him.

"Well?" Kramer demanded.

José shook his head sadly. "The old woman, she is dead, señor. The slaves want to bury her, at least that way she will be one with Mother Earth."

"Out of the question. There is no time and even if there was I won't waste time on a slave, especially a dead one. No, unshackle the corpse and toss it into the brush. The scavengers will have a feast this night."

"I don't think they will like that, señor Kramer," José said as he looked at his feet.

"I don't give a damn what they like! They are my property now and they will do as told or I will see them suffer! And that goes for the people that work for me. Do I make myself clear?"

"Si, si, señor, perfectly," José said as he turned to his fellow helper and they began unshackling the corpse of the old woman. No sooner did they begin then three of the slaves tried to stop the two Spaniards, pushing them away from the corpse.

José punched one away and the slave struck back. It was possible an uprising may have taken place right then and there if not for Kramer firing a shot into the air. Birds in nearby trees took flight and the night went silent as the report echoed throughout the forest.

"Enough! The next black bastard that so much as looks at one of my men cross-eyed will get a bullet in the head!"

He could see the slaves didn't understand him, but they understood the pistol in his hand. They knew it could kill without Kramer so much as blinking his eyes.

The slaves fell back, their desire to live overriding even their protection of the old woman.

Kramer pointed to the corpse. "All right, José, dispose of that now so we can keep moving."

José motioned to the other Spaniard and the two men quickly unlocked the manacles on the corpse. Once finished, they gathered the withered dark body and walked to the side of the beaten path, then carelessly tossed it into the shrubs. When the body landed roughly, it became impaled on a fallen tree, the broken branches like spears. The neck cracked and the head was nearly turned around, the eyes open and staring at the ground in death.

# DEAD HISTORY

As one, the slaves howled in loss and grief of their holy mother and José and the other helper moved closer to Kramer, fearing the slaves as they moaned and wailed.

As Kramer watched, they began to chant, a steady rhythm that conjured up the depths of the African continent. It was as if jungle drums could be heard, steadily pounding to the rhythm of a beating heart.

"What are they doing?" Kramer asked José as he began to sweat nervously.

"They are mourning their lost mother, señor. And..."

"And what?" Kramer demanded. "Out with it, what are they saying?"

"They are singing 'Death to Kramer, Death to Kramer'."

Kramer's eyes went cold and José nodded as he studied his worn shoes once more. "I am sorry, señor, but that is what they are saying."

Kramer listened for another few seconds, glaring at the dark sweating bodies, at the nineteen slaves he had left, and then he shrugged. "No matter, they can sing for my death all they want. As long as they march I am a happy man. Now, José, get them moving, we have a timetable to keep."

"Si, señor," José said and he moved to the rear of the slaves. He had a whip for times such as these and he used it now, whipping the closest bodies. The song went up in pitch as the slaves cried out in pain, but eventually they began to walk once more.

Kramer walked along side them, listening to the chanting the entire time.

*Let them sing! Let them sing all the way back to Charleston, for all the good it would do them*, he thought as he began to count his money in his head.


With dawn only hours away, Kramer finally led the slaves to his waiting ship.

Far from any coastal town, the ship was anchored just off the shore. After piling the slaves into the boat and making them row, Kramer soon found himself on the sturdy deck of the ship, the slaver-captain, McBride, standing next to him as he supervised the storing of the slaves in the ship's hold.

"We're ready to leave as soon as the tide rolls in, sir," McBride told Kramer. "And there is plenty of room in the hold for that lot you brought. A fine looking group, too, if I may say so, sir. I'll have my men take off those irons once they're situated."

"No, Captain, do nothing of the kind. Leave those manacles where they are," Kramer ordered.

"But, sir, slaves don't do well in shackles. They won't eat and they get sick, dampens their spirits, you see. Some may even die on the trip back to Charleston."

Kramer turned to stare the captain in the eye.

"I pay you for your expertise as a captain, my good sir, I thank you not to give me advice on how to treat my property."

"Aye, 'tis true, and I shall honor your wishes, sir." The captain cocked his head as if listening. "Sir, do you know what they are saying down there? They seem to be chanting it over and over."

Kramer waved it off. "Ignore it, Captain. One of their number, an old crone, died in the trek back to the ship. They are mourning her."

The captain nodded but then he cocked his head again. "But, sir, it sounds like they are saying your name as well. Is that true?"

Kramer knew it was but was not in the mood for idle chatter.

"Whether it is or not is none of your concern, Captain. Please make your ship ready to sail. It's a long journey back home and I wish to take my leave of this ghastly continent."

"Aye, sir, I'll do just that." The captain turned and began hollering orders as his crew began to work. Kramer eyed the removable floorboards that led to the hold, now replaced and refastened. He could hear the chanting easily through the decking, and though he refused to admit it, it made him shudder.


The following day, a few hours before nightfall, a white sail was spotted on the horizon.

Captain McBride stood at the aft deck with a telescope as he studied the distant ship. Still on the horizon, the ship would disappear with each wave it crested, only to reappear. But it was easy to see the ship was making good time in their direction.

"Dammit," McBride cursed, "'tis a British ship of war, sir. And she's seen us."

"So?" Kramer spit.

"No, sir, you do not understand. The British have sworn to stamp out slavery. If they catch us with what is in the hold, they'll scuttle the ship and take us all into irons. It will be over for us one and all."

"Then I suggest we lose them, Captain," Kramer said as he eyed the bouncing dot on the horizon.

McBride nodded and began yelling once more. His crew went into action, raising the sails and trying to squeeze as much speed out of the northerly wind. Kramer watched the activity with a nod, then paused as he heard the chanting once more. The black bastards were still at it, it seemed. Well, they could sing till they were hoarse, for all the good it would serve.

Captain McBride's crew did their best to coax more speed from the wind but in time, as night was about to fall, the British ship was much closer.

McBride stood at the aft deck once more, and when he lowered his telescope, he shook his head.

"It's no use, sir," he said to Kramer. "They'll be on us soon." He pointed to a flash of light on the British ship. "See that? That is the signal to lay to and wait for them to board us." He shook his head. "It's over. We'll spend the rest of our lives in the Queen's jail."

"No we won't, sir!" Kramer yelled. "Keep going, just till nightfall."

"But sir, they will catch us. They are sailing four feet for our every two. We have no chance of escape."

"Nay, good Captain, escape isn't my plan; just keep us out of their reach before nightfall and I promise you we will be safe."

Desperate and with little option, Captain McBride nodded. "Aye, sir, that I can do, but not by much." Then he went back to making his crew work harder. Kramer called José to him who was always within earshot.

"Si, señor?"

"José, get the slaves ready and have them on deck when I give the word."

"Señor?" José asked, not understanding.

"Just do it, José, no backtalk. Unless you would like to spend the rest of your life hanging in a cell in London?"

"No, señor, no I would not. It shall be done."

Captain McBride was true to his word and he managed to keep the British ship in their wake, and as night fell and the British ship wasn't able to discern what was happening on the deck of the slaver ship, Kramer called José to him.

"It's time. Get the slaves on deck, and hurry man, there is no time to waste!"

"Si, si," José said as he had his fellow Spaniard and a few of the ship's crew to help him.

In five minutes time, all nineteen slaves were on deck, each glaring hatefully at Kramer. None looked broken, each still holding the spirit of free men in their hearts.

Kramer chuckled as he walked to the first slave in line and picked up the hanging manacle from which the old woman had been affixed.

The slaves were amidships and only a few feet away was the ship's anchor. With a malevolent look on his face, his eyes gleaming in the wan light as dusk fell across the ocean, he clamped the open manacle to the chain of the anchor.

As he worked, the chanting began once more, Kramer now recognizing his name in the rhythm.

"Keep going, you black bastards, you won't be singing much longer. There is more of you in Africa, and when I return, I will recoup my losses from this voyage and still come out ahead." He stood up from the chain with a wide grin on his face. "Here, have a drink on me!" Without waiting for a reply, he kicked the anchor off the opening on the deck rail and watched it splash into the murky water. The coiled chain began to play out and at first no one understood what was happening. That is until the chain went taut and the first slave in line was tugged off his feet to slide across the decking, following the same path as the anchor.

As the slave began to slide, the rest of the chained slaves were pulled as well, a tug of war they could not possibly win.

One at a time, they were pulled from their feet, to slide across the decking, screaming and scrabbling for purchase. Fingernails broke and bloody trails were streaked across the decking as wails of torment and doom filled the night. One after another, the manacled slaves were pulled into the ocean depths, each one into the water adding to the weight so that the rest could never so much as attempt to halt their progress. By the time the last of the nineteen were sliding down the deck, the look in their eyes was absolutely chilling. The dread and fear was palpable, as each man in the ship's crew stood in utter shock at what Kramer had wrought, at the merciless murder of nineteen souls—no matter what color their skin.

As the last one went screaming into the ocean, Kramer turned, and his grin faltered when he saw the faces of the crew. "What! Stop looking at me like that. I did what had to be done. If they were found on this ship, we'd all be in irons with them? I saved you all. I'm a goddamn hero!" He pointed at McBride. "You told me the British would show no mercy. I saved your ship, Captain."

"Aye, sir, I guess you did, but at what price to our very souls?"

"Bah, rubbish, all of it. They were nothing but slaves. Now stay out of the British's reach until daybreak so they don't know anything is afoot."

Captain McBride nodded and did as he was ordered, staying just out of reach of the British warship.

As the dawn touched the horizon, the chase was over and the British ship fired a warning shot across the slaver's bow, and they were hailed and ordered to drop sails and be boarded.

McBride did as ordered and minutes later a small boat with four solders and an officer pulled away from the British ship and crossed the small distance between the two vessels.

Boarding, the British officer signaled the four soldiers to lower weapons as the man studied the deck of the ship and the crew men on display.

"We are here to search this vessel. Do you deny me permission?" the officer asked, though everyone knew the result if the answer was no.

McBride, standing next to Kramer, nodded respectfully. "My ship is your ship, go where you please, sir."

# DEAD HISTORY

The Englishman grunted and sent his soldiers to begin their search. He didn't need protection, for the British ship of war had its cannons trained on the slaver. One act of defiance and the slaver would be sent to the ocean floor.

Time passed and eventually the soldiers returned. One stepped up to the Englishman and whispered into his ear. When the report was made, the man looked at both McBride and Kramer. "It appears no slaves were found but the odor of men packed in your hold like cattle still exists."

Kramer weaved the accusation away as if he were at a tea party. "Nonsense, there are no slaves here. If there were, where are they now, my good sir? I think you should watch yourself before accusing good citizens of wrong doing."

McBride said nothing, though he was sweating profusely.

"Indeed," the Englishman said, scowling. "But we both know they were here, murderer, and where they went, and if I could prove it without a doubt what you have done, I would see you join me back in England to spend the rest of your natural life in a jail cell."

"Ah yes, sir, but you can't, because there were never any slaves on this ship. In fact, my good sir, I believe you should apologize and take your leave of us. We are on a tight schedule and don't have the time to lay about all morning in the middle of the ocean."

The officer pointed to where the ship's anchor should have been. "And how do you explain that? All ships have an anchor. Why is yours missing?" His tone of voice told Kramer he knew exactly where the missing anchor was and what it had been used for.

"It was..." Captain McBride interjected but Kramer cut him off.

"A simple mishap, sir, that is all. It will be replaced at the next port we moor at," Kramer grinned.

The Englishman looked dejected at having no case. "We will meet again, sir, I promise you that. And next time it is I who will be the victor. Your type of butchery *will* be punished. If not by me then by some other."

"That sounds like a threat, sir, I think you have overstayed your welcome. I now say good day to you," Kramer said indignantly.

# DEAD HISTORY

The officer and his men disembarked the ship and sailed back to the waiting British ship of war.

Kramer, looking smug, patted the captain on the shoulder. "Ah, well, Captain. Profit and Loss, profit and loss. Take me home, sir, I have had enough adventure for a while."

As the British ship veered off and headed south, Captain McBride got his ship underway.

Two weeks and a day later found Kramer at his home. His plantation was only a mile from the sea and on this night he found himself tossing and turning in his bed.

As he lay sleeping, he began to hear a familiar chanting. At first he remained asleep, lost in the nightmare, but something caused him to snap awake.

Looking around his bedroom, at first he thought himself back on the slave ship, after leaving Africa. And then he realized why.

The chanting.

It was the same one the slaves had voiced and had continued to voice after he had disposed of the old woman's corpse.

Sitting up in bed, he looked left and right, as if he expected to see the slaves in his bedroom, but though the chanting continued, there was no one in the room with him.

Sliding his feet into his slippers, he stood up and went to the window overlooking the northern side of his property. Over the trees, a mile away, he could just see the glint of the moon off the ocean and the footpath at the edge of his property that would take him there.

The chanting seemed louder now, as if it was coming directly from below his window. Opening it, he looked out into the darkness, but there was no one to be found.

Thinking it was some sort of trick, some prank by someone from the ship—a crew member perhaps who hadn't been able to live with what Kramer had done, he went to his mantle and opened the top drawer. Here he took out two pistols.

They were well crafted, with polished grips and hair triggers. He had practiced many a day in the fields behind his home and could shoot the wings off a fly at twenty paces. Many a man had also suffered the guns first hand when he was challenged to a duel. Five so far and he had not so much as suffered a scratch, while the men he'd gone up against were now six feet under the cold earth.

With dexterity made from constant practice, he poured in glazed powder from a small container, dropped in two leaded balls, then set percussion caps on the touchholes.

Now armed and feeling more confident, he turned up the light of the lantern on his bedside table and slowly crept down the steps leading from the second to the first floor of his home.

Passing the doors to the servants' quarters, he paused for a moment, wondering if one of them could be the originator of this ruse, but then decided it was impossible. No servant would dare play a prank on him, not if they didn't want to suffer twenty lashes in the courtyard when he found out.

No, it must be from an outside source.

Reaching the front door, he slowly opened it, feeling the coolness of the night touch his exposed flesh. In nothing but his nightclothes, he felt exposed and regretted not dressing before coming down. He considered returning to do just that when the chanting began anew, pulling him from his musings and deeper into the night.

The moonlight waxed down on the land and he turned off the lantern and set it on the footpath, thus freeing his other hand to carry a pistol more easily. With both hands now firmly holding a weapon, he thrust his chest out and prepared to send some fool or fools to their doom.

He wasn't worried about killing whoever it might be. They were trespassing on his land and so he had the right to use lethal force if necessary. And that was what he planned to do when he found the blasted fools.

Following the path leading from the house deeper into the forest, the chanting seemed to always float just out of reach. If he had time to consider his actions, he would have realized how foolhardy it was to enter the forest alone, but he was angry, and his emotions had ruled him since he was old enough to walk.

He made his way down the winding path until finally coming out onto a small beach leading to the ocean. Looking back, he hadn't realized he had come so far and now it seemed as if he had been in a daze the entire time. It reminded him of the story of the sirens, who called men to their deaths by making them crash their sailing vessels on the rocks before them.

Shaking himself to free his mind from whatever spell he'd fallen under, he was about to turn and return home, feeling quite silly for his midnight walk for no apparent reason, when he paused as he stared out onto the dark water.

Slowly, as if the figure was still walking underwater, a head appeared, breaking the surface of the water.

From where he stood, Kramer couldn't make out the features of the figure, but he gripped his pistols tighter as he watched in fascination. There was no thought to turn and run, no idea of perhaps leaving as fast as his legs would carry him. It was as if he was rooted to the spot.

With treacle-like slowness, another head broke the surface behind it, followed by another and another. In all, nineteen heads appeared, soon followed by their bloated, pale bodies.

In the darkness, the figures were all but invisible, only their outlines silhouetted by the wan moonlight of the crescent moon hovering in the sky, ignorant of what was occurring on the beach.

Kramer, still planted to the earth, could only watch in horror as the figures slowly took shape, and when the first one was close enough to see clearly, he realized who—or what—these figures were.

Snapping from his fugue state, he raised his revolvers and shot the first figure in the face. But if he expected the figure to go down, he was sorely mistaken.

A clear hole appeared in the forehead of the creature, and the head snapped back from the force of the lead ball, but other than that there was no sign of distress.

Slowly, the head righted itself and the figure continued to stumble forward.

By now the last figure had left the water, and Kramer saw each one was attached to the other by manacles. Together, all nineteen shambled up the beach, moving directly toward Kramer.

Filled with a terror he never knew could exist, he fired again at the next figure in line. His bullet struck directly over the figure's heart and a small hole was made in the torso, a larger one out the

# DEAD HISTORY

back by the force of the round as it continued onward to strike yet another figure.

The figure took a step back and seemed to rock on its feet from being shot. But the one behind it pushed it forward and it didn't fall down. Kramer could now see the moonlight filtering through the hole he'd made in its body, the heart still inside the ribcage, only now it was still.

When the first figure was close enough for him to touch, Kramer let out a loud gasp, still unable to believe his eyes.

The slave was a rotting, diseased-filled corpse, the body now pale as the white sand at its feet, the body bloated with sea water to the point of bursting. Pieces of the face were now missing, as if fish and other sea life had been picking at it as the corpse made its way across the ocean floor.

And Kramer realized that was what must have happened. These slaves, the ones he'd sent to a watery grave, had walked across the ocean floor for two weeks straight until finally coming out here on the shore of Charleston.

The chanting was louder now, and Kramer could hear his name in the voices, the voices now warped by disuse and decay. One of the figures stepped forward and its arm fell off, the flesh and sinew rotted to the point it could no longer remain attached. Another opened its mouth and a small crab crawled out with the corpse's tongue in its claws. It dropped to the sand and scuttled away.

Some had no eyes, the orbs, once tender and juicy, eaten by sea life more than a week ago. But they were chained to their undead brethren and so did not need to see, led like dogs on a leash.

Kramer shot twice more, each bullet scoring a hit, but the undead slaves ignored their wounds.

"No, this cannot be! You're dead! Dead!"

But the slaves didn't reply, only shambled forward with their irons clanking amongst them, the chanting never ceasing.

"*Kill Kramer, Kill Kramer,*" they sang in their native tongue.

Kramer finally snapped out of it and turned to run, but as he took his first step, his right foot became tangled in his nightclothes and he tumbled to the beach. Spitting sand, he rolled over to see the slaves bearing down on him.

# DEAD HISTORY

He threw his right pistol at the closest face glaring at him. The barrel of the weapon struck the slave's cheek, leaving a long tear in the flesh. As the skin opened, no blood seeped out, the blood long dried and congealed.

He threw his other pistol at a figure but it merely went wide, falling to the sand where it was crushed under the decayed feet of more undead slaves.

Crying out in terror, he closed his eyes and prepared to be torn apart, but after a full ten seconds and still no pain, he opened them to see the slaves surrounding him.

"What do you want? Revenge? Then go ahead and kill me. I did what I had to do and I would do it again, by God."

They said nothing, even the chanting halted. Only the sounds of the waves crashing on the rocks now filling the void of the night.

And then the last slave walked through the crowd, and Kramer saw what he was holding in his hands.

It was the empty manacles of where Kramer had attached the slaves to the chain connected to the anchor. The same manacles the old woman had worn before she had died.

He let out a scream then, understanding what they intended, and as cold hands grabbed and held him still, the slave with the manacles locked them to Kramer's wrists and ankles, then stood back.

Kramer stopped screaming, sobbing silently as he looked up at the dead faces of the men and women he'd killed mercilessly. His chest heaved with anxiety and his vision was filled with spots as adrenalin suffused his body.

And then the salves turned and began walking back to the sea.

Kramer heaved a sigh, believing he was safe.

One by one they turned and shambled back into the surf, bits and pieces of their rotting bodies left behind in the sand.

Kramer lay there, perfectly still, wondering if it was all a dream when the last slave turned and began to walk away. This slave, the last in line, was connected to Kramer.

He was yanked hard, and before he realized what was happening, Kramer began to be dragged across the sand.

"No, no! You can't do this to me! I'm your master, you hear me, I'm your master!"

But the slaves never slowed, as each one shambled into the water and back out to the waiting sea. Kramer dug his hands into the sand to halt his progress, but nothing could slow his descent to the ocean. No matter how hard he tried, it was like an anchor was on the other end, slowly pulling him into the cold, cold water. Nineteen water-logged bodies were more than a match for one man, and as Kramer screamed for help, his vocal cords soon raw, he was sucked into the water. Still he screamed, his hands flailing, his legs kicking, and as ice cold water filled his mouth, he screamed some more.

As his lungs were filled to bursting, he waited for death to claim him but for some reason he wouldn't die.

As the muddy ocean floor stirred up around him, he realized he was deep underwater, and though he should be dead, he quickly found out being alive was no blessing.

As the undead slaves continued their journey back into the murky ocean depths, Kramer realized he was spared death for only one reason, so he could suffer for all eternity with the same cursed souls he had sent to their watery graves. For now, he was one of them, a slave.

And they were all slaves of Death itself.

# SAMURAI ZOMBIE KILLER

## DAVID BERNSTEIN

Kenji Matsuko sat at his master's bedside. The old man was ill, dying of cancer. Word had been sent to Emperor Gashi. With great regret, he informed his most trusted warrior that his master was not long for the world. Kenji was given permission to leave, to go to his master and pay his last respects, honoring his teacher.

"Kenji, my finest student," Ari said. "You have come." His master lay in a red-silken robe, wrapped in covers up to his chest. His skin was pale, chalk-like, his eye sockets sunken.

"Yes," Kenji said, bowing, dressed in a cloud-embroidered white robe, his Samurai armor back in the room he rented at the Han-ho Inn.

"I'm glad you came. I would not have taken you from your sworn duties, for the Emperor needs you, but a great dishonor will befall the village.

Kenji's eyebrows arched, trying his best to show no emotion. He was already rattled to his core at seeing his master so weak and fragile. Ari had never so much as had a cold in all his years, his chi incredible.

"Master?"

"Your brother, Makito, is dabbling in the dark ways. He will bring dishonor to you, me, and the village." Ari reached out with a withered hand, gripping Kenji's wrist. "You must stop him and his quest for madness."

Kenji got down on one knee, placing his head on the old man's hand. "Forgive me, Master, but how do you know this?"

"He came to me last month, a look of ill-will in his eyes. He talked about bringing down the hierarchy, the Emperor. He is wise in the ways of death, and teachings, I'm afraid. I always had high hopes for him, but I was wrong." Master Ari closed his eyes in shame.

"I shall honor your wishes, Master. It will be done. I will not allow dishonor to befall us."

# DEAD HISTORY

"Go, see to your brother. I will not die this evening."

Kenji stood. "Heit," he said, bowing before his departure. Once he was clear of the room, he broke into sobs. He was a strong, noble warrior who had fought on the harshest battlefields, killing many men. But a true Samurai lives through his heart and denies not his emotions. As graceful and deadly as he is with a sword, he is equally as refined with the arts. All Samurai study drawing and poetry. There was no shame in feeling sadness for his master. Clearing his tears and composing himself, he left for his brother's cottage.

Kenji loved the countryside, with its beautiful landscape and wild life. Allowed to flourish, the bamboo grew tall around the village. Beautiful Sakura and cherry blossoms sprouted around the village. He passed the local koi pond; a man and his son were fishing. The local river, with its lucidness, bubbling with white froth, poured over jutting rocks, and flowed down the mountainside supplying the village with fresh water.

The trail to Makito's house was long, and a steep climb in areas, dotted with lilac, bamboo, and oak trees. Looking ahead, to the top of the mountain where the ground flattened out, he saw a man approaching. The person appeared as if he was drunk.

As Kenji neared the stranger, he saw his skin was pale and riddled with sores. Upon seeing Kenji, the man hurried his hobbled walk and began moaning. Kenji, sensing something was off, placed his hand on the hilt of his sword. He stood stationary, assessing the situation with his heightened perception.

A breeze blew inward, and as the man drew closer, an odor of rot and decay assaulted the Samurai's nostrils. Wanting to cringe in disgust, Kenji remained still. He saw the man's eyes. They were lifeless–dead. This thing that approached him was an abomination, this he was sure of. As the thing came within striking distance, Kenji drew his weapon, the blade hungry for a kill. He sliced diagonally across the man's chest, before sinking the blade into the sternum, piercing the heart. He withdrew the blade, wiping the weapon clean before placing it back in its sheath.

The man stopped for a moment before moaning loudly and reaching out for Kenji. With its eyes wide and mouth agape, Kenji drew his weapon and sliced off the man's arms. They fell to the ground, but the man didn't flinch. He showed no care, and kept coming. Kenji, shaken, backed away with his sword out in front. What kind of demon was this?

Kenji gritted his teeth, found the strength deep within his gut, took a step forward and sliced at the thing's neck, severing the head from the body. As the head tumbled to the ground, the body followed. Both pieces lay unmoving, dead. Kenji wiped the blade, returning it to its resting place.

Kenji examined the body. It was no man, its blood not fluid, but pasty and long dead. He didn't want to think about it, but he knew his brother must have had something to do with this. With his cheeks defining themselves in anger, he headed onward to his brother's house.

The cottage was nestled in a nook of thick bamboo. It was aged and weather beaten. The front porch clanged with moon-shaped wind chimes hanging from the thatched overhang. Statues of Fu-Dogs sat on either side of the entranceway. Smoke bellowed from the chimney and a horrible stench seeped from the open windows. The call of crows cawing among the branches of the oak trees gave Kenji a further sense of dread. He stopped before placing a foot onto the first step of the house. He gathered up his confidence, then continued forward, knocking on the door.

"Brother, I knew you'd be coming," Makito said from inside. "Come in."

Kenji slid the door to the side and stepped in. The odor was worse inside, his eyes tearing. "What is that smell, Makito?"

Makito appeared from the doorway of another room. He had long greasy hair and bags under his eyes. His robe was tattered and stained with red smears. He wore his sword at his side. "Come in. Come in."

Kenji closed the door behind him. He removed his sandals, not that Makito had such customs, but to show respect to another's home. Kenji took a seat on a cushion on the floor in the living room. His brother brought tea and biscuits before taking a seat across from him.

"It is good to see you, brother," Kenji said.

"You as well, Kenji," the man replied, his voice raspy.

# DEAD HISTORY

"Our teacher is dying," Kenji said. "You need to pay your respects."

"He and the rest of the town are dead to me," Makito said, waving his hand in the air dismissively. Kenji's eyes hardened at the gesture. "They side with the Emperor, the one you serve," Makito finished.

"Makito, I have not come to debate politics. I have come because our master requests it and tells me you are dishonoring our name and village."

Makito began laughing. "He speaks of dishonor? Brother, you have been brainwashed by the nobility, but no worries. I have plans to bring down the Emperor."

Kenji stood, placing his hand on the hilt of his sword. "You are my brother, Makito, but to speak of the Emperor in such a way will surely be the death of you."

Makito rose to his feet, venom in his voice. He showed no indication of wanting a fight, his hand away from his sword's hilt. "And you, brother, will die by his side if you return to him."

"Was that your abomination I ran into on my way here?" Kenji asked.

"Oh, you met one of my test subjects, did you?"

"What have you dabbled in now? The black arts? They are forbidden by law."

Makito walked away, but turned around before entering the kitchen. "They are your laws to obey and follow. I live amongst the wild. I bow to no emperor."

"He is a just and righteous man. He brought prosperity to our lands and peace among our villages," Kenji said.

"He's a rat, a coward."

"You will come with me and stop messing with the spirit world." Kenji took a step forward, reaching out for his brother's arm. Makito pulled away and kicked him square in the abdomen, sending him sailing backward. Kenji stumbled over the table, splintering it to pieces. When he looked up, Makito had vanished.

Kenji stormed through the rooms of the house, but his brother was gone. He found a trapdoor hidden within the floor of the kitchen. Lifting it cautiously, he descended a set of wooden stairs leading to an underground crypt-like room.

# DEAD HISTORY

Lit torches lined the walls. Men, undead, like the one Kenji killed earlier were chained to the walls, moaning and reaching out for him. His brother stood in the far corner behind a table crowded with vials full of strange liquids and jars containing rare herbs and animal parts. Some were moving.

"Makito, what have you done?" Kenji demanded, his face wrought with horror.

"My soldiers," Makito said, waving his arm proudly. "Behold, brother," he declared with open arms. "The start of my army of undead."

"Makito, you've gone mad," Kenji said, drawing his sword as Makito started laughing. "This must be stopped."

"Stopped? It's already in motion, you fool."

"What are you talking about?"

"Have you had a drink of water lately?" Makito grinned.

Kenji's face paled as the blood ran from it. His brother had pierced the armor of his soul.

"The water supply is tainted with the contagion," Makito explained. "Right now the change is taking place within you, brother. And did you really think our master was ill from natural causes? I poisoned him and a group of other fighters first. I had to test a batch of the substance on them, making sure no one would stand in my way. My undead soldiers will pass the disease onto everyone they bite; growing my army to immeasurable numbers once they get beyond the village."

"You lie," Kenji growled, lunging forward, but Makito was prepared, disappearing behind a stone door set into the wall. Kenji screamed in anger, pounding on the door, but it wouldn't open. His brother's cowardice and betrayal was too much for his soul to bear. He fell to his knees, tears rimming his eyes.

"Makito!" he yelled. He knelt in silence, the zombies chained to the wall moaning, clawing at the air to get at him.

The villagers were doomed, infected by Makito's poison and would become members of the undead. Kenji looked at his hands. They were clean, but soon they would be stained with the blood of people he cared for. Kenji gathered his will, focused his energy, and rose to his feet. Eight zombies were chained around the room. He approached the first, slicing its head off with a single strike. All eight were headless corpses within seconds. Sheathing his sword, he climbed the stairs to the house. Makito was nowhere to be found. His master would soon become one of the undead. He needed to get to him before the town was crawling with zombies. How many had drunk the water? All?

Kenji took a log from the fireplace upstairs, touched it to the thatched roof outside, and set the place ablaze. Everything would burn to the ground, including the corpses in the cellar.

He sprinted to his room at the inn, dressed himself in his samurai armor, and went to see his master. On his way, people were screaming and running about in the center of town. Two members of the undead had a woman in their clutches and were gnawing at her stomach, yanking out her intestines and eating them. Kenji ran over, pulled his sword out, and removed one of their heads with a quick stroke before running his sword through the other's skull. Both dropped lifelessly to the ground.

He stood as people watched him from shop windows and homes. A man ran up to him, shaking. "Great Samurai," the man said, bowing. "What is happening in our village?"

Kenji looked at the man, then at some of the people standing in the background. They all looked sick, with pale skin, emaciated bodies, and gaunt faces.

"I need a rider to deliver a message to the Emperor!" Kenji yelled to the crowd. He put a hand on the man's shoulder. "Please, sir, go with your family to your home. Lock the door and stay inside." The man went running off.

The dead woman the zombies had been eating began to stir. Kenji jumped back, amazed at how she was able to reanimate even in such dire condition. Makito's work was far more damning than he imagined. She sat up, reaching out, and tried to grab his leg. He drew his sword and quickly dispatched her by removing her head.

He looked around at the growing crowd, people creeping out of their homes and shops. "Someone, find me a rider," Kenji demanded. "I need to deliver a message to the Emperor." A scream broke out from within a shoemaker's shop. A man, blood seeping from his neck and drenching his clothes, stumbled from the store. Kenji ran over to him. Looking through the shop's doorway, he saw a zombie woman coming out of the store. With a quick move, Kenji

# DEAD HISTORY

sliced the top of her head off from the ears up. She twitched violently before falling to the ground. Upon impact, the half of her brain still left in the skull tumbled out, falling apart like shriveled, gray noodles. Kenji then brought his blade down on the man's neck, severing it from the body. The crowd screamed.

"People!" Kenji declared, standing. "There is an undead contagion amongst us. These undead things carry a disease. Do not let them bite you. Go to your home and stay inside!" Chaos broke out as people grabbed children and valuables to flee their homes. He knew most of them were already infected from the water, but maybe some of them had a chance.

"Samurai," a voice said from behind him. Kenji turned around to see a young boy standing before him. "I'm a rider, sir."

The boy appeared normal, his skin wasn't pale and he looked well-fed. "Come with me," he said, leading the boy into the shoe shop. Inside Kenji wrote a note to the Emperor, sealing it with wax he found within the shop. "Take this note to the Emperor, show the guards this." Kenji said and handed the child a medallion only he would have, indicating to the Emperor that the message was truly from his trusted warrior. The young boy departed from the store, heading for his horse.

Kenji left the store and looked around. People half his age were hobbling like elders. His brother had infected almost every villager. Only a few lucky ones, like the young boy, hadn't drunk the water. The shame could never be forgotten or erased. His soul weighed heavily on his body as he traveled to his master's house just outside of town.

"Kenji," Ari said. "How goes it with Makito?"

Kenji hung his head in shame. He could barely look at his master, knowing what he was to become. He sat by his teacher's side, telling him everything he knew.

"This is not your fault or shame to carry. Your brother..." he stopped, coughed up phlegm mixed with blood before continuing, "has disgraced both of us and the entire village. He is a lunatic and a mass murderer." Ari took Kenji's hand. "You must stop him. Our village was only the beginning for him. No one must be allowed to leave."

"I know, Master."

"And you know what must be done?"

"It is already in motion," Kenji said as a tear slid down his cheek.

"It will start with me, my warrior." Master Ari held out a shaking arm.

Kenji's face faltered with terror. "I cannot."

Ari's pale face reddened with anger. "You will. I command it." He lay back on the pillow, straightening his long white beard. "I am ready, for there is no defeating this demon that rides in my blood. I've been fighting it for some time, thinking it was cancer. Now that I know, I can die easier."

Kenji took out his tanto, handing it to his master. Master Ari would perform seppuku, a ritual of suicide reserved for samurai, allowing him to die with honor instead of by his enemy's hands. Ari held the bladed weapon, tip down, to his stomach. "Goodbye, my noble warrior," he said and plunged the knife into his gut, ripping it across and shredding the intestines. He let out a gasp, shuddered a moment, then fell still. Kenji cried out, plucked the tanto from his master's stomach, and placed it back in its sheath. The master's white robe lay torn and bloodied.

Looking at his master, crying, he saw the old man's eyes open. With lightning speed, he drew his sword and lopped off his master's head. Outside, screams erupted.

He ran out to see zombies walking with their arms out and attacking villagers. One was coming up the stairs at him. He cut its arms off before removing the head. Some of the villagers had pitchforks and swords.

"You must destroy or remove the head in order to kill them!" he yelled to the villagers.

From his right, he heard the air whistle and ducked out of the way of an arrow. Turning, he saw Makito holding a bow, readying another arrow.

"Hello, brother. Is the master dead yet?"

Anger coursed through Kenji. He growled in rage as he sprang to his feet. He drew his sword, calling upon all his samurai abilities to help him through what must be done.

# DEAD HISTORY

The next arrow sailed past him as he charged at his brother. Makito withdrew his own sword and raced forward, a horde of undead behind him. The brothers collided, the sound of metal clanging when their swords met.

They parried, each one taking swings at the other. Nicks and gashes lined their bodies within seconds. Zombies came at them, trying to eat their flesh. Makito had a confused look on his face. The zombies were attacking him as well as his brother. Upon dodging a zombie attack, Makito slipped up, Kenji's blade coming in and slicing his sword arm off. Blood spurted from the limb as he screamed in agony. He fell to the ground as Kenji cleared the area of zombies before pointing the tip of his blade at Makito's neck.

"Go ahead and run me through," Makito said. "My plans have been set forth and you can't stop them."

"I've already taken the necessary steps in dealing with this mess. I should have killed you long ago, but Master had hope for you."

"You would never kill your own brother, your own flesh and blood. You are weak, but slice me so that I may rise again."

"You really are demented, Makito." Kenji sliced his brother's legs off above the knees. Makito lay, writhing and screaming in disbelief.

"I leave you for the zombies, Makito. May they rid the world of your evil and devour every piece of you." Kenji left his brother on the ground as a group of undead began tearing at him and eating his flesh.

Kenji sliced his way through hordes of undead, some of them the villagers he'd just seen in town. He returned to his master's quarters. His knees ached and he had a fever. The disease was working through him already. Hopefully the Emperor's men would arrive soon and wipe out the town, stopping the undead plague from spreading across the lands.

Kenji knew he wouldn't be around to see the outcome, realizing it was out of his hands. He knelt by his headless master and bowed his head. Placing the tip of the tanto to his temple, gathering his chi with measured breaths, he shoved the blade into his skull.

The knife penetrated his brain, killing him, and making sure he would never rise again.

# THE COURIER

## ERIC S. BROWN

"Close the gates!" Captain Fisher screamed over the cacophony of gunfire all around him. He felt a cold hand grab his shoulder and he spun, delivering a bone-shattering blow to the dead woman's pus-leaking face with the butt of his revolver.

She stumbled backwards, black-looking, stale blood oozing from her broken nose. Captain Fisher brought his revolver's barrel level with her forehead and fired off a point blank round, sending her back to Hell with a single shot.

The dead were everywhere and his men were quickly being overrun. Retreat was not an option. Up until a few minutes ago, the fort had been one of the safest places left in the west. When he found the idiot who had ordered the gates to be opened, he swore to eat his heart himself.

The siege had lasted two weeks and supplies were running low, everyone's nerves strung tight. Captain Fisher had seen many a well-trained soldier fall apart from less than the horror they had been living in. The hungry moans of the dead never stopped, night or day. They just stood outside the fort and hammered its walls and front and back gates with their fists when the mood took them. He himself had stood watch many a night just to spare his men some of the misery inherent in staring down at them; enduring the ungodly smell of death and decay rising from their rotting flesh.

Many of his men believed the only hope of survival they had lay in getting word to the rumored, massive gathering of forces on the eastern shores of the Mississippi river, which was supposed to be preparing for a full-out offensive push against the dead. Such a thing would be suicide for whoever drew the short straw and rode out to deliver the word. And that was assuming a way could be found to push the dead back from the gates far enough to open them for the messenger to escape.

The best option presented so far was to drop a barrel of gunpowder over the side of the wall and hope the blast bought enough time to let someone out and close the gates. Captain Fisher believed he'd put a stop to such nonsense the night before but the sound of an explosion pulled him from his bunk this morning and let him know, he'd indeed failed in doing so. None of that mattered though. All that mattered now was getting the gates closed. The dead were pouring inside in staggering numbers and Captain Fisher's hope of achieving his goal was dwindling with each passing second. Until the gates were closed, the things would keep coming, too. There were hundreds if not thousands of the creatures surrounding the fort's walls that had waited for weeks for something like this to happen.

Captain Fisher fired his revolver's last round into the chest of a long dead Indian who leaped at him from the top of the fort's wall. He ripped his saber from its scabbard and gave a howling cry of war as he charged the latest wave of creatures pushing their way inside by crawling over each other. With a mighty swing, he took the head off the lead creature and watched as it bounced away.

"Sir!" he heard Private Hyatt yell as the young man rushed to join him. The private would have been a more welcome sight if his Winchester was loaded and working. Instead, the rifle looked to be barely holding together, and Fisher knew the private had been using it as a club against the dead, the stock smeared with blood which covered its length and drenched the young man's hands.

"Get the damn gate closed!" Fisher ordered. "I'll hold 'em while you do!"

The private slammed himself straight into one of the massive gates and shoved against it with all his weight as Fisher slashed another of the things, cutting off the hand that was reaching for him. His next swing caught a dead man in the mouth, slashing through the muscle and meat of his cheeks and leaving the dead man's mouth hanging grotesquely open like a disjointed snake jaw.

Captain Fisher continued to hack and slash at the army of the dead as they pressed forward, the black blood splashing onto his tunic and covering his medals. One medal in particular was a bright red square, Fisher having received it for bravery in the heat of battle.

His attention was so focused on the horde making its way through the gates, that he didn't notice the animated corpse of his second-in-command coming at him from behind until the man's teeth sunk into the side of his neck. Blood sprayed into the air as Captain Fisher cried out in pain and the dead in front of him surged forward at an even faster rate. A sea of grasping hands and stumbling legs took him to the ground as his saber was jerked from his weakening grip.

Two hours later and several miles east, gun smoke hung heavily in the air. Daniel pumped the lever action of his Winchester, chambering another round. His aim was rushed and desperate but the bullet still managed to strike home.

It slammed into the dead man's forehead and the body dropped to the ground and lay still as blood and brain matter seeped from the hole where the round entered.

Daniel counted five more left in the pack of creatures as they came stumbling out of the woods towards his camp. On the other side of the camp, his horse bucked and strained against the rope which held it tied to a tree. Between the stink of the dead and the gunfire, it was determined to get free and bolt if it could.

The fastest of the dead was almost on top of him. Not even the speed of his new rifle with its rapid rate of fire could stop them all in time. The fact that he'd already sent four of the monsters back to Hell did nothing to deter the others. Their snarls were angry, loud, and filled with hunger. Daniel was neither stubborn nor stupid enough to keep trying to hold his ground in the face of certain death. He leapt out of his bent knee firing position and whirled about, running for his horse. Cutting the rope with a deft flick of his knife drawn from his boot, he hopped onto the animal's back and took off, leaving the rotting abominations behind him.

When Daniel thought he'd put a safe distance between him and the dead, he slowed his horse and tried to take stock of his situation. It wasn't hard to figure out where he was. He'd ridden through this area so many times that he knew it like the back of his hand. Daniel was down to his last handful of rounds for his Winchester and had no desire to face the dead with only the Colt strapped to his side.

He'd never been much good with pistols. Thank the Lord, he was close now. The fort should only be a few more hours ride to the west. If luck was with him, he should be able reach its gates before the sun fell out of the sky and the moon rose.

Daniel reached the fort with little light left to spare. Strangely, there were no sentries posted to challenge his approach. His heart sunk when he saw the massive gates were partially open. As he drew closer, the smell of rotting flesh reached him on the wind. His instincts told him to turn around and steer clear of the fort but his sense of duty drove him on.

Daniel's orders required him to inform the men stationed at the fort to withdraw and join the forces gathering on the other side of the Mississippi River. He'd never failed to deliver a message before and he had no intention of failing now. If there was anyone left alive, they likely needed all the help they could get. Besides, he needed rations and more bullets if he was to have any real hope of making it back alive.

He pulled his Winchester from the holster strapped to his horse's side and checked it, reloading with the last of his bullets. With the rifle held ready in his right hand and the horse's reigns in his left, he prompted the animal on slowly towards the gates.

Bodies lay all around the fort's wall. The largest numbers of these corpses were clustered in front of the partially open gate. Daniel didn't bother to count them. Their number didn't matter, the only thing that did was whether they were really dead. His eyes scanned over each corpse as he passed it, making sure it had a head wound. It was the only way to know for sure and he wasn't taking any chances. He'd seen the dead play possum before and many good men lose their lives to the ruse.

The fort was in shambles. A part of its interior was burnt to the ground and spent shell casings lay everywhere. Daniel dismounted but kept a tight hold on his horse. There was nothing to be found here unless it was to be taken from the bodies of the dead themselves, a task he didn't look forward to. The sun was setting in the sky and the shadows were growing longer. If there were any of the creatures left in the fort, they would be waiting for him inside the remaining buildings.

# DEAD HISTORY

Staying in the open and looting the dead was much safer than going in search of the things he needed. He could forgo the rations if he could find ammo. He was used to hunting for food when the need demanded it. He poked the closest corpse wearing a uniform with the tip of his rifle. When no response came, he knelt beside it and began digging through the man's pockets.

After what seemed like an eternity of searching the bodies, he'd collected over a hundred bullets. It was now too dark to keep searching, so he gathered his loot and left the fort behind him, riding off in the same direction he'd used when approaching the fort.

The idea that so many men had died alone and in vain haunted him. He felt an irrational guilt for not arriving sooner with their 'withdrawal' orders. He did his best to shake off the feeling and focused on finding a spot to camp for the night. He was well past the point of exhaustion and knew that pushing on in the dark would only lead to mistakes and trouble. With the chance of the dead still in the area, a fire was out of the question. It would draw them to him like flies. Hell, sleeping on the ground was out, too.

Taking a bundle of rope and his Winchester with him, after securing his horse, Daniel found the most comfortable looking tree he could and climbed into it. He found a wide branch to serve as his 'bed' and tied himself to the tree trunk as he settled in for the night. He sat with his back against the roughness of the trunk's bark and closed his tired eyes.

Daniel awoke in the night to the sound of shuffling noises at the base of the tree. His groggy eyes opened and looked down into the hungry face of a dead man in a soldier's uniform as the creature scurried up the trunk toward him. The dead soldier growled when he saw Daniel's fear and began to climb faster. Daniel jerked up his Winchester from where it rested in his lap only to have it slip from his fingers. He watched it plummet through the darkness to land with a thud on the ground below. The man was almost on him. Struggling to draw his pistol, he felt an icy hand grab his thigh. The soldier's jagged nails cut into the flesh of his leg through the tough material of his pants. Daniel fought against the hold of his safety rope, trying to get into a kicking position. The heel of his boot lashed out, smashing into the dead soldier's face. The blow shattered the dead man's nose. Black, stale blood seeped from the wound. The soldier appeared to smile and came at him with renewed fury.

Daniel knew his situation was hopeless. Still unable to free his pistol, he panicked, snatching his knife from the top of his boot. With a quick slash, he cut the rope holding him in place and fell from the tree. He landed on his left shoulder to the sound of breaking bone. His scream was long and thick with pain. Before he could right himself, a heavy weight landed on top of him.

Gnashing teeth tore away the better part of his right ear and he felt warm blood wet his hair and run down his neck. He hurled himself to his feet, slinging the soldier off of him, then drew his pistol as the dead man leapt at him again. He shoved the barrel of the weapon under the soldier's chin and squeezed the trigger as the nails of a grasping, rotting hand slashed down his face from his forehead to his chin. The nails scratched his eyes horribly, leaving him unable to see as the soldier toppled over onto the dirt, this time dead for good.

Daniel sat still, his breath coming in gasps. Tears of blood rolled down his cheeks as he sobbed, knowing his life was over. He heard movement in the surrounding trees and the distant snarls of more of the dead as they drew closer. He smelt the stench of decay and death all around him.

Suddenly, several pairs of cold hands latched onto him, shoving him face first into the soft dirt. He screamed as the first set of teeth ripped a hole in his chest, taking away a chunk of his skin and meat. Daniel kept screaming until one of the things bit through his wind pipe and his heart finally stopped beating.

When the thing that was once a man lifted its head, the wan moonlight reflected off its uniform. The medals on the tunic were those of a captain, one bright red medal in particular seeming to almost glow in the suffuse light filtering in through the treetops.

Though now, the captain served in a new army, one he would never be discharged from.

An army of the dead.

# WILD WITH HUNGER

## LEE CLARK ZUMPE

"You'd not think it possible," said Noah Brownlow, one of three men elected to the Board of Guardians of Basingstoke and appointed by the Central Poor Law Commission to investigate claims of neglect and abuse at the workhouse in neighboring Ravenwood. The eerie serenity that met them in the village amazed them all, though the hordes of people skulking along the highway leaving town had provided adequate evidence to support reports of the mass migration underway. "Not a single soul about the place."

Shutters covered every cottage window on the outskirts of the village, confining the shadows to silent chambers and still corridors. Flower boxes, once brimming with brightly-colored, radiant blossoms, spilled over with brown, shriveled flora. As they proceeded, they encountered only cold autumn winds traversing vacant roads. "What has become of them all?"

They had questioned many of those they met fleeing the village. Some muttered indistinct warnings while others simply wept. Most had nothing to say at all, their spirits seemingly overpowered by some awful burden.

Their carriage led them through the narrow streets of impoverished Ravenwood, the noise of its measured passage ricocheting down dead-end alleyways. The three gentlemen scanned the ramshackle tenements crowding the village. Within the squalid lodgings dwelled generations of paupers—virtual slaves of the ironworks at the edge of town. Some buildings featured once prosperous store fronts, their doors now boarded and their hearts festering away with neglect.

"It's midday, and the streets are barren." James Naughton stroked the ivory grip of his cane, his apprehension manifesting itself in uncontrollable, uncharacteristic restlessness. Since hearing tales of the abandoned township, fears of plague had unsettled the noted physician. It had been little more than a decade since he had watched cholera ravage London. "Either they are all dead, or they hide from death."

"I'd prefer not to dig their graves just yet, Dr. Naughton." Sampson Digby patted his nervous companion's shoulder. "We may find that everyone is engaged in some local festival, or occupied by some other community affair."

Their carriage came to a standstill outside the notorious workhouse. Silence promptly filled the void, pouring in from every quarter. Overhead, terminally gray skies drifted over the marred landscape. The Hampshire countryside had been deforested and partitioned, allocated and apportioned over centuries of constant habitation and exploitation. After all, land—like people—had to be meticulously managed and manipulated.

Built to accommodate no more than one-hundred inmates, the population of the Ravenwood workhouse had exceeded three-hundred at last count. Its design lacked both imagination and grace, and its slipshod construction left its residents lacking basic facilities and any sense of wellbeing or security. Its shortcomings were by no means unique: Similar institutions across the country suffered from epidemic overcrowding and scandalous mismanagement. The purported severity of conditions at Ravenwood, however, accentuated its extensive deficiencies and magnified its disgrace.

"Let us see if we can find someone to answer all of our questions," Brownlow said, stepping out of the carriage. A glance toward the driver revealed a terrified youth prone to disturbing delusions and apt to be influenced by superstitions. "The administration block should be just through the gate. Perhaps the Master and Matron will greet us."

"Your optimism cannot curtail my trepidation, Brownlow." Naughton's gaze followed a solitary rat as it cautiously skirted the workhouse's perimeter wall searching for its next meal. Unimaginable filth had accumulated in the streets adjacent to the complex. Heaps of foul-smelling waste and debris attracted great black clouds of flies. "I am accustomed to sensing the presence of death, hovering like an unwanted shadow over a patient's bedside as I labor to keep blood coursing through his arteries." Naughton lowered his head as he set foot in the street, the weight of the oppressive sky pressing down on him. "Death is no guest in this place—he has dominion over it."

* * *

Peter Hawley peered out the window of the shop belonging to the village coffin-maker. Across the boulevard, three somber fellows marched right through the gates of the Ravenwood Workhouse—formerly a residence of all those unable to support themselves through more traditional means. The townsfolk once looked upon it as a blessing, since it removed from plain view all those unfortunate wretches whose unmistakable undernourishment and infirmity made those more privileged feel acutely uncomfortable. Hawley's own father, in fact, had habitually praised the limitless benevolence of English law for providing sanctuary to those whose blood and sweat greased the wheels of the empire.

The surviving villagers—those who had not fled or fallen victim to the predatory creatures inhabiting the workhouse—now considered the place a malignant pest house. Their commendations became condemnations when word of the first mutilated corpses spread through the parish. Young Peter had seen them, his father's former employer coughing up vomit as they packed the tattered mortal remains in shoddy caskets. Their flesh had been slashed and shredded, their entrails yanked through gaping breaches and their skulls split and emptied.

The workhouse custodians claimed wild dogs had gained access to the men's block, blamed the viciousness of the attacks on famine or madness, and distanced themselves from the initial victims by seeing to their swift and supposedly secret disposal. Neither the coffin-maker nor the undertaker could keep from recounting the scene when swayed by gin-and-water, and the tale quickly circulated around Ravenwood.

"Who's that lot, then?" Peter's friend Dudley Potter joined him at the window. Dudley, a few years older and wiser than fifteen-year-old Peter, had been out foraging for food all morning. The closure of the marketplace just before the exodus had left the boys few culinary options. "You'd think they'd know better than to go right into the bloody nest."

# DEAD HISTORY

"They're outsiders, I think," Peter said, watching the last man slip into the menacing darkness that had engulfed the workhouse. "They must not know what's happened." Peter hesitated, yearning for a return to normalcy but unable to dismiss the fear of venturing out into the open streets. Though the things generally slept during the day, their voracious appetites sometimes sent them into the shadowy alleyways before dusk. "We should warn them."

"Bah," Dudley answered, turning his back on the workhouse. "Let 'em go. At least two of them are rather plump," he said, thrusting out his midsection and patting his stomach. "They should make an ample feast—enough to keep the gorgers off the streets tonight, I'd wager."

"And tomorrow?" Peter looked to Dudley for guidance since no one else could offer it. His parents had both disappeared weeks earlier, most likely dragged off to the workhouse in the middle of the night by the gorgers. The coffin-maker had packed up his belongings earlier than that, predicting the suffering to come. "What will we do for food, for lodging? What will we do when they come for us? What will we do tomorrow?"

"We'll worry about tomorrow later." Dudley plucked a few wormy apples and a handful of moldy berries from his pockets. "Let's get something in our bellies right now."

* * *

"The stench is overwhelming." Brownlow held a kerchief to his face, covering his nose and mouth. "No one should live like this."

The architects of the Ravenwood workhouse devised the main segment of the facility in a cruciform pattern, with administrative offices in the base and the kitchen directly behind. The infirmary and lunatic cells lay at the opposite end of the section. At the intersection of the two wings, in the segregated dining hall, inmates would be fed paltry meals without the luxury of utensils or the comfort of conversation. The overlords demanded silence, even among family members.

The men's comments echoed through the vacant corridors as they approached the hub of the workhouse.

"Abandoned, just like the rest of the village," Digby said, cold indifference shading his tone. "Just like the poor to take flight at the first hint of hardship." Unlike his companions, Digby did not necessarily take issue with the accusations leveled at Ravenwood. He believed the worst scenarios would prove to be the result of undue overstatements of less inflammatory pieces of evidence. Authorities deliberately kept conditions at workhouses inhospitable to persuade as many people as possible to find employment elsewhere and to circumvent the inherent weakness of an overly generous welfare regime. "Sure to end up in London begging along the turnpike near Fortune Green or picking pockets in Saffron Hill."

"If so," Naughton said, turning an anxious eye toward the others, "they'll carry with them whatever ailment besieged this town."

"Digby, I believe," Brownlow said, "would have much preferred the poor await inevitable death here, by pestilence or starvation."

"It seems the only noble recourse, does it not?" Digby's aristocratic background effectively stripped him of all compassion and goodwill. "Out of sheer gratitude, one would assume they favor death amidst their peers to the shame of afflicting disease and distress upon their superiors."

As the men entered the heart of the facility through a heavy door on groaning hinges, the fate of at least some of the villagers became painfully evident. Bones lay scattered across the floor, meat and muscle indiscriminately stripped from them. Collected in vast mounds in the unlit corners, more substantial mortal remnants drew rodents and insects alike. Hundreds of disfigured and decapitated corpses congregated in that place, their limbs detached, their innards hollowed out and strewn across the long tables where inmates once dined on moldy bread, fetid soup and loathsome gruel.

Behind them, the door thundered as it closed. The tell-tale latch of the lock perished beneath the clamor.

"For the love of God," Digby said, covering his mouth as he choked on his own vomit. His eyes fell reflexively to the floor which he found damp with gummy blood and viscera. Arms and legs, half devoured, revealed gluttonous bite marks. "What manner of nightmare have we been fated to endure?"

"Plague is not the author of this slaughter, Naughton." Brownlow recognized his colleague's concurrence, though he expected no verbal reply from the physician. "Yet, such depravity and debauchery cannot be the work of rational men."

"Not of men, at all," Naughton said, less affected by the grisly scene than the others. He knelt down to inspect a half-eaten arm which had been ripped from its socket. He examined, too, a nearby skull—its cap smashed and removed. The recurring, petite, crescent-shaped wounds left him with little doubt. "Cannibalism is an aberration of nature and demonstrates degeneration of the soul. What makes this occurrence particularly unspeakable is the age of those involved. Children caused this carnage."

All the blood in Brownlow's heart dried up in that instant, and the faceless, nameless dead surrounding him ceased to exist as individuals. They became provender, forage, feed for famished cattle. Naughton's revelation sickened him, yet simultaneously he found himself validating the nightmare as necessity.

"So finally it has come to this," Brownlow whispered, his observations not intended for his colleagues. "Like animals driven to the brink of extinction, survival suppresses civility. We provoked this atrocity."

None of them noticed the shifting shadows displaced by a pack of lean, lithe predators stealthily gauging their prey. Little more than sinewy, swarthy silhouettes set against the immeasurable darkness of a somber, windowless institution, they moved with uncanny dexterity and speed. Coal-black and sprite-like entities, had the shade not thoroughly cloaked their advance, not one of the men would have mistaken these things for the children they once were.

"Stop! Stop!" Digby's panicked cries no sooner escaped his lips than he found himself engulfed in impenetrable darkness. Sharp-clawed, tiny hands carried him along cramped passageways so confining his struggles proved futile. "They have me," he screamed, the first moist mouth nuzzling his flesh. In an instant, their fingers tugged at his vestments and their teeth ripped at his skin. "Oh, God, please help!"

Naughton thrust his open palm against Brownlow's chest, stopping him dead in his tracks.

"Surely, you don't intend to pursue them?" The doctor showed neither fear nor agitation. He remained cold and detached, drawing on his scientific background to help him maintain his composure. "Anything that can take down a man of Digby's girth that quickly and quietly would certainly have the two of us for dessert."

Retracing their steps, they each muttered unintelligible curses when they found the door through which they had entered the chamber locked and impassable. As Digby's fading cries reverberated through the darkened hallways, Naughton scanned the room, searching for another route of escape. He spotted a pass-through window that led outside into a courtyard. "Follow me, and be quick about it."

Brownlow helped the doctor through the tight aperture. Outside, the sun still shown, though the gray skies stifled much of its brilliance. Eager to join his colleague, Brownlow pushed his upper body through the swinging door.

"No!" He felt the nails tear into his lower leg, pulling him back inside. "Naughton, help me!"

"Here," Naughton said, handing him his cane. "In the head! Strike it in the head, Brownlow!"

Having tasted the light of late afternoon, the chamber seemed that much more inundated by darkness as he let himself fall to the floor. Brownlow rolled over quickly, saw the thing that had frustrated his retreat. Its jagged teeth, discolored by blood, protruded over its scabby lips. Its saucer-like white eyes housed a narrow, vertical sliver of black. It kept its filthy hands near its chin, fingers fidgeting incessantly as it studied its intended victim.

The hunger in its expression reminded him of the rat he had seen outside the compound searching for sustenance. Though physically repellent, its wretchedly emaciated frame and its feigned frailty temporarily beguiled him, entrancing him with the same deadly proficiency a cobra employs to paralyze its prey.

When it lunged toward his face, Brownlow shrugged off his momentary stupor and swung the cane, burying the ivory grip deep in the thing's skull. A rush of frothy black blood spurted from the gaping wound.

# DEAD HISTORY

\* \* \*

They had killed one.

Peter Hawley watched wordlessly through a breach in the curtain wall surrounding the workhouse. Two of the strangers had somehow eluded the voracious gorgers—descended right into their den and escaped back out into the light of day using the very aperture the monsters used when they set about prowling the town for victims after dusk.

And they had killed one.

The two men hauled the twitching corpse away from the building, deeper into the light of the declining day. Peter recognized its gaunt and wiry frame, its sunken cheeks, its unsettling blue-black pallor and its elongated limbs terminating in razor-sharp claws. Though want and untimely death had transformed it into this hideous creature, Peter knew it had once been a small boy of perhaps five or six years of age.

"D'ye see, it Dudley?" Peter squatted in a dark recess, hugging his knees tightly against his chest. His companion rested an arm on his shoulder, watching the unfolding scene with negligible interest. "D'ye see what they've done?"

"Hush, please," Dudley said, smothering any further commentary for the moment. "That's a good lad."

One of the strangers knelt over the body, inspecting it methodically, poking at its extremities and prodding its torso. Clearly a learned man, Dudley expected him to reach the same conclusion the workhouse nurses had come to before they had fled the facility. In the children's ward in Ravenwood, the dead had developed a habit of not staying dead for very long.

"Never said you couldn't kill one," Dudley admitted, though he had certainly inferred it when he spoke of the horrors he had seen before meeting Peter. "Problem's getting one on its own, away from the pack. Like wolves, they is."

"What should we do, then?" Peter inquired.

"What's there to do," Dudley answered quickly in a hushed tone. "I let you drag me here to show you that they're like all the others." Dudley, an orphan who had spent ample time in workhouses across the English countryside over the short but exhausting span of his lifetime, felt no attachment to the strangers. Unlike Peter, he regarded most adults with disdain and distrust. "If they're smart, they'll leave; if not, they'll die when night falls. Either way, they'll be neither a help nor hindrance to us."

"We could go with them..."

"Go if you want, I don't care," Dudley said, but his grip on Peter's shoulder suggested his apathy lacked substance. "I rather like having the run of the town to myself. And I prefer being hunted by animals to being ill-treated by masters and matrons and beadles and chaplains."

By now, Naughton had made his shocking discovery and recoiled in revulsion. He stood back from the disabled corpse, jabbing it repeatedly with his cane, ensuring that the semblance of life would not again return to it. Brownlow, visibly disturbed by his companion's revelations, reflexively scanned his appendages, searching for open wounds.

"The hour is late, Dudley. If they go back inside, the gorgers will have them." Peter saw the men searching their surroundings for an alternate route of escape. A mound of firewood entangled with leafy, creeping vines concealed the narrow fissure in the wall where the two boys hid.

"They've no hope unless we act," Peter said.

The men had stumbled on the facility's self-contained bone yard. A great basin rested at the center of the weedy lawn. Nearby, the rammer—used to pummel the animal bones into gritty dust for fertilizer—lay dormant in unchecked vegetation. "Let me show them the way," Peter said.

"Why? So they can deliver us to a workhouse in some other town? You're like me now, Peter," Dudley said, pinching the younger child's ear. "No home, no family; a sad little orphan. Do you want to end up like those things in there?"

"No..." Peter scowled. "But, if we help them, they might take us in..."

"Listen to me," Dudley said, pointing toward the strangers. "They're not to be trusted. They'd sooner see us rot in some workhouse than welcome us into their own homes."

Dudley had never known the love of a parent or the generosity of a stranger. He had, however, experienced all of the most deplorable traits of guardianship, including derision, neglect and the depravities of exploitation and abuse. "Stay with me, Peter," Dudley said, almost pleading. "I'll take care of you. Promise."

* * *

"That firewood," Naughton said, gesturing toward the perimeter wall. "We need to haul it across the yard. We can build a fire beneath the pass-through window. If we can keep it going all night, it may keep them from our throats." His companion, Brownlow, stood idly, his gaze fixed upon the small corpse sprawled across the ground. Its uncanny eyes stared vacantly skyward. "Do you hear, man? We must act promptly to save our hides!"

"What is it?" Brownlow nudged it with the tip of his black shoes, noticing for the first time the bloodstains spattered over the bottle-green of his redingote and light gray trousers. "Beast or boy?"

"Both," Naughton said brusquely, minding the advance of eventide. "In life, it had been a child; in death, it becomes an animal driven wild with insatiable hunger. It is an uncommon phenomenon, but one that has precedence in the annals of medicine."

"Gratuitous neglect," Brownlow muttered, repelled by its protruding ribs and pelvis, its sunken eyes and skeletal limbs. "An overriding attitude of apathy affected their mortal degeneration, left them lacking the nourishment and affection any child deserves."

"After death liberated their underprivileged souls," Naughton added, somewhat less disposed to ascribe blame, "their unchecked hunger reanimated them and incited them to acts of cannibalism and cruelty." Naughton wiped blood off the ivory handle of his cane on a kerchief and tossed aside the soiled linen. "Tonight, Brownlow, unless we act now, we will join Digby and the countless others who have become victims of these bestial predators."

"We must survive," Brownlow said, finding strength in his resolve to not let the Ravenwood atrocities go unpunished. "We must expose the source of this incident; warn others that the path our society has chosen can only lead to more suffering, more malice and more death."

"If thoughts of retribution will fuel your instinct to survive, so be it."

Quietly, but with a hurriedness generated by equal parts fear and disgust, Naughton and Brownlow began to stack firewood beneath the pass-through window. When they had conveyed a sizable amount, Naughton broke off and began collecting dead vegetation to use as kindling.

When darkness threatened to smother Ravenwood, the doctor knew the time had come.

"I think I hear movement in there, Naughton," Brownlow said, heaving one last bundle of wood onto the pile. "I hope you have devised some method of lighting our bonfire or this night may be quite short for the two of us."

Naughton dug through the pockets of his cassimere coat, finally retrieving a small cylindrical tin.

"Fortunately, I picked these up on my last trip to London," he said, a mildly conceited smile stretching across his face. "Surely you have seen them in apothecary shops," he continued, plucking a small bit of wood and coarse paper from the container. "They call them 'friction lights,' or 'lucifers' depending on who you ask. It's a wood splinter tipped with a mixture of antimony sulphide and potassium chloride. Gently rub it across the surface of the sandpaper, and ..."

A wavering flame danced on the end of the splinter, its assertive defiance of endemic darkness symbolic of the inherent arrogance of science and its crusade against the unknown.

An hour later, an inferno raged in the bone yard, sending fiery tentacles across the brick face of the workhouse. Once the flames were established, but before the blaze became unapproachable, Naughton managed to open the pass-through window with his cane so that smoke and flames spilled inside the edifice.

"This fire will do more than keep the things from making a midnight feast of us," Naughton said boastfully. "It will rid the town of them once and for all."

Some time after midnight, a handful of creatures tried to escape—or perhaps they simply could not bear the suffering any longer and opted for a more abrupt end. They scuttled out through the passage, engulfed in flames, and shambled into the courtyard where they finally collapsed.

Naughton, not fully satisfied with the finality of their termination, beckoned Brownlow to follow him.

"Take up the rammer and follow me," he said, pointing toward the basin where bones were once crushed by workhouse inmates.

Brownlow strained as he lifted the heavy iron rammer. He turned to his colleague for further instruction, but found none necessary. Naughton was engaged in the grisly business of crushing the skulls of the smoldering things, and Brownlow soon followed suit.

Dozens more spilled out over the ensuing hours; shuffling, crawling and writhing. Most appeared singly, though a few seemed to approach destiny hand-in-hand or in small groups. Naughton and Brownlow tended to each in the order of its departure, permanently relieving the pangs of unappeasable hunger that had constituted a preternatural semblance of life.

"May God forgive me," Brownlow whispered. He alternately fumed and wept as he participated in the extermination. "May God forgive us all."

Being a man of science, Naughton initially remained detached and unaffected by the gory scene. Either fatigue or the burden of involvement gradually tainted his perception, and—much to his astonishment—he began to take certain pleasure in dispatching the creatures.

When two figures of slight build and slender frame scurried from the darkness along the fringe of the courtyard, it was therefore unfortunate that Naughton was the first to react. Instinctively, he raised his cane and struck with animalistic speed and ferocity. The first boy fell at his feet, a crimson fountain spewing from the fractured skull.

The second boy vented a chilling scream that drew Brownlow's gaze.

"Naughton, no!" Brownlow could see clearly by the morning's light that neither child had been transformed; Naughton, though, saw only monsters. "They are not like the others!" Brownlow cried, but Naughton's eyes revealed his madness. "Leave him be!"

Peter Hawley had convinced poor Dudley Potter to trust the strangers, to leave their hiding place and seek refuge. Now Dudley had a hole in his head, and a wild-eyed man towered over Peter, ready to strike a deadly blow.

Peter ran toward the second stranger who seemed to understand that something terrible had just happened. The boy hoped he would make the other man understand, too, but, as he approached, he saw a wealth of anger, frustration and distrust in Brownlow's eyes.

Brownlow lifted the heavy rammer high above his head as Peter tried to arrest his momentum. It came down with crushing force, catching Naughton in the forehead as he affected one last, ineffective swipe at the boy with his cane.

"It's over," Brownlow said, holding out an open hand to Peter.

The dawn illuminated Ravenwood, exposed the pillar of smoke still rising from the burning workhouse. Other survivors, if there were any, would see it as a sign of hope. Brownlow rejected hope, considered it a precursor of complacency and apathy. Hope, without action, was an empty promise.

"Don't worry," Brownlow said, patting Peter's head. "We'll find you something for breakfast. I'll see to it. I'll take care of you."

# LEGACY OF DEATH

## MARK RIVETT

Basilio had never gotten used to the jungle. During the day the insects and constant bird calls clouded his hearing, which in turn, clouded his ability to think clearly. At night, things were worse. Not only were the sounds of the jungle amplified, but he could hardly see. In one hand he held a torch which lit the way through the treacherous terrain, in the other he held his pistol ready to fire at anything that might jump out from beyond his meager illumination. He had been in the New World for a month now and had spent every minute of his time in abject misery and if not for his brother, he would have been happy to live out his days in Spain.

"Basilio, put your pistol away. You're shaking so hard you're liable to shoot someone," Eduardo said. He pulled the donkey behind him and seemed impervious to the environment Basilio found so unbearable. Eduardo was a beast of a man who towered over everyone around him and seemed to behave as if he was always about to slam his fist into the jaw of the person he was speaking to.

"You don't need that thing, Basilio. The jungle is more scared of us than you are of it," Basilio's brother, Carlos, said. He led the group along the trail with a torch in his hand and a long, heavy steel blade in the other, chopping at leaves and vines to clear the path as they went. Carlos was of average build but somewhat chubbier, having allowed the generous spoils of his slave trading business to fatten him.

"I doubt that, Carlos. I have seen snakes as thick around as my leg and cats as big as a donkey. I will be keeping my pistol out at all times. You'd be wise to have your pistol out and powdered as well," Basilio hissed back. "Who knows what's out here?"

"It's not the snakes or the cats that bother me…" Isandro said, bringing up the rear of the group immediately behind Basilio. He also held a torch in his hand and had a long walking stick in the other. "It's the bugs. They never stop." Isandro rarely spoke but seemed to possess a demeanor of confidence.

"Quiet. I see it. Let me do the talking. Eduardo, be ready if I signal," Carlos said as he motioned for everyone to stop.

"No problem." Eduardo turned to the donkey laden with numerous bags and packs, and Basilio could hear the rattling of something metal–perhaps coins–being removed from one of the packs.

The night was as black as Basilio had ever seen. There seemed to be no moon in this part of the world and the cloudy sky always seemed on the edge of a downpour. Basilio had barely seen the sun since coming to this place, and there was no moon to relieve the utter blackness of the night. He watched his brother creep up to the animal hide tent ahead, his form nearly vanishing in the darkness if not for the red glow of the fire light set before the tent.

"Follow quietly." Eduardo nudged Basilio onward and gently pulled on the donkey's leash. Isandro followed silently.

As they approached the fire-lit camp, the form of a man could clearly be seen sitting before the fire with his back to the tent. Nearly naked save for a loin cloth, the man crouched on a log. His eyes were shrouded in shadow but Basilio got the distinct impression that the man was well aware of their approach. With open arms, Carlos emerged from the jungle and stepped into the firelight. Everyone else approached but stopped short of entering the camp.

"Hello. I am Carlos. We are looking for Hutzen. Are you him?" Carlos spoke loudly and enunciated each word slowly. He made sweeping motions with his arms in an attempt to express his words.

The Aztec man who sat before them was silent. His wrinkled skin seemed to exaggerate an expression of malice. His tattooed chest heaved with quiet breaths and he picked his teeth with a sharp animal bone.

Carlos took another few steps forward and his torchlight, added to the campfire light, revealed a macabre dwelling. Tall wooden sticks decorated with animal bones and feathers jutted out from the ground. Animal skulls littered the ground and strange symbols covered the animal hide of the tent.

# DEAD HISTORY

"We were told you could help us. We will pay you," Carlos said.

"Leave," the old man said. His deep voice rasped with the wear of age.

Carlos reached into his belt pouch and removed a gold coin. He crouched down on a log next to the old man and held the coin out before him. "You know what this is?" Carlos phrased the question more as a statement.

Basilio knew what Carlos was showing the man. Carlos had shown him countless times before. His brother was in charge of a slave trading outpost on the coastline. One of the slaves that passed through the outpost on his way north had attempted to buy his freedom with a collection of strange gold coins. After questioning the man, Carlos had somehow come to the conclusion that the coins had come from the mythical El Dorado, the city of gold. From that moment he was determined to trace the coins back to their origin, and that is what led them to this hermit's tent in the middle of the jungle.

The old man reached out with his hand and precariously gripped the coin. His wrinkled face pealed back into a gruesome half-toothed grin, and Basilio couldn't help but sense an undertone of malice.

"El Dorado," the old man said.

"Then you are Hutzen? You've been there?" Again Carlos spoke his questions as statements but with added excitement.

Hutzen reached out with an ancient finger and pointed westward. With eyes on Carlos he said, "River." He then picked up a stick and began drawing in the white ash at the base of the fire.

"No, no, I don't want a map. I want to hire you as a guide." Carlos rattled his coin purse.

Hutzen didn't seem to understand and continued to draw. Carlos reached out and gripped the old man's wrists to stop him. Hutzen recoiled and spoke something in his own language that sounded spiteful.

"You guide us." Carlos rattled his purse again. "I'll pay you."

"No," Hutzen spat back. His malicious grin had returned. "River." He pointed again and resumed drawing his map in the ash.

Carlos poured a handful of coins from his purse into his hand and tried to hand them to Hutzen. Hutzen regarded the coins for a moment as if Carlos were handing him a fist-full of animal dung. "Guide us. Guide us to El Dorado." Carlos was desperate to make sure Hutzen understood what he was asking.

"No." Hutzen gestured to the map he had drawn. "Follow."

Carlos stood up abruptly and turned toward the group and called out, "Eduardo."

Eduardo stepped forward and Basilio could see what he had removed from the donkey's pack. It was a heavy iron set of shackles and a pistol. It became clear to Basilio what Eduardo's job was in Carlos' slave trading outpost.

"Come hear, you old pile of bones." Eduardo held his pistol out toward the Aztec and took a menacing step forward. The old man was slow to realize what was happening, and before he could react, Eduardo leapt over the campfire and smashed the butt of the pistol down on Hutzen's head. The ancient man landed face down on the dirt behind him and Eduardo roughly gripped Hutzen's wrists and slapped the shackles on him. He then gripped the old man by the arm pits and hoisted him to his feet. It wasn't until that moment that Basilio realized how powerful a man Eduardo was and Hutzen groaned with pain as Eduardo kicked him in the back to force him in the direction of the group. Blood from Hutzen's forehead ran into his eyes and down his cheeks.

"You know better than to try and reason with these people, Carlos. We should have just taken care of this to begin with and gotten some shut-eye. You know you can't reason with Aztecs," Eduardo said. He seemed to take pleasure from his work and began tying Hutzen's shackles to a nearby tree.

"I know, Eduardo. But we had to make sure he's who we're looking for. He's liable to tell us how to get to the Pearly Gates and back again if he thought it'd buy his freedom." Carlos began to unpack his bedroll from the donkey. "Let's get some rest. We'll get breakfast here in the morning and then we'll get going. Are you *cabrones* ready to be rich beyond your wildest dreams?"

Basilio quietly removed his bedroll from his pack, grateful for an opportunity to rest.

"I thought we were making pretty good money in the slave trade," Isandro said as, he too, prepared his bed roll.

"*Si*, but how'd you like to live like royalty?" Eduardo said. "We'll make ten times what we could in a hundred years working the trade. No more cleaning up after worthless old fools like him." He gestured to Hutzen.

Hutzen sat silently with his back against the tree. His forehead was wrinkled into an expression of seething hatred and his eyes, concealed in shadow, stared into space with quiet rage.

\* \* \*

Basilio awoke to the smell of eggs and sausage on the fire. Isandro was preparing breakfast and the morning light revealed how macabre the hermit camp actually was. In addition to the bones and feathers, all sorts of strange objects were strewn about: snake skins, black bird corpses staked upon tall spears, and a jaguar pelt hanging over the tent.

"Today is an exciting day, Basilio! It's the first day of our expedition to El Dorado. Our family will be wealthy for all time because of what we begin here. Can you picture it?" Carlos stood rolling up his bedroll.

Eduardo interrupted Basilio's reply: "Hah, I don't care about my family. I just want to live out my days drowning in drink and fattening myself with all the food I can eat. I want to buy any woman I want, maybe two women! It's so real I can see it."

The group ate the breakfast prepared by Isandro, and the entire time Carlos and Eduardo boasted about the fantastic life they would live once they were rich beyond rich. Basilio could not help but be distracted from his breakfast, his eyes darting over to Hutzen who sat staring at them with a piercing, silent stare.

After breakfast, it took a few moments to pack up and begin making their way in the direction Hutzen had originally indicated: west. The trek through the jungle was slow and hazardous and the insects seemed to be even more persistent and thick. As usual, Carlos was in front and Isandro was at the back. Eduardo had fastened Hutzen's shackles to the donkey which forced Basilio into the uncomfortable position of walking next to him. The old man marched silently, and it seemed as if the rugged jungle terrain didn't hinder him in the least. Basilio thought that, despite the Aztecs age, he would be much faster traveling through the jungle than even Isandro who was an accomplished naturalist.

A half-day walk took the group to a river bank where Carlos decided to take an opportunity to rest, eat lunch, and consult his new guide on the next course of action. The sky was still gray but everyone was grateful for an opportunity to rest as the hot and humid weather wore quickly on all of them.

"Isandro, lunch," Carlos ordered, even though Isandro had already anticipated the order and began preparations.

Basilio watched his brother remove a water skin from his belt as he approached Hutzen. After taking a deep drink, he offered the water to Hutzen who, despite his reluctance to take anything from his captor, accepted and then drank deeply. "Which way?"

Hutzen stood for a minute, staring at Carlos before pointing down river.

"Thank you." Carlos turned, leaving Hutzen with the water skin. He took a couple steps toward the river, pealed off his tunic and pants, and wadded into the water. "I need to cool off."

"How do you know he's telling the truth about what direction to go? Maybe I should smack him around a little just to make sure." Eduardo said and followed Carlos' lead and made his way into the river.

"He's telling the truth. See, to him, you're the bad one and I'm the good one. I do the same thing with the slaves back at the outpost. I let them think I'm protecting them from you just long enough to get them to happily shuffle into a ship destined for God-knows-where... how do you think I maintain order when half the time we're outnumbered by natives ten to one?" Carlos stretched out in the water, floating. "Besides, why would he lie? He knows his only hope is that we'll cut him loose after we find what we're looking for."

"Will we?" Basilio stood at the shoreline, watching his brother.

"Will we what?" Carlos asked.

"Will we let him go after we get to El Dorado?" Basilio watched as Hutzen lay in the grass on the shoreline and closed his eyes.

"Probably not. He's old, but he can still carry a good amount of gold. Once we're home, I can try to sell him up north but I doubt I'll be able to. I can set him free then." Carlos had clearly thought this through, his experience in his trade aiding in the formulation of his plan.

Before long, Isandro had prepared lunch and the group ate hungrily, the effort from their journey sapping much of their energy. Carlos made sure Hutzen received a portion of food, and the group set out again, following the river downstream. As they made their way along the shoreline, the random rocks and stone outcroppings began to look more and more like carved structures of ruins from a time long ago. Carlos' eyes darted about with excitement.

"There's a camp up ahead" Isandro, from the back of the group said as he was the first to notice a collection of four tents on the river bank ahead of them.

"Get down! We approach slowly and quietly! Get your pistols out. Eduardo, keep the donkey and Hutzen here and keep watch with your musket," Carlos ordered.

The group did as they were told and Basilio could feel the rush of excitement and fear. The camp was clearly European but they were a very long ways away from any Spanish or Portuguese settlements. It was likely that whoever occupied the camp was here for the same reason they were, to find El Dorado. If that was the case, it was much more likely they would prefer to just kill competitors than to cooperate and have to share the spoils of their expedition.

Isandro broke right and crept along the vegetation on the shoreline. Basilio followed his brother to the left, and he hugged the jungle; attempting to keep trees and tall grass between him and the camp as he approached.

"What on earth is that smell?" Basilio gasped as he was slammed with an overwhelming stench.

Carlos heaved in an attempt to hold his breath "Something's rotting," he gasped.

The group crept closer, Carlos and Basilio on one side, Isandro on the other. A cloud of flies swarmed about the carcass of something long dead lying by a nearby tree.

Abruptly Carlos broke his attempt at stealth, stood upright from his crouching position, and marched into the camp. "There's no one here, look."

Isandro left his hiding place on the shoreline and approached Carlos. "It looks like they had about three pack animals, probably donkeys, tied to that tree. They must have been killed by animals not too long ago." Isandro said and gestured to the heavily decomposed remains lying near the tree. The flesh had grown black and peeled away from the yellow bone as scavengers took their turn since the animal's demise. Maggots and flies gorged on the rotting meat.

Basilio waited for a few moments before following his brother into the camp. He had gotten somewhat used to the smell at this point but was hesitant to get much closer if he could help it.

"Why'd they leave all their equipment, their tents?" Basilio asked while glancing around. He noticed the camp didn't appear to be abandoned; cooking pots, bedrolls, even a musket lay about as if the owners were about to return at any moment.

"Maybe the jungle got them," Eduardo said and made his way to the rest of the group, his musket in one hand, the donkey and Hutzen in tow. "Anyone who doesn't know how to survive out here is just prey for something that does."

"Take a look around, take whatever may be useful and we'll set up camp downstream once we get the hell away from that stench." Carlos began rummaging through a tent, followed by the rest of the group.

Hutzen stood shackled to the donkey and glanced around the camp, at the donkey corpses, and the jungle. A wide grin crossed his face and he nodded in approval.

"Look. They were here to find El Dorado!" Isandro held up a coin identical to the ones Carlos carried with him.

Carlos stopped his scrounging for a moment and took a few steps over to Isandro to observe his find. "Maybe they were." Glancing over to Hutzen he held up Isandro's coin "How far?"

Hutzen looked over to Carlos and began speaking in his Aztec tongue.

Carlos shook his head and picked up a handful of pebbles from the riverbed. He held one up. "This is a day." He made a broad

# DEAD HISTORY

motion with his arms at the sun. "How many days until we reach El Dorado?" He held up the coin to emphasize the city of gold.

Hutzen reached up with his shackled hands and took the pebbles from Carlos. He stood thinking for a minute and then held out three stones.

"Thank you." Carlos patted Hutzen on the shoulder. "Three days! We're not far now."

"One of them must have gotten hurt," Eduardo said as he held up a bloody bed roll and gestured to some bloody rags lying on the ground within the tent.

"That's a lot of blood," Basilio said, feeling somewhat light-headed at the gruesome sight.

Carlos thought for a minute. "We don't really know what happened here or to this group, so we'll have to be extra cautious from here on out. Let's get away from this place and set up camp."

The group finished scrounging and moved downstream until the abandoned camp was out of sight. The sun began to set, and when a suitable location was found, they prepared to rest for the night while Isandro prepared a fire and dinner. As Basilio waited to eat, he couldn't help but sense that the jungle had grown much quieter since their expedition began, and as night fell, the noisy jungle that was just becoming familiar seemed alien again.

Hutzen sat chained to a tree with the donkey. He didn't seem overly concerned with having been torn from his home and cast into shackles to guide the group to a place no European had ever found. El Dorado was, of course, famous. However, while there were many expeditions that set out to find it, most never returned.

Suddenly, the donkey began braying loudly and pulled his chain taught against the tree, backing away with all its might.

"What'd you do?" Eduardo thundered as he stomped over to Hutzen with one hand balled into a fist.

"He didn't do anything. I was watching him," Basilio interjected before Eduardo could slam his fist into Hutzen. The donkey's braying became louder and more frantic.

Thinking for a moment, Eduardo paused before opening his fist and slapping Hutzen across the face and then kicking him in the leg. Hutzen glared at Eduardo with hatred but sat against the tree, resigned to his helplessness.

# DEAD HISTORY

"Eduardo, get your musket. Something's spooking the donkey," Carlos said, his pistol already out as Isandro began lighting torches and sticking them into the ground around the camp to provide more light. Basilio drew his pistol and peered into the darkness beyond the torchlight.

"Shut that damn thing up! What a horrible sound!" Carlos gestured to the donkey which was insane with panic. It's braying nearly drowned out his orders.

Eduardo, clearly as annoyed with the donkey as the rest of the group, knew that a spooked animal was far beyond reason to be calmed. With his musket in hand, he smashed the butt of the gun into the donkey's forehead. The beast collapsed in a heap and fell silent.

Almost in reaction to the silence a hollow moan rose up from the darkness and the group stood with their backs to the campfire, looking out into the jungle for the source.

"What the hell was that!?" Basilio had never heard anything like that in his life.

"Shhh... listen," Carlos hissed. He seemed to have pinpointed the origin of the moan and trained his pistol on a swath cut between some trees on the edge of their camp.

The rest of the group aimed in the same direction, as the unmistakable sound of something shambling through the jungle toward them became louder. Hutzen himself edged to the side of his tree, opposite the emerging sound.

The torches cast enough light to distinguish the form of a man slowly emerging from the jungle. The man walked clumsily and his arms hung limp at his sides.

"Stop! Who goes there?" Carlos spoke sternly but uncertainty tainted his voice.

"What in God's name is that smell?" Eduardo hissed through clenched teeth.

The approaching stranger's only reply was a horrifying moan as it drew into the torchlight to reveal itself. The man's flesh was badly decomposed and his clothes hung as rags. His lips were gnawed off and an array of broken teeth shone through black-stained gums. His eyes, glazed white, seemed fixed on the group with purpose.

Carlos pulled the trigger on his pistol, followed by Eduardo who fired with his musket. The shots smashed into the stranger's chest and he toppled backwards to lay still.

"What on earth..." Eduardo took a step toward the corpse as if to investigate and then jumped back in fright. The haggard man slowly rolled onto its stomach and awkwardly began to bring himself to its feet.

Isandro took one step toward the intruder and aimed directly for the man's heart with his pistol. After the briefest of pauses, he fired his pistol and the bizarre man swayed slightly as the shot penetrated his body but, unphased, continued to lift himself off the ground.

"Reload!" Carlos drew his blade and stood between the stranger and the camp as Eduardo and Isandro began to hurriedly powder and load their weapons.

The stiff, uncoordinated man who resembled a creature, brought itself to its feet with its back turned to the camp and slowly leered around to face Carlos. With one rotten hand it reached out and Carlos swung with his blade, lopping the creature's arm off at the elbow. The thing seemed oblivious to its wound and lumbered toward Carlos as he backed away.

Two shots again pierced the night as Eduardo and Isandro fired their weapons into the creature, its posture counterbalancing the force of the blows and merely swaying backward slightly. The mutilated man seemed not to notice the impact of the balls and reached out toward Carlos with his one boney hand.

Basilio stood paralyzed with terror but the sight of the creature in full firelight brought him to his senses. Its horrific form was reaching for Carlos and its mangled maw gaped open hungrily for his brother's throat. Seeing the creature focused on Carlos, Basilio saw an opening. Quickly, he stepped toward the creature and placed the pistol against its temple. A flash of powder and sparks erupted as the pistol fired and the invader toppled to the ground face first.

Isandro and Eduardo stood back from the corpse but continued to load their weapons. Carlos stood staring at the rotting figure, his blade ready to strike. Basilio took several steps back and began to reload his pistol as well. Hutzen sat against his tree with a wide grin on his face. A strong wind rustling through the jungle was the only sound to pierce the black night.

"It's dead. Help me get this putrid thing out of camp," Carlos said, the first to break the silence.

"I'm not touching that foul thing! How do you know its dead? We put six shots into it and cut off its arm and it didn't even seem to notice." Eduardo was uncharacteristically panicked. He was used to being the scariest thing around and having that illusion shattered was not a pleasant experience for him.

Isandro grabbed the figure's legs and Carlos did the same to its remaining arm and they hauled the corpse out of the camp.

"What was that thing?" Basilio addressed Hutzen who looked up at him.

Basilio walked over to where Hutzen sat and crouched down. "What was that?" he asked again, hoping to bridge the language barrier. Hutzen's only response was a deep, sinister chuckle and a wide, confident grin.

"I think that was the injured man from the abandoned campsite. His clothes were rotting off him but they were clearly European. I've never seen anything like that before," Carlos said, having returned from his grim task of disposing the body.

"Who's keeping first watch?" Eduardo asked.

"That's a good idea, Eduardo. I'll keep first watch. You can take second, Isandro third, Basilio can be morning watch," Carlos said. "Okay, I know everyone's a little shaken up but we have a big day ahead of us tomorrow. Get whatever sleep you can and we'll talk about what happened in the morning."

Despite Carlos' orders, no one was able to sleep that night and the morning came far too early for everyone.

\* \* \*

Breakfast was eaten in silence and camp was packed up without a word. No one was in a mood to discuss anything, but despite their horrifying experience, they continued on. The sky was overcast and the clouds threatened to give way to a heavy downpour at any moment.

# DEAD HISTORY

Eventually the sound of rushing water could be heard in the distance, and as they made their way downstream, it was unmistakable that they were approaching a waterfall. The ruins had become more elaborate and collapsed stone buildings could be seen poking out from beneath overgrowth. Before long, they found themselves at the edge of a cliff where the river terminated as a beautiful waterfall into the jungle below.

"Where to now?" Carlos first words of the morning addressed Hutzen.

"Down." Hutzen spoke as he motioned to the cliff edge.

"Figures," Carlos said and turned angrily and continued with the group toward the waterfall. As they neared, a large structure could be seen adjacent to the water; a raised stone platform flanked by four pillars on each side stood in nearly perfect condition at the edge of the cliff. A long table sat in the middle of the platform and the pillars, floor, and table were covered with carvings of strange symbols. The symbols were similar to those they had seen on Hutzen's tent and Basilio shot the old man a wayward glance just in time to catch an expression of excitement vanish from his face.

Climbing onto the platform one by one, they looked out over the cliff to assess their first real challenge of the expedition. A sharp drop descended roughly one hundred feet below, down a stony cliff face. The donkey would have to be left behind and the supplies divided up and carried by the group from now on.

"Look," Isandro said. He had climbed atop the table in the middle of the platform and pointed at something on the ground before him. The rest of the group walked over and looked.

A rope was tied to the base of one of the pillars and lay coiled up on the ground. Next to the rope were two words scrawled in some sort of brown-black substance – **DEATH BELOW**

"Nice of them to leave us a rope," Carlos said as he began to unload the donkey and tie the packs to the end of the rope.

"They also left us a warning, Carlos. Was that nice of them, too?" Basilio asked with apprehension at how cavalier his brother was about their next course of action.

"If you found a city laden with treasures beyond measure would you leave a sign at your doorstep that said *gold below*?" Eduardo asked as he took off his backpack and peered over the edge down to the jungle below. The base of the cliff immediately below the stone platform had a small grass clearing that would make an excellent landing.

"No, but I wouldn't leave a rope at my doorstep either, Eduardo," Isandro replied. He seemed to take a cautionary view similar to Basilio. "And if they're down there, how'd the rope get coiled up here?"

"I don't think it's important," Carlos said. "Whoever came before us isn't here any more and we're a few days away from our destination. Take Hutzen's shackles off. He can't climb down with them on. Tie up the donkey next to the river; we'll come back for it." Carlos began to lower the packs down the cliff face with the rope.

Eduardo stomped over to Hutzen and removed his shackles. Hutzen looked up at Eduardo, his face expressionless.

One by one, they made their way down to the clearing at the base of the cliff and put their packs back on. They divided up the equipment from the donkey and stood for a moment, observing their surroundings. The rush of the nearby waterfall was the only sound of the jungle, and as they glanced about, small unusual looking rocks could be seen jutting out from all over the ground.

"Bones," Isandro said. He was the first to recognize what the rocks actually were. "Must be hundreds of them."

"Pistols and muskets out," Carlos said. "These bones look like they've been here for a long time but I'm not taking any chances." Carlos held his blade in one hand and his pistol in the other.

"Should I put the shackles back on Hutzen?" Eduardo asked. He already had the shackles in his hands, eager to put them back on the old man.

"No, let him walk at the front with me. He's our guide now," Carlos said casually as he walked over to Hutzen. "Which way?" Carlos asked.

Hutzen massaged his wrists as he watched Eduardo disappointedly put the iron shackles into his pack. Looking back at Carlos, he gestured in a direction and the group began to make their way through the jungle.

# DEAD HISTORY

The jungle canopy was dense and the overcast sky made for little light. Carlos, excited to be making progress, elected to eat lunch on the road, and as dusk approached, they had to light torches well before the sun went down to find their way. The sounds of the jungle were almost non-existent and the sky began to roll with thunder.

"It's going to be a wet night," Eduardo remarked.

"Should we make camp before it starts to downpour?" Basilio directed his question at Carlos, but his eyes caught Isandro who stood motionless at the back of the group. Isandro's eyes squinted as they focused on something in the jungle off to the side.

"That's probably a good..." Carlos began.

"Not here," Isandro interrupted.

Carlos saw that Isandro had stopped and was peering into the dense thicket. As Carlos walked from the front of the group to where Isandro stood, Isandro lowered his torch and motioned for the rest of the group to do the same.

"What's going on? Why are we stopped?" Eduardo bellowed, having failed to notice the change in Carlos and Isandro's demeanor.

"Shhh!" Carlos chided Eduardo and stood closer to Isandro.

Isandro slowly raised his blade, pointing into the jungle and Carlos attempted to direct his eyes to where he was gesturing.

Eduardo and Basilio moved closer to Isandro and Carlos in an attempt to see what the two men were focused on.

"I don't see anything," Basilio whispered.

"Keep watching and you'll see it," Isandro whispered back.

Then Basilio saw it... the dense thicket would have made it impossible to see anything if not for Isandro's keen eyesight. There, wandering through the jungle, were several men shuffling about. They were too far away to distinguish them clearly but they seemed to be wandering haphazardly without direction.

"What should we do?" Basilio asked.

"It's not safe to make camp tonight. I don't think they've seen us so if we continue along where we're going we'll avoid them," Carlos said quietly.

"I can make my way into the thicket close enough to shoot them," Eduardo suggested. "Take care of them before they alert anyone else."

"No... the musket shot will alert anyone else for miles. Let's leave them...where's Hutzen?" Carlos asked. He took his eyes off the figures in the distance and glanced about.

Isandro, Eduardo and Basilio were stunned. Their attention had been on the figures in the distance for only a moment but apparently a moment was all Hutzen needed to slip away.

"That bastard! I knew I should have kept him shackled," Eduardo snapped as he looked around frantically for any sign of the old man.

"Dammit!" Carlos growled. He stormed about, peering through the jungle for Hutzen, hoping in vain that the old man would reveal himself.

A loud thunder crashed through the jungle and a gentle rain began to fall.

"It's okay. I remember the map he was drawing back at his camp," Carlos said. "When we get back to the trade outpost, remind me to send an expedition to find that son-of-a-bitch." Carlos was furious but couldn't let his anger discourage the men he was leading. Hutzen's escape was his fault and he knew it. His overconfidence in his ability to gain Hutzen's trust cost him a guide.

"So we continue on?" Isandro looked questioningly at Carlos.

"Yes. Let's get moving. It's going to be a miserable night." Carlos turned his back on the group and began to march along their original path through the jungle. One by one the rest of the expedition followed suit.

As night fell, the blackness of the jungle, accompanied by the relentless downpour and rolling thunder was unforgiving. The torches struggled to stay lit against the howling wind and torrential rain and the moonless night threatened to engulf them in shadow. The group marched on in miserable silence, hoping their efforts would pay off with the wealth of El Dorado.

Basilio was startled when he felt a strong grip on his shoulder. He turned around to see Isandro staring off into the jungle again.

"Carlos, Eduardo! Stop!" Isandro whispered as loudly as he could. Eduardo and Carlos glanced behind and saw that Isandro was once again focused on something important. They hurried over to where Basilio and Isandro stood and attempted to locate what he was focused on.

"Listen," Isandro whispered.

The group stood silently for a moment. The patter of rain, the wind rushing through the jungle, and the occasional thunder, made listening difficult but there was a sound that was unmistakable echoing beneath the more prominent sounds of the environment. Numerous hollow moans overlapped one another into a single terrifying undertone.

"I hear it! What the hell is that? It sounds like..." Basilio was cut short by the very loud, very close, moan of something terrifying lumbering out of the jungle near their position.

The group positioned to face the sound, extending their pistols and muskets, now ready to fire. The human-shaped creature was far more rotten than the one they had encountered before. The walking corpse-like thing stumbled along on thin legs that were laden with numerous gruesome cuts and tears. The chest cavity was splayed open, displaying a heartless torso and black gore; dried blood caked the creature from the shoulders down. A lazy head wobbled on a thin neck and sunken white eyes stared at the group with a soulless hunger.

The living corpse reached its arms out toward the group and shambled towards them. Isandro, Basilio, Eduardo, and Carlos fired their weapons. The shots made black pitted holes in the creature's shoulders and chest but were otherwise ineffective in stopping it.

As before, Carlos stepped forward with his blade as everyone else reloaded. This time, however, the blackness of the night hid other dangers. Another form dove through the jungle and tackled Carlos. The attacker and Carlos rolled to the ground, the torch Carlos was holding hitting the wet grass to be extinguished in an instant. With one quarter of their light gone, the night seemed all the more black.

Isandro drew his blade and attempted to hold off the original attacker. Eduardo took the butt of his musket and smashed it into the side of the creature's ribcage. The force of the blow made a sickening crack but the thing seemed unaffected and stayed focused on driving its jaws into Carlos' throat. Basilio hastily reloaded his pistol as he glanced about. The dim torchlight vaguely distinguished the forms of several dozen additional bodies emerging from the jungle toward them.

Eduardo brought his musket back for a second blow. He swung hard again, connecting with the creature's skull. The thing went limp and rolled off of Carlos and onto its back. This one also had a ribcage splayed open, revealing an empty cavity, black gore coating its naked body.

Before Eduardo could turn to help Isandro, another corpse dove into him, wrapping its rotten claws around his waist in an attempt to drag him to the ground. Carlos stood up and swung his blade into the back of Eduardo's attacker. As before, the creature seemed to ignore the wound. Eduardo placed the butt of his musket between himself and his attacker in an attempt to use it as leverage to peel the corpse off him.

Three more of the dead and rotting, yet walking, corpses had emerged from the jungle to engage Isandro, and he was being overpowered quickly. The ghouls seemed to possess no sense of self preservation or reasoning ability. It seemed they only sought to overpower their prey with sheer numbers. Isandro, with blade in one hand and torch in the other, had lopped off hands and arms, but there were too many clawing, scraping hands and hungry snapping jaws to fight off. Isandro was quickly being overpowered. With a fast step, Basilio extended his loaded pistol and pointed it directly at the head of the one who was getting a grip on Isandro's neck, then pulled the trigger.

*Click.*

The impotent sound crashed like a hammer into Basilio. His powder was wet. His pistol was useless. Before he could make another move to help Isandro, the creature bit down on Isandro's neck and his scream drowned out the sound of the rain and thunder. A torrent of gore erupted from the wound and Isandro's struggles grew less. His scream weakened and the torch slipped from his hand and went dark as it hit the ground. Instantly his four attackers became six, then eight, and before Basilio could intervene—if he could intervene—Isandro was lost beneath a ravenous pile of bloodthirsty, soulless attackers. They were distracted, at least for the moment, with their new-found prey.

Another scream erupted.

Just as Carlos pulled Eduardo's attacker off, two more gripped Carlos from behind. One locked onto his shoulders and sunk its shattered jagged teeth into his arm. Another wrapped its arms around Carlos' legs and tore into his ankle. Eduardo was off balance, and before he could regain it to help Carlos, the one that had just lost its grip on his waist turned and slammed into Carlos' knees, sinking its teeth into Carlos' thigh. Carlos fell backward beneath the weight of three attackers, his screams gurgling as his mouth filled with blood and rainwater.

Dozens of additional bodies poured into the dim torchlight. Basilio dove toward his brother but was caught by the powerful arm of Eduardo.

"He's gone Basilio! We have to get out of here!" Eduardo screamed, his hair plastered to his face from the rain.

Basilio struggled in vain for a moment against the brute holding him, but more and more figures shambled into the light. It soon became clear there was nothing that could save Isandro or his brother now.

The only choice was to run.

Basilio and Eduardo turned and ran as quickly as they could. Their torches threatened to blow out, but the terrifying prospect of being lost in a pitch black night was enough to keep them moving with a mind on their only light. The screams of Isandro and Carlos ceased beneath the sound of countless moaning.

The ghouls were in turn eventually drowned out by the sound of the rain and thunder. After a run that seemed to last for hours, Eduardo and Basilio slowed then stopped.

"Where are we?" Basilio asked.

"I have no idea. I just ran. I feel like those things are right behind us still. We can't stop," Eduardo said. He paced around in a circle, peering through the dark jungle at every angle.

"We have to stop, Eduardo. We have to get back to the cliff. It's north. Do you know which way is north?" Basilio looked up at the starless night sky.

"No, we can't stop! Those things are after us. We have to keep going!" Eduardo was still in a panic.

"Eduardo! When the sun comes up we can figure out which way is north, but until then if we're running in the wrong direction, we're going to have to spend that much more time in this jungle with those things." Basilio didn't have his brother's talent for leadership.

Eduardo stormed over to Basilio and towered over him. "I'm not staying still for those things to catch up with me! If you want to stay here, that's fine. You'll slow them down for me if you do, but I'm going!"

"Okay, Eduardo, okay. Which way are we going?" Basilio had already lost his direction.

Eduardo backed off of Basilio and began to storm into the jungle while Basilio stood still.

"Are you sure that's not the direction back toward those things?" Basilio asked, hoping Eduardo wouldn't rush back to him in a rage and pummel him.

Eduardo seemed to have lost his sense of direction also and stopped dead in his tracks. The idea of walking straight back to his doom hit him in a place that forced him to listen to Basilio's reasoning. He turned and marched a few steps in the opposite direction before stopping again. He stood for a few moments, studying his surroundings. "Then which way do we go?"

"I don't know, Eduardo. We have to wait until morning. Sit down. Drink some water. Rest. As soon as the sun comes up, we'll head north and get the hell away from this place." Basilio was relieved he'd gotten through to the brute. After a moment of contemplation, Eduardo sat down next to Basilio with his back to a tree.

"I don't want to blow our torches out but I think that's what drew them to us earlier," Basilio said. "But I think if we're going to stay in one place for the rest of the night we should extinguish them. Our eyes will adjust to the darkness. It's safer that way." Basilio hoped this last nugget of reason would get through Eduardo as well.

Eduardo sat silently for a moment before extinguishing his torch. Basilio did the same and there they sat, exhausted but

# DEAD HISTORY

unable to sleep in the pitch blackness of the jungle night. The sound of the rain and thunder pounded ceaselessly through the otherwise silent jungle.

Once or twice, though they couldn't be sure, the sound of what seemed like a distant moan shot fear down their spines as they struggled to come to grips with their situation.

* * *

"Wake up," Basilio whispered as he nudged Eduardo.

Eduardo groaned and then jolted out of sleep. "What? Did you see them?"

"No," Basilio looked around and then slowly got up. He was soaked and so was most of his gear. But he was alive, which was more than he could say for half the expedition, including his brother. "They're out there, though, I can hear them. It's morning. We need to get moving."

The sun was again concealed by thick dark clouds and the jungle beneath the canopy was cloaked in shadow. The ground was wet with the previous night's rainfall and the trees dripped a constant stream of water droplets which felt like gentle rain.

Eduardo stood up. He, too, was soaked, and his clothes and equipment was all the more heavy for the water they had absorbed. "That way's north."

"Yes. Keep alert. I heard…" Basilio was interrupted by a distant moan. He glanced around quickly but couldn't pinpoint its origin.

Eduardo stiffened and his eyes darted left to right. "Go!"

Basilio and Eduardo began a light jog through the thick vegetation. It was difficult going, the ground uneven and soaked, but fear drove them on. Occasionally they would stop for a few minutes to rest. The jungle all around them was as silent as the grave. There were no animal sounds, only the gentle patter of water from the trees and the quiet rustle of the wind.

But then, all too often a hellish moan could be heard. Sometimes it would be distant, and Eduardo and Basilio would be unable to locate its origin. Occasionally the sound would be much closer and they could see the clumsy ghouls, often shambling together in groups of three or more, staring at them with lifeless white-glazed eyes. Their chests torn open and their torsos were smattered with black gore.

Eduardo and Basilio continued their jog, easily outpacing the slow, mindless corpses, but they couldn't shake the sensation that with every moan they heard, there was another addition. That the relentless nightmare mob was growing in numbers as it pursued them. Their occasional, but necessary, rest stops became shorter and shorter.

"We're almost there!" Eduardo exclaimed as the cliff face loomed larger through the jungle.

It was late afternoon and both Eduardo and Basilio were utterly exhausted by the time they made it to the base of the cliffs. They collapsed on the ground and laid there for a few moments, grateful for being so close to their escape from their living dead pursuers.

"So, is the way out east or west?" Eduardo asked. His reasoning ability seemed to have a stronger hold on him than the previous evening. He rubbed his chin as he thought.

"It's west but I don't know how far, Basilio said. "We never crossed the river that the waterfall fed into so it has to be west." Basilio lay on the ground. The darkness of the jungle wasn't nearly as dense near the cliff edge and, although the sky was still overcast, he was grateful for the additional light.

"I need to rest, Basilio. Those things are far behind us now and at least we know they won't be approaching us from the cliff face. Let's take advantage of it for a few minutes." Eduardo had considered dropping his equipment a long time ago to lighten his journey, but they still needed to make it back to civilization after their escape and thought better of it.

"Okay, Eduardo, but only for a few minutes. We may be protected from one direction, but remember the directions we can run if we need to are also limited by the cliffs." Basilio didn't have the strength to even think about not taking advantage of an opportunity to rest. He didn't consider himself in a situation where he was any safer than before but his body just burned with a need for rest.

A long while passed and the gray clouds above began to rumble.

"Eduardo, we need to get out of here before night fall. I don't know how far away the rope is and we can't scale this cliff face without it," Basilio said as he picked himself off the ground.

# DEAD HISTORY

Eduardo stiffly followed suit. "Let's get going then. I'm not spending another night down here."

The two began their walk westward along the base of the cliff. As night approached, they stopped to light torches, and moments later, the sky opened up with a torrent of rain as heavy as the previous evening.

"I'm going back to Spain when I get out of here," Basilio said. "The slave trade doesn't appeal to me and I was comfortable in Europe."

Basilio made small talk with Eduardo to lighten the dour mood. They were both miserable, but had gone through quite an ordeal together. Passing the time through talk was a good way to keep their minds off their situation.

"Your brother had a very good setup; think about it again when we get back to the trading post. It's easy and you can make a lot of money." Eduardo's livelihood was now threatened with Carlos' death. He was uncertain if he could run the slave trade, and a partner would certainly help to ensure it wouldn't fall apart.

Basilio was about to answer when he stopped, cocking his head to the side. "Did you hear that?"

Eduardo nodded. The overlapping moans of a dozen or more ghouls were barely audible over the clatter of rainfall. "Let's go!"

Eduardo and Basilio held their torches out as they began jogging along the base of the cliff. Nightfall had descended but their escape couldn't be far away now.

A half dozen of the ghouls came into view from the tree line. They regarded Eduardo and Basilio for a moment as they jogged past, then moaned as they raised their arms and lumbered forth in pursuit.

"Do you hear the waterfall? We're almost there," Basilio gasped and quickened his pace as much as his exhausted body would allow. The unmistakable crash of the waterfall rose above the rainfall and thunder.

A minute later they were there. The rope dangled where they had left it, and without hesitation, Basilio gripped his torch in his teeth and began climbing. Eduardo did the same.

About ten feet up, the rope suddenly went slack. Basilio realized in terror that he and Eduardo were falling. His mind snapped immediately to the reality of the situation. The rope had broken under their combined weight and their only escape route was now cut off.

Eduardo slammed into the ground first, followed by Basilio. The torches fell into the wet grass and everything went black. Coming to his senses, Basilio's only sensory input was the sound of the rain, the rumble of thunder, and the chorus of undead moans growing louder and louder.

Lightning flashed and for that split second of illumination, Basilio could see the cliff edge. Desperately he launched himself at the sheer rock, hoping beyond hope he could claw his way to the top. Eduardo did the same but it became immediately obvious that even if the stone wasn't slick with water, their efforts were futile. Spinning around to face the jungle, another bolt of lightning revealed the endless throngs of living dead corpses, each one moving forward with outstretched hands and hungry, jagged teeth.

Eduardo screamed in agony as he was ripped apart and a heavy force slammed into Basilio, spinning him around. Desperate for some last, slim opportunity for escape, his eyes caught something in the lightning.

Another illuminating crash confirmed what he'd seen. The rope had not broken, it had been cut.

Standing atop the cliff, framed by two stone pillars, stood a figure, blade in hand, glaring down at them. Hutzen's silhouette was unmistakable. As Basilio was overwhelmed with the sensation of a half-dozen powerful jaws driving sharp fangs into his body, he was certain that despite the fact he couldn't see his face, Hutzen was watching from above with a smug satisfied grin on his wrinkled face and a sinister chuckle on his lips.

# THE CASE OF THE SPITTALFIELDS

## G.R. MOSCA

**S**pittalfields, London 1888

Her footfalls echoed against the brick buildings as she quickened her pace through the moonlit alley. She stared again over her shoulder, observing the shadowy figure half a street away. It had been following her for two streets, refusing any intention of interrupting its pursuit of her. She darted into a darkened alleyway, hoping to elude her hunter. Streetlights disappeared and the back alley was lit only by the grace of an autumn moon. Even now, a light fog surrounded her, the autumn night sending a quicksilver shiver down her neck and along her spine. Her breathing became harsher, heavier and faster as her eyes darted along the brick backs of the Whitechapel tenements and industrial buildings. Pickets of wooden fences lining the yards appeared to her to become the teeth of an unrelenting monster bent upon crushing her in its yaw. She had almost reached the end of the alley when the scuffle of feet brought her head around again.

It was the thing; it no longer hid its intentions but stood at the mouth of the alley, openly staring and mocking her with cold, bright eyes. Her heart pounded under her corset as her hands reached out for the alley gate. As she stared, it reached into its overcoat and pulled out the longest knife she had ever seen. She would have screamed if she had maintained the presence of mind to be afraid but her instincts told her to run.

She flew through the gate into yet another alley. If only she could find a constable or perhaps a gentleman who might offer some protection. Still she ran on, looking over her shoulder to gauge her pursuer's progress. It, too, had begun to quicken its pace but it did not flatter her with anything more than a leisurely trot. The blade glinted in the moonlight, daring her to stop long enough for it to test her mettle. She dared not relent.

It was a moment later when she spied a figure in the distance of the alleyway, standing with its back to her. Hope reigned within at the prospect of this ordeal ending. She was certain the gentleman would observe her plight and would chase away the monster with righteous words and good breeding. She knew in her heart that this was her moment. She turned towards the gentleman, becoming curious at his persistent inattentiveness. She opened her mouth to utter a cry of distress but nothing issued forth except a low hiss of breath, like a dog panting. She hated herself at that moment, feeling like some low animal, pursued and revealed as such by that *thing*. She dared one more glance behind her before she might reach her savior. The thing behind her now stood openly in a shaft of perfect moonlight. It remained as still as a statue, and although it revealed itself in the luminescence of a perfect silver orb, its features remained secret with the exception of its cold eyes. She nearly stopped to catch her breath but again observed the glowing blade the thing held.

She turned and ran the few steps remaining to her savior, reaching out to him with her delicate hand upon his shoulder. He wore a thin topcoat, underneath which she could feel his bones. It struck her as odd that in this weather a gentleman would be without proper attire against the chill. Unsettling still was the sharpness of his frame, unlike the well-bred and rotund gentlemen of her acquaintance. She grasped the shoulder with more insistence until the man turned to acknowledge her. In the glow of a full moon, the red-stained eyes met her own whereupon she recoiled in horror as she took in the desiccated countenance and deathly pallor. When the man opened his mouth, his yellowed teeth yawned with hunger and his breath carried a thousand corpses on a silent howl.

She felt only a moment of pain as he sunk his teeth into her throat, biting and chewing her flesh. Eternal midnight came quickly as she died while this horror gnawed, chewed and ripped the skin from her face, ingesting her young life into his decayed mouth.

As the creature who was once a man feasted, the knife-wielding pursuer put away his blade and slowly advanced towards his ward with the knowledge that he was more akin to a sheep dog; coaxing his anxious sheep to their pen; than to a killer. The task of killing was left to his ward and always at the pleasure of their master. A sudden stifled scream caught his ear. He smiled at how busy the evening had become.

Less than a quarter mile away, near Mitre Square, Catherine Eddowes was quietly bleeding from her slashed throat before being disemboweled by Saucy Jack. In the fall of 1888, this was just another night of terror in Whitechapel.

*  *  *

Richard Downes held the Times at arms-length as he surveyed the headline:

### *Two Dispatched By the Hand of Saucy Jack. More Deaths Feared in Autumn of Terror.*

His eyes moved down the column of type, taking in the details of the latest murders. He seemed visibly moved by these atrocities in his city. Richard Downes, late of Scotland Yard, had been one of its more prominent inspectors. He was thin and diminutive with jet-black hair and piercing black eyes above an aquiline nose. He often twirled his handlebar moustache when thinking through a problem or piecing together seemingly disparate clues. He possessed a keen eye for observation and a nimble and rational mind that when brought to bear on a case, proved a formidable combination in finding the truth and keeping Britain safe. He reached for his cup of tea as he read on. Through the drawing room door entered his manservant and companion, Colin Toller.

Mr. Toller stood six feet tall, sturdy of frame, with ham-sized fists and a quiet demeanor. He had thrice been Britain's bare knuckle's boxing champion until an unfortunate accident in the ring cut short his career. He now took care of Richard Downes and served as his assistant whenever the need arose.

Richard looked up from the paper. "Have you read the latest about this bloke?"

"Yes, sir. Sounds like a real nobbler if you ask me, sir."

"Yes, well, nobbler or not, this is quite a pickle our city is in and there's not a damned thing I can do about it, dear boy."

"I hope he never catches me in a dark alley, sir. I would knock his block off. More tea, sir?"

"No, Mr. Toller. I think this calls for a whiskey. Be a good lad and fetch us some, eh?"

Colin turned and left the room, leaving Richard Downes to ruminate further on the newspaper.

A moment later, Colin returned. "Someone here to see you sir."

"Early enough, too. Who is it?"

"Inspector Fleming, Scotland Yard."

At that, Inspector Fleming was led into the room, and after shaking Richard's hand, took a seat near the fireplace. Inspector Fleming was well known to Richard, having been a colleague with him in the force for many years before Richard's leave. They respected one another and Inspector Fleming often came to call for advice with difficult cases.

Colin brought a brass tray with three glasses of whiskey and they settled into their chairs while facing the early morning glow of an autumn fire.

\* \* \*

Later, they stood in Mitre Square, surrounded by constables, reporters, and the curious. Inspector Fleming escorted Richard to the unidentified body of Catherine Eddowes, which was slumped near a wall of an industrial building and covered with a burlap cloth.

Inspector Fleming bent down next to the body. "She was found in the wee hours of this morning. I warn you, Richard, it's not a pretty sight. The killer took liberties with her that most common killers lack the imagination for."

The inspector lifted the burlap away from the body. The first thing Richard was aware of was the immense amount of blood loss. Catherine had been bled almost white from her wounds. He observed the cut across her throat, which had certainly been the killing stroke. The cut was clean and exposed her gullet clear to the spine. The killer was most certainly a powerful individual. Richard also observed that both of the victim's ears were missing. The inspector next lifted her skirt to expose her abdomen. Bystanders audibly gasped at the site now exposed. Most of the woman's abdomen had been lain open by several strategic cuts while her internal organs lay surrounding her. The sight of this caused one onlooker to faint dead away and several others to give up their morning breakfast. Richard Downes took all of this in with quiet contemplation. His face was a stony mask, never slipping or giving way to the horror with which he was observing. His mind catalogued everything.

"Inspector, is there anything missing from the body?"

"What do you mean? Money or jewelry?"

"No, Inspector. I mean any body parts aside from the ears. Are there any organs missing from her abdomen?"

"I don't rightly know guv'nor. I suppose we will have to wait for the doctor's rendering."

"Any idea who she might be?"

"We suspect she might be one of the ladies of the night who parlay in this area for their bread and butter. We're still inquiring about this."

Richard nodded for the body to be covered again. He looked around the square at the buildings, specifically the entrances and egresses to and from the area where they now stood. His keen eyes flitted across the faces of the gathered crowd of onlookers. He shook his head as a bracing wind whipped across the square.

Richard turned to Inspector Fleming. "You said there was another body, Inspector?"

"Just a few streets away. Follow me, Mr. Downes."

They headed off with Mr. Toller following behind, the big man clenching his fists.

* * *

Even in the daylight, the Eccles Street alley seemed dark and brooding. Inspector Fleming led the two men towards a high wooden fence deep within the alleyway. Unlike the Mitre Square crime scene that had been full of spectators, journalists and police, the area they were in now was populated with only a few Bobbies and one or two onlookers. At the foot of the fence lay another burlap covering. Richard observed a pool of congealed blood

# DEAD HISTORY

bordering the burlap. Inspector Fleming bent down and lifted the coverlet, revealing the remains of the previous evening's victim.

Richard viewed the body. To his eye, the two crime scenes could not have been more different. This victim was in pieces, with body parts heaped one atop the other in a disorganized and haphazard way. Richard bent closer, taking in the condition of the body. He then observed the woman's dismembered hand, which appeared to be clutching something. He opened the hand and found a piece of bandage lying in the middle of her palm. He took this into his own hand and stood upright.

"Inspector. Why do you think these women were killed by the same individual?"

"I have to assume that we have only one killer in this city capable of such a heinous crime. Why, Richard, are you saying we have more than one madman loose in London?"

Richard bent down over the body again. "Inspector, think back to the previous crime scene. The body was intruded upon in a deliberate fashion. The dismemberment and disembowelment was accomplished with precise strokes of a blade with almost surgical accuracy. There were few, if any, ragged edges to be observed. Look at this body. There is no deliberateness to the horror here. There are no cuts of any kind, Inspector. On the contrary, these are teeth marks. This individual was attacked and ripped apart as if by some wild animal. I say that not to disparage your investigation, nor to suggest this attack is the work of an animal, but merely to contrast how utterly different these two attacks were from one another."

Richard Downes stood up again and faced the inspector. He held out the yellowed piece of bandage retrieved from the victim's hand. "And this, taken from the dead hand of this poor soul. May I hang on to this? I might be able to tell you more if you allow me to analyze it."

"Yes of course, Richard. What are you telling me then, that we have more than one fiend at work in Spittalfields?"

"Yes, Inspector. That is exactly what I'm saying."

# DEAD HISTORY

* * *

Less than one week after his examination of the victims, Richard Downes stood in a darkened alley in the East End of London with Colin and Inspector Fleming. It was Richard's strong opinion that either killer would claim another woman within the fortnight. His belief was deduced from a study of the crimes committed within the last three months of the area and the results of his tests from the curious piece of cloth found at the second crime scene.

Richard recalled summoning Inspector Fleming to his residence a few days earlier. He had met the inspector at the door and led him straightaway to his laboratory. There he had summarized his findings from the fabric. The first curious piece of evidence had been the material's age. If Richard's test results were correct, the cloth was close to two thousand years old and made from a material found in the delta region of Egypt. The second curious piece of evidence to be derived from his examination was an unidentified chemical that had permeated the cloth. It was of an unknown extract, however when Richard completed a partial synthesis of the compound, he discovered it had extremely curious qualities. The foremost quality being that it rejuvenated anything it came into contact with: rusted metal became as new, dried wood regained its original constitution and luster. Even applying it to a gray hair plucked from his head—one of only a few to be found—restored the follicle to its original color and shine. What this meant, he couldn't say. For the moment it was another puzzle piece awaiting the time when it might be added to a larger picture.

The wind howled as midnight approached. The three companions secreted themselves behind a building on Hansbury Street, close to the vicinity of the previous murders. Inspector Fleming felt in his pockets for a flask of whiskey, and having retrieved it, took a generous swallow to fortify himself against the cold. He proffered the flask first towards Richard, who waved it off with a smile, then to Mr. Toller, who waved it away as well.

Inspector Fleming nodded agreeably and helped himself to another snort. In the meantime, Richard pulled a police revolver from his pocket and checked the chamber, then put it away. Next he fingered his cane and applied pressure to a catch on the handle,

## DEAD HISTORY

pulling the lower part of the cane away to reveal a hidden saber. Satisfied that all was in order, Richard closed the cane back onto the blade with a snap and leaned on it for support.

"You're not one to come to one of these parties without bringing a box of chocolates, are you guv'nor?" Inspector Fleming remarked with a sense of pride. He pulled his police revolver out and checked the chamber as well. He then put the gun back in place and pulled out a lead sap. "I prefer one of these beauties if I'm going to the dance."

"You always were a good dancer, weren't you Jack," Richard smiled.

Inspector Fleming grinned in reply and then looked over to Colin. "What did you bring for the kiddies?"

Colin looked back at the inspector and first held up his right fist and then his left fist. "I brought John and Bull." At this they all laughed and then settled back to waiting.

It happened suddenly, at almost one hour past midnight. They heard a woman's scream from across the fence, no more than an alley or so away from the spot they were standing in. Colin was the first to run in the direction of the voice, followed closely by Richard and Fleming. Colin appeared to fly through the alleyways as he displayed an encyclopedic knowledge of the twists and turns of the maze-like back streets of the East End.

Moments later, they stood at the entrance of an alley spying three figures frozen in a curious dance. Richard could see a lone figure in shabby clothes seeming to observe a woman and her attacker. This lone observer was small, with long hair covering its face and wielding a long knife in its gnarled arm. Further inside the alleyway, the woman who had screamed now lay in a heap, a few feet away from the third figure.

Richard, Colin and Fleming hoped that the woman was unharmed, however, the assailant drew nearer and staggered slowly towards her supine body. Curiously, this figure wore a thin topcoat that covered most of its body. Where the moonlight shone through the fog, they could glimpse that this figure looked as though it was wrapped in bandages.

As they continued further into the alley, the man standing guard over the scene finally took notice of them and let out an unearthly hiss so vile, it sent shivers down their spines. It then raised its knife threateningly at the three of them. The inspector pulled his badge from a coat pocket and shouted, "Halt where you are, Scotland Yard!"

In response, the figure raised its knife and rushed towards Fleming. Richard already had his saber free from the cane and parried deftly with the thing. While the two dueled, Colin ran around them towards the girl just as the other creature was almost upon her. It became aware of Colin's approach and faced him. The shock of this thing's features threw Colin into a brief state of confusion. Its eyes were blood red, it's face was that of dried flesh, no more human than a hornet's nest, but its teeth were alive with a fury that was unsurpassed by any wild animal, be it here or in the deepest heart of the jungle.

It lunged towards Colin, all teeth and corpse-like breath. Colin gathered his wits and automatically raised his ham-fists up into a boxing stance. As the thing closed in upon him, Colin cocked back his right fist and let fly with all the might and energy in his possession. His blow connected with the thing's jaw and its head flew off its shoulders as the body crumpled to the ground.

Meanwhile, Richard parried and counter-parried the guardian's knife thrusts as Inspector Fleming reached into his pocket for his revolver. The thing was an excellent fencing adversary but as he caught sight of his ward giving up the ghost, he must have decided it was time to leave the fight for another day. The guardian quickly turned and jumped towards the fence behind him, but not quickly enough. Richard grabbed a hold of his coattails and held on with all of his might. For a moment the two figures were locked in an interminable tug-of-war until the thing shirked itself out of the coat and was lost to the darkness.

Richard and Fleming now ran to Colin who was gently cradling the woman's head in his hands. She appeared unharmed, and as Colin and his companions bent over her, she opened her eyes. They went wide for just a moment and then visibly relaxed as she realized that she no longer needed to fear for her life from the loathsome thing that had attacked her. Inspector Fleming looked over at the remains of the creature and remarked, "Your boy Colin knocked that creature's head clean off, Richard."

Richard smiled at Colin and replied, "And that's exactly the reason why they won't let him in the ring anymore." Richard looked back over at Colin. "Isn't that right Mr. Toller?"

\* \* \*

News of Saucy Jack's victims continued to make headlines through the month of October. It was nearly November when Richard, Colin and Inspector Fleming arrived at the British Museum. They quietly passed down corridors filled with objects of history intent upon one destination only–the Egyptian Wing.

When they arrived, they asked for an audience with Dr. Liebestod, the visiting professor of Egyptology and esteemed professor of Occult Linguistics at Berlin University. When the doctor arrived, he was surprised then puzzled by this odd collection of individuals who had come to seek his counsel. He acted nonchalant until Inspector Fleming flashed his badge and requested a private room for their conversation. The doctor's expression quickly turned from boredom to worried and he immediately suggested his office in the museum for their meeting.

The doctor's office was actually a laboratory filled with various tubes, vials and Bunsen burners as well as glass cases containing the bodies of what looked like mummies. Richard was envious of some of the doctor's equipment and wondered for what purpose Liebestod might have use for all of this paraphernalia.

They sat around a large oak desk and Richard took a parcel from his coat and unfolded it on the desk's surface.

"Doctor, do you have any idea what this might be?" Richard asked.

Lying on the desk was the swatch of fabric found at the second crime scene. The doctor seemed a bit relieved at the question and picked up the fabric to study it for a few moments.

"Ya, of course. Look around you gentlemen. Each of these mummies is kept in almost pristine condition because of a process that the Egyptians perfected but has since been lost forever. These are the sacred wrappings of a pharaoh's mummy warriors."

# DEAD HISTORY

Inspector Fleming guffawed and blurted out, "Mummy what, you say?"

"Ya, ya. Werklich, mein Inspector, the mummy warriors of Pharaoh Im-Hotep the second. The legend tells us that the pharaoh possessed an army of fearless warriors. They looked like men but in battle they felt no pain, feared no man and gave no quarter. They were not like regular men. They were more like animals. It is said they would rip apart their enemy in battle and literally devour them."

Richard looked the doctor in the eye. "Why then would anyone bring these things back to life?"

The doctor smiled and continued. "You are mistaken, Herr Downes. These things were not alive to begin with. Legend says that they were the 'army of the dead'. This was the secret to their victory in battle. One cannot kill that which is dead."

Richard pressed on. "How does one raise an army of the dead, doctor?"

"We cannot know. Perhaps they are a phenomenon of nature. Perhaps these things were made. What we do know is that at some time during the reign of this Pharaoh, a meteor appeared in the sky. It was shortly after this event that mention of an army of the dead begins to appear in the scrolls."

"Doctor," the inspector interrupted, "how is it that we find this cloth at a murder scene in East London along with your card in the pocket of a criminal who may or may not have been instrumental in causing at least one death that we're currently investigating?" With this pronouncement, Inspector Fleming placed a card of introduction bearing Dr. Liebestod's name onto the table next to the swatch.

"I assure you, I cannot tell you what the circumstance's surrounding this unfortunate coincidence may be."

"We have your monster, Doctor. We're here by no mere coincidence," Inspector Fleming said.

Richard could tell Dr. Liebestod was becoming anxious so he interjected. "You said these things are dead. I assume you mean that they cannot be killed. Why then shouldn't the mummies in this room sit up and attack us?"

# DEAD HISTORY

The doctor became very excited again. "Simple, dear sir. They are dead and cannot be killed by normal means, however, the Pharaoh had them mummified and then put into a deep slumber using a serum of great alchemical potency."

"What are you saying, Doctor?"

"My friends, I'm saying that these creatures surrounding us are merely asleep and given the counteragent would again awaken to serve their original intention."

"As agents of death?" Richard hazarded.

"Very good, Herr Downes. Ya, that is as good as any description I have heard." The doctor stood up and walked to one of the laboratory tables. "May I show you gentlemen something?" He looked at each of them in turn. Inspector Fleming nodded in agreement. "With your permission I shall call my assistant. Hans," the doctor shouted and moments later the guardian they had encountered in the alley during that late October evening walked into the room, carrying his long knife in one hand and a small revolver in the other. The three men stood almost simultaneously and faced the doctor and his assistant.

"Now, now, please do not take any hasty action, my friends. Please sit down. I have something important to show you."

Dr. Liebestod picked up a syringe from the laboratory table. The syringe contained a serum that seemed to glow as if it were brimstone from the depths of Hell. "This synthesis took many years to perfect. It is derived from the alchemical formula contained in the book of Al-Hazred the Mad Arab. When I inject this into the sleeping bodies of these warriors, you shall see with your own eyes their rebirth. There is but one drawback. They are hungry upon awakening and remain hungry forever after."

At this, Dr. Liebestod began injecting the smallest amount of diabolical fluid into the neck of each figure. When he was finished, he had injected no less than fifteen of the sleeping monsters.

"And now, I must leave you. Auf Wiedersehen." He exited the room while his assistant stood near the doorway, still pointing his pistol at the three men. The assistant said nothing but his eyes sparkled with malice.

Interminable seconds passed like minutes to no effect; the bodies remained inanimate. Colin looked at Richard questioningly at

# DEAD HISTORY

how long this should be allowed to go on. Richard glanced over Colin's shoulder at the doctor's assistant and whispered something very quickly and pointedly to Colin. Inspector Fleming wasn't even aware when Colin spun around and threw a small but lethal knife that struck the assistant in the shoulder. He howled in pain and fell towards the laboratory table, throwing burners and tubes of fluids into disarray. In moments, a small conflagration had begun to quickly spread throughout the laboratory. Colin and Richard were again on their feet and speeding towards the assistant. He saw them coming towards him, turned, and leapt through a closed window, breaking glass and landing hard on a brick sidewalk outside of the museum. Richard and Colin continued to the window but turned when they heard Fleming exclaim with a startled gasp, "Help me, they're alive!"

Richard and Colin now saw several pairs of desiccated hands grasping the sides of their glass display cases. Several other mummified creatures were sitting up in their cases and hissing loudly at the interruption of their long sleep. Richard and Colin could scarcely believe their eyes as the things rose from their glass coffins and slowly began shuffling towards them, jaws clicking menacingly.

Inspector Fleming was the first to react by drawing his service revolver and firing several bullets into the walking horrors to no effect. Meanwhile, the flames from the fire grew, bathing the room in a soft orange glow. Several of the creatures nearest the fire spontaneously burst into flames. Richard let loose his saber cane and took the heads clean off of two of the closest monsters. Colin, affecting his best boxing stance replicated his infamous roundhouse punch and took the head off of another ghoul.

"Follow me, lads. Out this way!" Richard shouted as they alternately dodged the demons or dispatched them ruthlessly. They fought their way outside as smoke and flames shot through the windows of the museum. By the time they reached the street, constables and fire brigade wagons were arriving on the scene.

Richard looked about the grounds but could find no sign of the doctor or his ghastly assistant. The three heard a distant hissing and screaming from the fire within the building, and recoiled at the thought of what they had narrowly escaped.

Inspector Fleming, still shaken by the ordeal, looked at Colin with amazement and said, "Let me guess, a circus knife thrower as well?"

Colin smiled in reply.

Richard wondered if he would meet the good doctor and his assistant again at some point in the future. If so, he vowed he would be prepared.

* * *

It was cold in Miller's Court in the wee hours of the November morning. A well-dressed gentleman was leaving the tenement lodging of a young woman named Mary Kelly. As he closed the door behind him, he looked into the courtyard tentatively, pressing his hand against the front of his overcoat while the other hand carried a large leather case. He then walked out of the alcove into the gloom of Miller's Court.

"Hang about, my son," a voice boomed, catching the man by surprise. A ham-sized fist clamped onto the shoulder of the gentleman.

Colin turned him around and inquired, "And where do you think you're going at this time of the morning, my good sir."

"It's alright, boss. I'm just minding my own business." He nodded towards the building while curling an index finger over the crease of his nose.

Richard stepped out of the shadows and into the courtyard. "Hold him there, will you, lad," he asked as he stepped towards the doorway. As Richard opened the door, the scent of blood and gore wafted from the flat the gentleman had just exited.

Richard disappeared inside the flat for just a moment but when he returned, his demeanor had completely changed. In all the years they had known one another, Colin had never seen him as angry as he now appeared. Richard's hand went to his cane and in a moment he freed the rapier from its sheath.

The gentleman looked at Richard with apprehension and whispered, "Is there no help for a widow's son?"

Richard looked back at him with burning embers in his eyes, and in a voice quaking with anger spat out, "Certainly, sir. Why don't I do you the kind favor of sending you straight to Hell." He raised his saber and ran the gentleman through. The man crumpled to the ground, exhaling his dying breath.

"Help me throw this piece of excrement in the Thames, would you please, Mr. Toller."

With that said and done, they disposed of the body.

Richard and Colin were to share many other adventures during their career as advisors to Scotland Yard; however, they never spoke of the events that occurred during the autumn of 1888. But, neither Saucy Jack nor the Spittalfields Horror ever darkened the streets of London again.

# ONLY THE DEAD WILL STAND

## KEVIN JAMES BREAUX

Lane had followed him from town to dusty town; through three states and over six long months. He had to make sure he was targeting the right man. He had to make sure his vengeance would be proper. They called the gunslinger by many names; Reaper, Widow Maker, even Mr. Death.

Lane simply referred to him as the Silent Man, because in all this time tracking the man, he had never heard the man make a sound.

Upon reaching the small town of Three River Junction, New Mexico, Lane became overwhelmed with nostalgia. His home was a lot like this sun beaten little place; a combination of farming fields and a single main street running through a collection of staple shops.

As he entered the city limits, he swore he could hear his late mother cry; her sobbing adrift atop the wind blowing from the largest of the three rivers that cornered the town. Her endless weeping; he remembered it well. *She cried a lot.*

It had been nearly ten years ago, 1870, when Lane's father died. He was a well-known hunter and shootist living in a small trading post just outside of Carson City, Nevada; a good, caring family man, say-all. He promised his wife, son and daughter, with all his heart and soul, that he would win the yearly gunfighter's contest in the big city.

Lane dredged up a memory of when his mother pleaded his father not to go, her tears raining upon his old deer skin coat. With a shiver that ran all the way down his body to his toes, Lane also recalled how drawn-out and severe the winter had been that year; the deer and rabbit scarce, his father had to find a new way to provide for his family.

No living man could match his speed with a six-shooter, his father said time and again. He was *right*–and *dead wrong*.

# DEAD HISTORY

\* \* \*

On the day of the big contest, Lane witnessed his father put two slugs in his opponent before the man in the filth-stained and tattered clothing raised his arm and fired back. His mother screamed as his father fanned his arms backwards, spinning like matching windmills while he fell slow and steady. Lane sprinted to his father in time to hear him speak his last words. Six short sentences he would not soon forget.

"I hit 'em, son," he said gritting his teeth through the pain. "*I know I hit 'em.*"

"Oh, no! Dakota! No!" Lane's mother wailed.

"Poppa?"

"I've been shot in a bad place, son, a bleeding spot. I'm not gonna live long, so it's up to you to take care of your mother and sister."

"Poppa!"

"I hit..."

Turning to the sharp-dressed business men who orchestrated the contest, Lane watched the man who slew his father receive his monetary prize. His face covered with a blood stained bandanna, the duelist showed no expression of victory. Standing slowly, Lane hoisted his father's gun to his hip. It was heavier than he would have ever imagined, so he steadied it with his other hand.

Reaching his tiny finger to the trigger, he braced himself, like his poppa taught him; one foot slightly ahead of the other. Before he fired the gun, the man, his target, turned his gaze away. As much as he wanted to shoot, his father's teachings would not allow it. "Never shoot a man in the back, son," his father always said. "No place for cowards in our Lord's Heaven."

\* \* \*

Nine years had passed from that day to today. Three thousand, five-hundred and seventy-nine days; Lane had scratched each one into his left arm with his father's old hunting knife. Not a day passed he did not wish for this moment. Tomorrow there would be a gunfight; tomorrow he would have put the Silent Man in the ground where he belonged.

Stepping tall, Lane entered the Three Moon Tavern with his eyes squinted and hat lowered; the hunter could not risk being discovered by the prey he stalked. In each town, the Silent Man sat with his partner, a skinny gentleman with grey-splashed hair who handled all the of the gunfighters affairs as if he was some sort of child. The man could have been his father, for all Lane knew, but in all these month's he had not heard such gossip. He only knew the Silent Man and his friend would come to the tavern populated with the best whores the night before his fight.

The collective whispers of spectators, tavern owners and whores from place to place told the story of a deeply suspicious man. The gunfighter would not eat or drink the night before his fights. He would just sit quietly, while his partner did business with the establishment's owner.

A wager would be placed. If the Silent Man won his duels, he would get his pick of whores. The doors would be shut to normal patrons and the night would belong to him. If he lost, he would hand over his entire winnings from his most recent fight, a total Lane learned was quite a treasure.

Sitting at the bar, Lane kept his back to the Silent Man and his partner. He ordered a drink, the biggest mug of dark ale he could afford. Shy to a fault, Lane would not look anyone in the eye, not until morning; not until he placed a bullet in the Silent Man's head. Not until he earned it.

Lane wished he would have arrived sooner, before the combatants of the five fights were determined. He wanted to be on that small list, to not only slay his father's killer, but make his victory official. As it turned out, this town would be awarded with a sixth, unexpected, fight tomorrow; one final draw down.

"Come now, honey, don't be shy!" the man who accompanied the gunfighter often called Reaper said to a passing whore. "Don't cha want to play with a legend?"

"He stinks is all," the overweight, chestnut-brown haired woman squealed. "This one needs a bath."

The tavern owner, who had been tending bar at the moment, joined her in a chuckle before Reaper's partner spoke up.

# DEAD HISTORY

"My friend here never bathes before a fight. It's bad luck."

"He smells like something died," the whore pinched her nose, soliciting another laugh from the patrons of the bar.

"It's been a long ride, my love, please understand."

"My girl, Peaches here, thinks you two been sleeping with the pigs," the tavern owner yelled over Lane's shoulder.

"Reaper does like his girls a little plump, but I dare not call the women he chooses to spend his time with pigs for risk of insulting him."

Tapping the table, the man drew Reaper's attention around to the tavern owner. Staring through the tiny slot of space where his soiled bandana and moth-eaten hat met, Reaper held perfectly still.

"I wasn't..."

"What do you think, pal?" Reaper's partner said as he tapped him on the shoulder.

Reaper released a guttural moan that lasted through the count of three. Lane would have spit the ale from his mouth out on the bar counter, had he not choked it down the moment he heard the sound come from the Silent Man's mouth.

Lane shuttered; that tone, it was like hearing a tornado for the first time; a curious sound you instantly regret. Suddenly everything dropped silent; still, something very bad was about to happen, Lane could sense it.

"Better give him another drink," Lane whispered to the tavern owner.

"What?"

"Get him another drink, before he gets angry."

Snatching up a mug of ale he had just poured for another patron, the tavern owner rushed across the room to Reaper's table.

"Compliments of the house, my friend," his voice shook with fear.

Erupting in a deep belly laugh, which instantly cut the tension building in the room, Reaper's friend tapped the table, shifting the gunfighter's attention back down.

"My thanks to the house! Now let's get down to business, my good man."

# DEAD HISTORY

"Josie, tend the bar," the tavern owner ordered one of his whores.

A tall, skinny blonde with straggly hair jumped at his command, rushing behind the counter from her spot atop the lap of a man who looked like he had been working deep in a coal mine all week. Before addressing the two thirsty men at the far end of the counter from Lane, the young woman took the time to button her blouse and dust off the seat of her dress. It was during this time one of the two men screamed out his order, causing Lane to nearly jump from his barstool.

"Sorry, sir, coming right up."

Tapping the empty shell of a .44 cartridge on the soft surface of the worn and discolored wood of the counter, Lane fell deep into thought, almost missing the flash of cleavage the new bartender offered up when she came to attend him.

"Keep it up and you'll have yourself a hole?"

"Excuse me?"

"You're tapping the counter like a man with something serious on his mind."

Looking down at the rut he had made in the near-rotten wood, Lane apologized.

"No worries, this bar's seen worse."

"Another?"

"Coming up," the girl said with a squeak in her voice that made Lane wince. "You here to watch tomorrow's fight?"

"You could say that."

With a smile that would have lit up the small establishment, had her teeth not been stained from tobacco use, the barmaid handed Lane his drink.

"Oh, wait, are you one of 'em?"

"One of who?"

"One of the gunfighters; I should've known. All gunfighters are fine as cream gravy," she winked.

"You don't say." Nodding his head back over his shoulder, Lane motioned to the other gunfighter in the bar. "You think he's all daisies?"

"Oh…"

# DEAD HISTORY

"You hear that girls? If this man wins all his duels tomorrow, he gets his pick o' the lot of ya," the tavern owner announced after making a deal with Reaper's partner.

"Shit," Josie said under her breath.

Looking up, the tavern owner locked eyes with Josie as she stared past Lane to the dirty-covered gun fighter who looked like he walked the whole length of the Llano Estacado.

"Hey, Josie, maybe you'll learn a few new things, huh?" the tavern owner called.

"As I said, my friend here likes the plump ones, but you never know when he might want an appetizer before his main course," Reaper's friend said.

A few of the older whores laughed, knowing Josie lacked the experience needed for such a challenging job.

"What do you think, Josie?" the tavern owner asked.

"Yeah, Josie, gotta spread those pretty young legs for someone other than the boss to keep your job, sweetie," Peaches snipped.

"Oh," Reaper's friend's eyes opened nice and large. "She's new?"

"Used to only tend my bar, but the poor things made some bad choices," the tavern owner scratched his prickly chin. "In for a bundle of money, needs to pay it off somehow, right?"

"Well then, you up for a toss, *Josie*?" Reaper's partner adjusted the crotch of his pants while staring at her.

"Ha, poor Josie, you gonna run her through the mill?" Peaches joked.

Lane spotted Josie's eyes well up with tears before she could turn away to wipe them. Seeing her trembling hand as it poured another drink, he wondered what hurt was hidden inside her.

"You're mine for the evening," Lane slapped down a handful of papers.

"Wha…?"

"You're busy tonight." Lane shot her a glance he hoped she would understand as the opening of a falsehood.

"Oh, sorry, mate, looks like I'll be entertaining this fine gentleman tonight," she said.

Breathing a sigh of relief, Josie smiled at Lane, yet before she could thank him, a man from the opposite end of the counter interrupted her with his demands for another shot of whiskey.

"I..."

"Say no more."

Stepping smoothly from his barstool, Lane hoped to make a quick and unobserved exit. He had already drawn more attention to himself than he ever wanted to. In full stride to the door, he kept his gaze down and away from the gunfighter, until the tavern owner called him out.

"Hey! Hey, you!"

Lane knew he was the target of the caller, but he kept walking; the door was just a few steps away.

"Hey!"

Not wanting the entire bar to turn their attention his way, Lane stopped so the man would stop yelling. Peering out from under the brim of his hat, he peeked at the bellowing man.

"Don't cha break poor Josie!" the man broke out into a belly laugh after saying.

"I'll take fine care of her," Lane said. His full bladder was putting pressure on his gun belt, so he turned sharply out the tavern door to the stalls. His mind ablaze with self-doubt, he questioned why he had to speak up, why he had to intervene, why now? He was so close to his goal, why take such a risk? While pissing in the dry, rancid smelling hay, he slammed his left fist against a beam above his head.

"What were you thinking, Lane?"

"Thank you," a sweetly feminine voice whispered at the stall entrance.

Lane waited till his stream had tapered off before giving his dick a good shake and answering the skinny broad who invaded his moment of privacy.

"No worries."

"Why did you..." Josie asked curiously.

"'Cause."

"'Cause why?"

Lane wanted to tell her. He wanted to scream at the top of his lungs, to release the pent-up frustration he had held locked up in his chest since he was a boy, but something told him doing so would only further jeopardize his plan. Everything was lined up as he needed it, everything would be over tomorrow at high noon.

"I couldn't bear the thought of getting some dirty old man's sloppy seconds," Lane outright lied.

"Oh... well, you paid; you ready?" Josie asked, running her fingertips down his arm to his hand.

"Little later, okay? Just go to your room and wait for me."

"Fine, then."

Lane watched Josie leave the stalls. The swing of her hips, the bounce of her hair; *now* he wanted her. It had been too long since he had held a woman, and the trepidation of dying tomorrow caused him to wonder if the previous woman he laid with months ago would be his last.

Accustom to the love of whores, since they were as emotionally vacant as he was, he wondered if fucking Josie this night would give him anything other than immediate gratification.

"No, Lane," he told himself.

Again he questioned himself why.

Why was he allowing these other thoughts in his head? There was only one reason he was here, now, and that was for revenge.

Looking at his father's pocket watch, he read the hands. They read past midnight; it was a new day. Retrieving his father's hunting knife from his belt, he carved a new line in his arm while walking towards the exit of the stall.

"Dead man..."

Lane looked up from his bleeding arm as the Silent Man shuffled in, blocking his egress.

"Eat..."

The voice, it sounded like it belonged to a man in desperate need of water, with a mouth as dry as the Arizona desert. Raising his arms, Lane spoke slowly so as not to agitate the gunman. "Look, mister, I don't want any trouble."

"Girl..."

"Yeah, sorry, but I want to party with the girl tonight."

Stepping towards Lane with his arms out stretched like two stiff, wooden boards, the Silent Man closed the distance. Sans his bandana for the first time in all the months Lane had tracked him, his mouth was visible. Although dark in the stalls, what little light seeped in through the cracks gave Lane's keen eyes a glimpse at something seriously wrong.

"Your face, what... what is that?"

"Dead." The spoken word stretched out twice as long as normal and dropped off to a low murmur at the end. As the Silent Man spoke, Lane could see what was wrong; the gun fighter's lips were missing and the surrounding flesh was discolored like rotting meat.

"Mister, what kind of plague do you have?"

Having held his ground while the Silent Man slowly approached, Lane was suddenly close enough to smell him over the pungent aroma of urine in the air. Lane recoiled when the outside breeze slipped into the stall at the back of the Silent Man; collected the stink that was stuck to the man's skin and clothing, the odor punching Lane right in the face.

"Christ, man!" The smell made Lane's eyes water.

"Eat."

Lunging swiftly forward, the Silent Man grasped Lane by his shoulders in a squeezing grip. Bleary-eyed, Lane shoved the man back with all his might, knocking him to the ground near the exit.

"Touch me again and you better be ready to draw down."

Lane wiped his eyes with his sleeve as he walked a wide birth around the man. Nearing the door, the light from the torches outside illuminated the Silent Man's face even further. Ensnared by the sight of the man's grayish-green skin and the craterous hole where his absent nose should be, Lane stopped and gasped. He had seen men like this before, only they had lain motionless; departed from this world, months past.

"What the hell?"

Standing slowly, the man moaned loudly. He must have been sick, Lane thought; stricken with some deadly disease. Covering his mouth with his bandana, Lane tried to back away out the door but was caught again in the grasp of the Silent Man. Shoved hard against a pair of thick beams that made up the side wall of the stall, Lane watched as his six shooter spilled from his holster to the hay-covered ground.

# DEAD HISTORY

Leaning towards him, Lane's adversary opened his lipless mouth; a cavern full of jagged brown stalactites and stalagmites. Sensing he was going to be bitten by this man who was clearly ill, Lane drew his father's knife and plunged it into the belly of his attacker. The Silent Man showed no pain as Lane pushed the blade deeper and deeper into his flesh. He should be howling in pain, Lane thought, but the man was not, he was still trying to snap down his jaws.

Spinning around so he could redirect the Silent Man's force and use it against him, Lane broke free of his grasp.

"Whatever has made you ill has made you forget what pain is, hasn't it? That's how you were able to keep standing after my father hit you. *He knew he hit you.*"

"Dead..."

"Bastard!"

Stabbing wildly, Lane gouged two more holes in his nemesis's chest before grabbing him and shoving him out of the door and into the empty street.

Huffing loudly, Lane stood silently over the man who had killed his father years ago. He knew the wounds he had just delivered would be fatal, it was over, not as he intended, but over still.

Wiping his father's hunting knife with his bandana, Lane drew a deep breath and held it in his lungs. Not a sound could be heard, no coyotes howling in the distance, no music or merriment seeping from the tavern down the street; total, blissful quiet.

"Rest in peace, Silent Man."

"Hey! Gunslinger!" a woman's voice shattered the silence.

Lane turned around, it was her, the young whore from the tavern. She was calling to him, waving her arms like a long lost relative.

"How long you gonna make me wait, buckaroo?"

She was as impatient as she was pretty and not a bit subtle.

"What happened here? Oh, shit, he looks cold as a wagon tire!" Josie blurted out.

Her volume made Lane cringe. He did not want to explain his actions to the local sheriff.

"Would you shut your cock holster just a moment?" Lane snapped.

"What did you do?"

Lane sighed. "He attacked me."

Josie's eyes widened as Lane quickly explained what happened. All the while thinking it was his story that thrilled her, it was not. The Silent Man had stood back up, his head rolling back and forth over his shoulders. When he shuffled his feet forward, his second step dragged deep in the dirt, alerting Lane to his presence. Spinning around, Lane deflected the Silent Man's hands before they reached his throat.

"*My gun!*" Lane yelled to Josie while pointing in its general direction.

Keeping his eyes on the stumbling man before him, Lane only caught a glimpse of Josie as she dove into the hay.

"Shit!" he exclaimed after catching another good look at the Silent Man's decaying face.

There was no way this man was alive; it was worse than he first thought. This man was dead but somehow still moving. When his adversary released a grumble like he did earlier in the tavern, Lane jumped.

"Girl, where's my gun?" Lane yelled while pointing his knife at his enemy.

Josie dug through the piss-soaked hay on her hands and knees. The metal gun should have been easier to find than this. The barrel itself extended to eight inches long, large and shiny; the wan light should have made it sparkle like a diamond in a lump of coal.

Josie yelled over her shoulder, echoing his tone of urgency. "I can't find it!"

"Fine then."

"What do we do?" she cried out.

Lane raised his arm, elbow bent, turning the blade of his hunting knife forty-five degrees downward. He had seen his father take this stance once when he was a child and a brown bear had them cornered during a hunt. He remembered holding his father's rifle; offering it to him repeatedly, but his pop did not reply.

Just like he was not replying to Josie now; he just stared at the rotting corpse of a man and stepped closer and closer. When the Silent Man was close enough to touch Lane, he turned his hand over with a fast and hard flick of his wrist. Three fingers from the

# DEAD HISTORY

Silent Man's left hand landed atop the hard ground like spilled shells from a six shooter.

Unwilling to waste his concern on the Silent Man's lack of physical response, Lane circled his swipe downward, slicing deeply across his dirt-covered torso. Left hand up, Lane barely held the man back as he fell limp into him, the contents of his stomach spilling out like ash from a hearth.

"Is he dead?" Josie asked again.

Dogs from all over town began to bark while voices emerged from the shadows in every direction. In no time there would be a mob of people flooding the streets, Lane knew it.

"Go! Go distract whoever walks the street. I'll get rid of this body."

"Then what?" Josie wiped her hands on her skirt as she spoke.

"I will return," Lane huffed while catching his breath, the odor from the Silent Man making it hard for him to breathe "I'll find your room."

"And then what?" she asked while fiddling with the buttons on her blouse, still waiting for a certain answer.

Glaring at the moonlight as it tickled Josie's breasts, his decision was clear.

"You owe me a toss."

"Oh, baby!" she grinned.

\* \* \*

Josie woke Lane when she returned to her room carrying him a fresh cup of coffee. The scent reminded him of home, years ago, when his mother would brew his father a cup every Sunday. No sooner did the recollection hit him, then a sense that things were still unfinished arose.

"How do you feel?" she asked with a kindness in her voice that made him smile for the first time in months.

"I slept well, thank you."

"I didn't ask you how you slept," she smirked as she handed him the hot mug.

"I feel better, thank you."

# DEAD HISTORY

"Good for you." She plopped herself down on the corner of her tiny bed with a moan. "Me? How am I this morning? I woke up sore in the loins, with bruises around my waste from your meaty mitts."

"Sorry, I didn't mean to hurt you I..."

"It's okay, could've been worse, I could've spent the night with..." Josie stopped herself when the image of the rotten-faced gunfighter entered her mind. "You never did tell me what you did with the body last night."

After taking a long sip of the sour coffee, Lane replied, "I buried it."

"Huh?"

"I took the body up in the hills and buried it deep."

"Oh."

A moment of silence passed. Lane wondered what she would ask him next; he could see her mind at work.

"You always go three times?"

"I haven't..."

"I'm not complaining, you're a fine man; prettiest I seen in this town."

Lane felt embarrassed to admit this to her, a whore nonetheless, but he felt compelled to speak regardless. "I haven't lain with a woman in a year."

"Really? That explains it, I suppose."

"Been busy."

"Busy or you haven't found the right one." She sat up and smiled, primping her hair.

"I like you," Lane smiled again, it was a new experience for him, this happiness, he was beginning to enjoy it.

"The contest is going to start soon, are you interested anymore?"

Sliding his feet out from under the sheets, he planted them firmly on the rough, wooden floor and stood up.

"That part of my life is over now."

"So you will *not* attend then?"

Buttoning his pants he motioned for his gun belt.

"I didn't say that."

# DEAD HISTORY

\* \* \*

Lane rested his back against the outside wall of the tavern while Josie scrubbed the dry dirt off his boots. He told her to stop, that it was unnecessary, but she wouldn't listen to him. He was learning quickly that the young woman needed to keep herself busy when she was anxious, but what, he wondered, was making her so nervous?

Standing still and quiet, Lane watched the tavern owner meet with the other men who held the gunfighter contest. There was some great discussion going on not a hundred feet from him, in the middle of the closed down main street.

Lane figured, by the looks of concern, and frantic hand gestures, that these men were looking for a last minute replacement for the Reaper, as they called him; a way to salvage the contest, and the numerous bets placed upon it.

"We have an announcement," one of the men called out in a deep bellowing voice.

Here it comes, Lane could sense it.

"One of our fighters..."

Yes, Lane knew what the man was going to say.

"One of our fighters has dropped out and we're now looking for a replacement."

As a smile formed on his face, Lane spotted Reaper's handler. The man walked confidently out of a shop across from the tavern. As a deep breath of satisfaction filled Lane's chest, he saw the impossible. Walking slowly, the man so many called Reaper, exited the shop, not ten steps behind his handler.

"What the hell." Lane couldn't believe his eyes. Although this man was dressed similar to Reaper, he couldn't have been him. Lane's mind flashed through the events of the previous night; he cut that man's fingers off, gutted him, twice, and buried him in the hills. That was not Reaper.

When Josie looked up from her position kneeling at Lane's feet, she saw the same sight he did. Feeling suddenly faint, she fell hard to her seat.

"T...that can't be I...I thought you buried Reaper," she shook her head in disbelief "...um Silent Man?"

# DEAD HISTORY

"I did. That ain't him. I buried him. That's someone else, a faker."

"Any man out there brave enough to enter the contest step forward," the man running the gunfighter's contest further announced. Before another word could be spoken, Lane stepped forward. He had seen and heard enough, this ended here, today.

"Enter me in the contest!" Lane roared.

"No!" Josie screeched, grabbing the back of his duster.

Shaking her loose as he walked steadily down the street towards the announcer, Lane focused his eyes on his soon to be target.

"Wonderful! The contest will continue as scheduled!" the announcer yelled loudly. "First up…"

"He and I," Lane said as he stepped up to the men organizing the contest.

"You want to die first, do you?" Reaper's handler spoke, approaching Lane from the other side of the men.

"How's those fingers?" Lane looked past the handler, to the man who he figured was pretending to be Reaper.

"So it *was* you?" the handler's voice peaked with the revelation.

Shoving the skinny man to the side, Lane stepped up to Reaper, who was wearing his usual dirty costume, with a handkerchief covering the lower half of his face. Snatching the man's arm as it hung still at his side, Lane raised the man's clinched fist up to reveal the missing digits.

"No, this can't be."

Reaper's handler spoke one word, calm and clear, and with that the rotting man attacked. Snapping like a snake, the dead-alive man latched his mouth onto Lane's neck. The bite cut through Lane's bandana and straight into the bare flesh of his neck. Howling in pain, Lane swung his fists wildly, staggered back, until one struck its mark. Dazed by the impact, Reaper also took a step backwards, giving the men who ran the contest enough time to fully separate the two combatants.

"Stop!"

"Save it for the gunfight you two!"

Reaching up to his neck, Lane felt warm blood oozing from the holes where the disgusting man had sunk his teeth.

"No, we go now!" Lane yelled while being restrained by two more men.

"Fine. Is it agreed?"

"Agreed."

"Your funeral, boy."

"Then take your twenty paces, each of you."

As Lane counted out his steps, he double checked his firearm. The Smith and Wesson 999P gripped firmly in his right hand had been in his possession since he was very young, bought with the money he made cutting timber over the course of three summers. It was the first gun he owned and it had served him right for many years. Today, it would bring him justice.

"Twenty," Lane whispered to himself before turning around.

"Lane, don't!" Josie shouted from the crowd forming at his left side.

He didn't answer her or acknowledge her in the slightest. This was not a time for women; revenge was men's work. The announcer cleared his throat before making his final statement.

"On the strike of twelve noon, you two men draw and fire. You have a spare moment, so I'd suggest you both pray, but I doubt either of you are holy men."

"Lane!"

Lane didn't hear the multitude of cheers from the crowd, or the singular scream of a panicked woman, all he heard was the chime. Drawing his gun with a swiftness that surprised even him, he fired.

*Bang! Bang! Bang!*

He felt the hot lead burning in his left shoulder; no more painful than the throbbing from the bite wound on his neck, but neither concerned him at the moment. All that mattered now was that the Reaper dropped.

Lane's first bullet had struck the dirty man's chest, not fazing him a bit; however the second hit the bull's eye. Splitting Reaper's skull down the middle, the slug broke open the rotting man's head like an overripe melon.

Lane did it; he had won!

Was this a sensation of excitement making his stomach turn over? Was it relief, or was it something far worse? His head suddenly spinning, Lane tried to wipe his brow, but in a blink of an eye

# DEAD HISTORY

he was no longer standing, but had fallen fast to the seat of his leather pants in a cloud of dust.

"Lane, are you hit?" Josie yelled as she ran to him.

"Shoulder." The nausea kept his words short. "He only fired once, right?"

"Yeah, just once," she said.

"What's wrong with me? I feel ill."

Lane shifted his eyes from Josie's face to the two approaching men. The man in charge of the contest walked steadily, with Reaper's handler just a step or two behind him.

"You okay, son?" he asked with a sincere concern.

"Not sure."

"Well, you did a bang up job there; you won the round, get yourself well, okay? Tomorrow's another fight."

"Yes." Lane nodded.

"Wait, hold up!" Josie called and chased after the tournament official, trying her best to convince him that Lane should no longer compete. While she spoke, Reaper's partner knelt down by Lane's side.

"You're fast, boy. Faster than the Reaper and you're gonna cost me a pretty penny, but that's all fine. You'll pay me back when you're dead."

"What? What are you talking about?" Lane asked, feeling sicker by the minute.

"You got the disease Reaper had now, boy, that's what I'm talking about. You'll be dead by sunset, and back on your feet by sunrise."

"That's mad talk."

"Okay, son, I been down this road before. This *Reaper*, and the ones who came before him, they may all be the walking dead, but they're still perishable. I'll train you just like I trained the last three. You'll be doing my bidding soon, too," he chuckled.

"You need a hand there?" the announcer asked as he approached, interrupting the tense moment.

Standing slowly, Reaper's partner took a moment to straighten his vest and overcoat before speaking again.

"Congratulations on your win," he said to Lane while tipping his hat. "Enjoy your prize."

# STALAG 44

## JOSE ALFREDO VAZQUEZ

**M**arch, 1945
**Somewhere in the Bavarian Forest, Southwestern Germany**

Whoever said war was hell was definitely right. That was the only thing private first class John Miller had in mind as he dropped the heavy radio equipment backpack to the ground and fell heavily alongside it. The equipment seemed too heavy for the skinny kid from Brooklyn to carry, but this was the army, and you did as you were told. Besides, there was a good reason for having the position of platoon radio operator assigned to him. He had been born Johann Muller, son of a German immigrant that worked at Brooklyn's harbor. His father wanted to make his only son as American as possible, so he was registered with the English version of his Teutonic name. And a good thing it was, as America joined the war against their former mother country. He was as patriotic as the next guy, so he volunteered for the army as soon as he turned eighteen. It didn't matter that the war was ending soon, he still wanted to do his part; his fluency in both English and German landed him the job of radio operator. It wasn't too bad. In fact, life had been good until the last few weeks.

When Lieutenant Keeler was killed by a German sniper, their platoon fell under the direction of First Sergeant O'Rourke, a bull of an Irishman from Boston. He was doing a fine job until Major Arthull appeared.

The day Major Arthull arrived, life in the platoon became miserable. The pompous ass came off the jeep that left as soon as he stepped out, and earned the special look from Sergeant O'Rourke immediately. That is, the special look he gave when he had this sudden instinctive dislike of something. Miller had seen that look before. It usually came before they were about to run into an ambush, and had saved the lives of many men on countless occasions. This time, Miller felt the hairs on the back of his neck rising in dreaded anticipation of how events would unfold.

Their platoon was forty men strong, divided into four squads of ten men each. Miller was in the command squad together with Sergeant O'Rourke. He basically followed him everywhere, and he knew that deep down, the old warrior had developed some affinity for his eager young shadow.

That was why when Major Arthull rounded up all the NCO's for a full briefing, O'Rourke noted their long faces and knew something was wrong. He had known even before they called for quarters and every man did their best to stand in line and listen to the speech.

Major Arthull addressed the assembled men like a schoolmaster teaching mischievous pupils. He apparently descended from a long line of southern aristocrats, and saw the war coming to an end as the signal that he hadn't done something heroic enough to brag in high society when he returned home.

He needed something, anything, to prove everyone back home what a wonderful leader he was. Probably that was the reason he came out with such a hair-brained idea as the one he presented to the men.

He stated that the Allied Intelligence Services had found the location of the famous Eagle's Nest, Hitler's prewar fortress. But he was convinced from what he had heard from townsfolk nearby that there was a second nest. There were rumors of a top secret military installation hidden in the area, and by God he would be the one to find and capture it intact. He had convinced someone along the command chain to have a platoon directly assigned to him, and they had the misfortune of having lost their Lieutenant just in time to be available for immediate dispatch. Probably someone back at HQ was breathing easier now.

Miller listened in stiff attention as the major rambled on about the importance of capturing the second nest intact, and the supposed glory that awaited those that achieved the feat. But they had to hurry before another advance unit beat them to the prize.

Sergeant O'Rourke also listened stiffly, while staring into the distance during the sermon. He knew the Germans were being squeezed by the Allied Forces on all fronts, and that it was just a matter of time for the hammer to fall and the war to end. He had seen more than his share of young blood being spilled already, and now this maniac wanted to have them go on a wild goose chase in hostile territory, well ahead of the advance battalions? Definitely there was something wrong with this picture. But he had been in the Army long enough to know when to keep his mouth shut.

That scene had happened several days before.

Now, they were getting ready to camp for the night, after having marched through forest country, always in the direction of the snow-covered mountain peaks ahead. They were way off the marked paths but to the major's delight, Hopkins, the leading point man, had shown them a clear space where tracks could be seen clearly under the thick-leaf layer that had been placed on top of them. The tracks were multiple and all headed in the same direction the platoon was heading, too. The major was talking excitedly about how correct he was all along, while O'Rourke stared at the prints and spoke softly to Private Whitecloud, their Navajo scout.

"How many?" O'Rourke asked laconically.

"Many, with a heavy load carried by some," was the equally soft answer.

"Don't like this," O'Rourke said.

"Neither do I," Whitecloud said.

"Hey, Sergeant!" Major Arthull yelled. "Leave the chief alone and organize camp for the night."

"Yes, sir," O'Rourke answered, after glancing at Whitecloud, who just stared at the tracks for a few more seconds before leaving to do his chores.

"Well, gentlemen, this is exactly what you would expect when you get a Redskin and a Mick together–plain laziness," Major Arthull said, earning a few chuckles from the entourage of non-coms surrounding him. It seemed that everywhere, there were always some idiots that followed whoever gave an impression of authority. But they all were insane if they believed he would remember them when he went up in glory through the ranks.

Later that night, the camp was formed. Miller found a soft spot near a tree, actually away from the central perimeter, where the glorious Major Arthull was reviewing his grand strategy one more time. There were gunshots heard in the distance, their location impossible to pinpoint. Guards were placed around the perimeter of the camp, and the other men got some rest.

Miller was about to fall asleep, when he heard a sound coming from the bushes behind him. Some leaves were being moved, and he lay still, as he slowly stretched his arm and grabbed his Garand carbine, pulling it closer to him.

When he heard the rustling again, he rolled on his stomach and pointed the rifle towards the bush. "Halt! Who goes there?" he screamed.

There was more movement from the bushes, and a lone figure came out, hands outstretched in the air, face wreathed in shadows.

"Please, don't shoot," a voice said in German.

Several men came running and grabbed the lone intruder, bringing him out of the bushes. All the officers came immediately, and stared into the figure that wore a striped black and white prison uniform, similar to what prisoners wore back home.

"Well, look what the cat dragged in," Major Arthull said. "I think we got ourselves a Jerry escapee."

"With all due respect, sir, he looks like someone whose been in one of those concentration camps we've heard so much about," Sergeant O'Rourke said.

Everyone had heard stories about the Nazi concentration camps, especially the one at Dachau, north of Munich, which had been recently liberated.

"In fact, sir, he may even give us some Intel on the nest we're looking for," Whitecloud added to the line of thought.

The major glared at him, as if telling him how dare he address a white man directly, but then he closed his eyes, as if he was thinking.

"You know, the chief here may be onto something," the major stated, refusing to acknowledge Whitecloud's reasoning. "Now we have to find someone that speaks German to interrogate him."

"We do have a German interpreter here with us, sir," O'Rourke added.

"We do?" The major actually sounded astonished.

"Yes, sir," O'Rourke answered, while at the same time thinking. "And you should have known that, at least if you took some damn time to know who the men are fighting under you."

"Who is the German interpreter here?" Major Arthull asked angrily, letting the comment slide.

"I am, sir," Miller answered meekly.

"Well, then, get to work, boy."

Miller turned to the German, and started a conversation with him. Everybody else looked at each other, and Major Arthull interrupted them impatiently, demanding to know what they were discussing.

Miller turned to him and said, "The prisoner wants to tell us something, but that's based on two conditions."

"And those conditions are...?" Major Arthull asked.

"First, not to interrupt him until he's finished with his story, no matter how incredible what he tells us sounds."

"And the second condition is...?"

"He wants a smoke."

That drew a hearty laugh from the soldiers. Even Major Arthull managed to hide a smile, and then agreed that they could spare a Lucky or two, which someone quickly provided. After taking a couple of heavy, long puffs from his cigarette, the prisoner began to talk, while Miller translated to English at the same time.

"My name is Johan Streissmann. I was born in Munich. My mother died when I was a boy, so it was only my father and me struggling for dear life. My father was a hunter, like his father before him, and he migrated to the city looking for a better future for me. He still managed to teach me his hunting skills during the spare time he managed to spend with me. You see, Germany, a few years before the war, was a terrible place to be. Everyone was poor, and food and jobs were scarce. And to make things worse, the Nazis arrived and began to make their presence known. You see, my father was there during the Pustch, and then he heard about Kristalnachen. We are, or were I guess, Jewish. My father had a gut feeling; call it hunter's instinct or something that told him things were not going to be okay for us Jews in the near future. He decided to travel to the mountains south of Munich, to the estate of a certain Baron Von Braun. You see, during the Great War, apparently they had served together, and my father had saved the good baron's life there. He went now to his estate, and begged the baron to hide me there for the time being.

"The baron was a man of honor, and despite his aristocratic origin, he had nothing against Jews. He agreed, and told my father that there was a very old cabin on the estate, very high in the mountains, that no one knew about. It was apart from the regular roads and thus difficult to spot. He told us that we could use it for as long as we wanted. As for himself, he would deny knowledge of our existence to anyone that asked. My father thanked him, and told him that he would take me there, and since I was about to be fifteen, he would leave me and go back to Munich to gather personal belongings and then return. That day, after we traveled and found the cabin, he said his goodbyes to me, made me promise to take care of myself no matter what, and to resist the temptation of going back to town to find out what was happening. He then smiled, and left. It was the last time I ever saw him.

"I learned to survive by hunting, using traps and drinking from a nearby creek. The Black Forest is abundant in life, and the cabin provided comfort against the harsh winters. It took me a while to get past the depression over the loss of my father. You see, I knew he had been lost for he would never leave me without coming back as soon as he could. So when he didn't, I had to assume the terrible reality that he was dead.

"I was informed about how things were around town because the baron used to send an old man, a hunter himself, to check on me. He brought me things I needed but the most important was current news. That is how I found out that we were at war, and that the Jews were silently disappearing from everyday life. Everybody commented, but nobody spoke publicly or asked about a person that did not show up for work or school.

"Everything was fine for a while, until the day that the old man came and told me that the baron's estate had been 'nationalized', though the baron had protested to no avail. In fact, his protests earned him a heart attack, and the old man died. The hunter told me that it would be his last visit, as he planned to leave the estate now that the army was taking over. He wished me luck and went on his way.

"He had been mistaken in one thing. It was not the Wermacht, the army, that had taken over. It was the SS, those black shirt bastards that were Herr Hitler's shock troops. It was not too long before they found me. They were apparently surprised to see a young Jewish man in such excellent physical shape, and I heard them talking by phone about having a 'good specimen'. They then took me to a place that I knew existed but never dared to go near. It was a large crack in the mountain that I had years before explored. It was a long corridor with solid rock fifty feet high on both sides, wide enough for four men to walk comfortably side by side. It ended in a small valley, keyhole shaped, surrounded by stone walls so sheer they could not be climbed. I guess erosion caused this strange formation to occur in the mountain. The top part of the valley had been covered with a huge camouflaged net, making it impossible to be seen from the air. There was the entrance of a cave at the end of the cul-de-sac which I had never cared to explore. Now I regretted not having done so.

"At the entrance to the small valley, once you left the stone funnel, there was a tall, large, wooden palisade with only a central double door. There was a single sign at the side–**Stalag 44**. I had heard about concentration camps, but the fact of me actually entering one was sobering. The camp inside the palisade had two areas, each side cordoned off by wire. There were two small cabins and a latrine area on each one. I was taken to the one on the left and was given this striped uniform to put on, and then pushed inside. I saw that I was in an area with men of different ages, but all were physically fit, unlike the emaciated forms on the cage on the right, which looked like souls half-starved to death. In my cage, there were actually men in uniforms. Some I recognized as being Italian army. I knew because before the war, some servicemen had traveled to Munich, back when Herr Hitler was eagerly following Herr Mussolini's steps like an apt pupil.

"One of the Italian men happened to speak German. He told me that his name was Gino, and he was actually very nice. He told me that his unit, the Ariete Division, had been serving alongside the Germans and Romanians in the Eastern Front against the Russians, when word came that Italy had changed sides after IL Duce was deposed. They had been quickly surrounded by Hungarian and Bulgarian troops, and then disarmed and marched into concentration camps, in the same way they themselves had marched so many Russian prisoners before. They had been rotated for several months in different camps, and he had noted that only the men in best physical form were still part of the group whose numbers kept dwindling until there were only a handful of them left. He pointed at some strange uniforms, and explained to me that they were American and British pilots that had their planes brought down, and that some others were German political prisoners.

"I asked Gino about the cave, and he lowered his voice. He told me that he had heard a story along the grapevine. It had been told by another prisoner, an Italian General, who did not care for his rank anymore, as he was as much a prisoner as everyone else. He had told them that the Romanians had been digging deeper and deeper at their oil fields, and that they had hit a very deep natural gas vein. But apparently there was something strange with that vein. Their particular digging area had been sealed by German SS stormtroopers, and no one was allowed to get nearby. The general had told them that the gas had been funneled and taken to a secret installation, deep in a cave system in Germany, for further experimentation. He now believed they were at that installation, and that they were in some sort of control group, and the starving prisoners on the other side were the other group about to be exposed to the gas. I asked Gino what the gas did, and he said that he did not know, but that probably it was something not very good.

"The next day, the call for formation came earlier than usual. I felt something raising the hairs on the back of my neck, so when I went to the latrines, I stayed there, and then jumped into the hole, hiding in the shadows, swimming in the foul stuff that made me gag from the stench. And I had been right. After the German guards checked the latrines, I climbed out and saw through a peephole that the groups of prisoners were being marched in formation to the cave entrance. I saw Gino glancing back, only to earn a slap in the face from a guard. They entered, and I stayed still and motionless in the latrine area, wondering what to do, since sooner or later the guards would come in and would then find me.

I decided to take advantage that the guards would probably be lax after having emptied the prison cages, and I chose to make it to freedom at the first opportunity.

"I did not have to wait long. That afternoon, gunshots were heard from the cave, and the guards left outside ventured in to find out what was going on. There was the sound of screams and more gunshots coming from inside the cave. I could see that the guards were really nervous now. The SS captain on the outside kept his cool, though. He rallied his men, and told them to be prepared to repel a possible prisoner riot. The guards formed a semicircle, with their guns pointing at the interior, and were about to set up machine guns at precise positions when a German soldier came stumbling out of the cave. His black uniform was shredded and bloodied. Several men ran to help him, but he fell face down onto the ground...and so did the hand grenade he held in his hand. The grenade exploded, sending his would-be helpers flying in all directions in bloody forms that fell in comical positions all around him, bones protruding from legs and arms due to the force of the explosion. The captain yelled for order, and I peed myself, having never seen so much blood and gore before.

"And it was then that I saw it. From the cave, a dark mist was coming out, keeping its height to about one foot above the ground, and was definitely expanding at the entrance. Also, I saw that a few men were trying to come out of the cave, one of them wearing a white lab coat. They screamed as they were suddenly seen to be pulled back inside, like ropes had been tied to them and then yanked back. The soldiers tried to look inside, but the captain yelled for them to maintain formation.

"It was then that they came out. Torn uniforms and prisoner pajamas were seen hanging off the gray-skinned figures that stumbled out of the cave and into the dimly illuminated area. Their eyes were as black as night. And I mean the whole eye. There was nothing of the white you normally see in someone's eye. It was just blackness, and an oily fluid oozing out of their eyes, ears, nostrils and those open, hungry looking mouths. The captain ordered his men to open fire, and the fusillade became almost unbearable. But the figures kept moving forward. They were rocked back by the gunfire, and some even fell, but then they just regained their footing and started to walk again.

"Then the mist reached the broken bodies of the soldiers killed by the grenade explosion. By God, the corpses started to twitch, and then began to get up. They had the same black eyes as the attackers, and they started to ooze fluids from their faces, too. The captain called one of his men, a combat engineer, and yelled for him to run and rig some of the rocks at the entrance of the valley with explosive charges. The engineer ran off with some men, and took from a small hut some boxes that were taken back to the entrance as the captain kept firing his gun at the approaching bodies.

"I saw this as my chance, and ran out of the latrine. The feces covering my clothes made them look dark, and in the dim late afternoon light, no one glanced at me. I ran with the men carrying the boxes, and saw them placing dynamite charges under some large boulders, and making a hastily assembled trigger mechanism at the far end of the entrance. One of the men told me to stay and watch the trigger. I don't even think he noticed my striped prison uniform; such was the sense of panic on his face. The men ran back to the cave and I heard the screams and the gunshots slowing down after a while. With my curiosity overriding my fear, I slowly made my way back to the cave opening, and went to the double wooden doors and peeked inside.

"There was blood everywhere. One of the huts had caught fire, so I could see more clearly what was going on. The things were actually *eating* the defenders. Some men had been torn to pieces by groups of the creatures. And there was the mist, hovering across the ground. I held the urge to vomit, and began to slowly push the doors closed wanting to lock the entrance to the Stalag forever. I was about to close the doors when I saw a lone figure walking towards me. By his uniform and the reflection of the fire on his face, I could make the outline of my friend Gino as he slowly came towards me. I wanted to call out to him, to tell him to come with me before I locked the nightmare inside, but the look on his face told me he was not my friend anymore. He moaned, and some figures near him raised their heads and began to look around. And I swear to God Almighty, the mist shifted in my direction, as if it

# DEAD HISTORY

had a life of its own. That was enough for me. I closed the doors and barricaded them with everything I could get my hands on, as I heard the pounding of fists on the wood getting louder. It was then that I ran as fast as I could and hid in the forest until I heard the noise you were making, deciding to seek your help."

The Americans looked at each other with blank faces.

Sergeant O'Rourke then asked how long ago it had happened. The prisoner only answered, "This same night."

"I think this is just a set up," Major Arthull said. "I think this is the nest we've been looking for. Tell him to take us there."

"Sir," Sergeant O'Rourke said. "With all due respect, I think we should get some reinforcements before investigating the area."

The major glared at him.

"Sergeant, I honestly don't care for your opinion. Now get this platoon moving, on the double!"

"Yes, sir," Sergeant O'Rourke answered stiffly.

About one hour later, they reached the area described by the prisoner. They entered the funnel, and saw the hastily prepared charges still on the rocks, with the detonator near the entrance. O'Rourke softly told Miller to stay near the detonator, and in they went, with the prisoner leading the way. Upon reaching the entrance of the small valley, the palisade was in front of them. Major Arthull had a camera prepared for the opening of the gates, and ordered the men to stand in line in order for the camera to get the entrance of the liberators to the concentration camp.

Near the door, the major stood proudly, the first in line, while two men removed the debris placed in front of the doors. The major turned back and smiled triumphantly at O'Rourke.

That was the last thing he managed to do as the doors suddenly exploded outward violently and a great mass of rotting humanity spilled over the shocked men. Screams of terror were muffled by the sheer number of black-eyed things pouring out, and the few guns that managed to be fired were swiftly silenced.

The German prisoner had stayed at the end of the line, and he now ran towards the entrance, followed by the shambling figures.

Miller saw him coming, and also saw how he fell down, to be torn apart by the figures that still continued to advance towards Miller. Without thinking, Miller leaned forward and pressed the detonator.

The deafening explosion collapsed the walls at the entrance, and the entire area became covered in a cloud of dust as it was buried under tons of rocks and debris.

**Present day**

The relief for the guards on duty entered the compound through the reinforced bridge built over a deep excavation that had thousands of sharp metal pieces pointing up. They had passed through the signs on the fence around the mountain that said in many languages **Danger: Unexploded War Bombs. Stay on designated paths only.**

The two soldiers took their positions and the guards presently on watch left, glad to be done for another day

"Hey, Frank, did you check on the old man yet?" one of the guards said.

"Nope," the other replied. "But he's probably in his corner, as usual."

The two men walked fifty feet to their right to see, as always, a very old man, over ninety years of age by his looks, sitting on a wooden chair in a corner. He had been standing guard for as long as anyone could remember, and it had been decades since the area was sealed off by the Allied Forces.

The old man looked at them and smiled, the old rifle resting between his legs still well maintained. He was unaware that his presence was no longer necessary. About a decade ago, the thermonuclear device buried under the control room had had its trigger set to automatic, so if the rock wall that stood in front of the large, bullet proof reinforced glass was ever moved, the sensors would trigger a ten kiloton explosive device.

Miller grinned to himself, thinking that if it ever did happen, the last thing the black eyes would see before being vaporized was his smiling face as he raised his finger at them in defiance; before he was sent into oblivion with them.

# ABOUT THE WRITERS

**David Bernstein**, a.k.a. MacabreZombie, is still writing horror for various anthologies and magazines, but has finally made major progress on his zombie oriented novel--Amongst the Dead, which the first three, maybe four by the time you read this, chapters are available online at Tales of the Zombie War. He is also proud of winning the MacabreZombie award for best horror fiction of 2009 and feels he'll win it again in 2010. He lives in the NYC area with his girlfriend of eight years.

**Kevin James Breaux** is a published artist and author. He is a member of the HWA and EAA. Along with having written many short stories Kevin's first novel, Soul Born, an epic fantasy, will be released in the fall of 2010. Please visit www.kevinbreaux.com .

**TW Brown** refuses to "grow-up and get over his zombie obsession". He has an upcoming short story in Living Dead Press' "Book of the Dead 3 Dead and Rotting: A Zombie Anthology". His first full-length novel "Zomblog" drops in January 2010.
Upcoming projects can be followed at www.maydecemberpublications.com.
Contact him via email at twbrown@maydecemberpublications.com

**Eric S Brown** is the author of numerous zombie novels and collections such as Season of Rot, War of the Worlds Plus Blood Guts and Zombies, Barren Earth (with Stephen North), and World War of the Dead to name only a few. Some of his upcoming books slated for release in 2010 include The Human Experiment (Altered Dimensions Press), Bigfoot War (Coscom Entertainment), Tandems of Terror (Library of Horror Press) and Anti-Heroes. Some of his more recent and upcoming anthology appearances include the first three Dead Worlds anthologies, the first two Zombology anthologies, Dead Science, War of the Worlds: Frontlines, Gentlemen of Horror, Creature Features, and The Best of House of Horrors 2009. He was also featured as an expert on the zombie genre in the book: Zombie CSU: The Forensics of the Living Dead.

**Nickolas Cook** lives in the beautiful Southwestern desert with his wife and three pugs. He is an editor (The Black Glove Magazine), a horror critic and reviewer, with close to a hundred articles in print, the author of a couple of dozen published short stories and three novels, THE BLACK BEAST OF ALGERNON WOOD (Dailey Swan Press), BALEFUL EYE (Stonegarden.net Publishing) and ALICE IN ZOMBIELAND (Coscom Entertainment).
To contact the author: Nickolasecook@aol.com.

**Anthony Giangregorio** is the author and editor of more than 40 novels, almost all of them about zombies. His work has appeared in Dead Science by Coscomentertainment, Dead Worlds: Undead Stories Volumes 1-5, and Wolves of War by Library of the Living Dead Press. He also has stories in End of Days: An Apocalyptic Anthology Vol. 1 - 3, the Book of the Dead series Vol. 1-4 by LDP, and two anthologies with Pill Hill Press. He is also the creator of the popular action/zombie series titled Deadwater.
Check out his website at www.undeadpress.com.

# DEAD HISTORY

**Mark M. Johnson** enjoys writing as a hobby. By the grace of good editors, his short fiction and poetry has appeared in Bits of the Dead, and Vicious Verses Zombie Poetry, from Coscom Entertainment. Zombology 1, from Library of the Living Dead Press, and the upcoming Horrorology from Library of Horror Press. Dead Worlds, volumes two & three, and Book of the Dead volume two, Love is Dead, and the upcoming Zombie Anthology Book of the Dead volume 3, from Living Dead Press. Born and raised in Detroit, he currently resides in Warren MI with his loving and supportive wife Cindy, one: wish she was in college daughter, one: high school son, one crazy dog, three cats, and a python.

**G.R. Mosca** was born in Birmingham, England and is a graduate of Bard College. He currently resides in Thomasville, Pennsylvania with his companion Annalisa and their five cats. If you wish to contact G.R. Mosca, you can send an email to: grmosca@aol.com.

**Mark Rivett** possesses multiple degrees from The Art Institute of Pittsburgh and lives in Pittsburgh Pennsylvania where the city's long zombie history inspires his writing. In addition to writing, Mark paints, builds models, and works as a web developer.

**Tony Schaab** is a 31-year-old fledgling writer, currently living in Indianapolis with his wife and dog. In addition to having short stories published in vampire, science fiction, and apocalyptic anthologies, Tony has a special affinity for the shambling undead: he runs a zombie-centric review blog, "Slight of the Living Dead," and is currently working on his first full-length novel, "Zombies Can't Dance." In his free time, Tony works as a private-event DJ, is Troupe Manager of Indianapolis' only independent improvisational comedy troupe "IndyProv," and volunteers at his local Humane Society. Visit Tony and read more of his work at http://tonyschaab.wordpress.com.

**Jose Alfredo Vazquez** is an eye surgeon in private practice. Has written the best selling Living Dead Epic, "The War Against Them", and his work also appears in "Dead Worlds 5". He can be reached at Thewaragainstthem@Hotmail.com

**Spencer Wendleton** is the author of "The Body Cartel," written under his pen-name "Alan Spencer." He has also completed a number of other projects about zombies, super vampires, grave diggers from hell, psychologists helming deadly machines, and b-horror movies come to life. The author welcomes e-mails at alanspencer26@hotmail.com.

**Lee Clark Zumpe** earned his bachelor's degree in English at the University of South Florida, and then began working with Tampa Bay Newspapers as a proofreader. In addition to his various responsibilities in the editorial and production departments, Lee is now the publisher's chief entertainment columnist. His short stories and poetry have appeared in a variety of publications such as Weird Tales, Space and Time and Dark Wisdom and in the anthologies Horrors Beyond, Corpse Blossoms, High Seas Cthulhu, Arkham Tales, Abominations, Frontier Cthulhu, Withersin's Unkindness and Cthulhu Unbound, Vol. 1. Lee's work has earned several honorable mentions in the annual Year's Best Fantasy and Horror collections. Visit http://muted-mutterings-of-a-mad-poet.blogspot.com/.

# DEAD RAGE
by Anthony Giangregorio
Book 2 in the Rage virus series!

An unknown virus spreads across the globe, turning ordinary people into bloodthirsty, ravenous killers.

Only a small percentage of the population is immune and soon become prey to the infected.

Amongst the infected comes a man, stricken by the virus, yet still retaining his grasp on reality. His need to destroy the *normals* becomes an obsession and he raises an army of killers to seek out and kill all who aren't *changed* like himself. A few survivors gather together on the outskirts of Chicago and find themselves running for their lives as the specter of death looms over all.

The Dead Rage virus will find you, no matter where you hide.

## CHRISTMAS IS DEAD: A ZOMBIE ANTHOLOGY
Edited by Anthony Giangregorio

Twas the night before Christmas and all through the house, not a creature was stirring, not even a. . . zombie?

That's right; this anthology explores what would happen at Christmas time if there was a full blown zombie outbreak. Reanimated turkeys, zombie Santas, and demon reindeers that turn people into flesh-eating ghouls are just some of the tales you will find in this merry undead book. So curl up under the Christmas tree with a cup of hot chocolate, and as the fireplace crackles with warmth, get ready to have your heart filled with holiday cheer. But of course, then it will be ripped from your heaving chest and fed upon by blood-thirsty elves with a craving for human flesh! For you see, Christmas is Dead!

And you will never look at the holiday season the same way again.

## BLOOD RAGE
**(The Prequel to DEAD RAGE)**
by Anthony Giangregorio

The madness descended before anyone knew what was happening. Perfectly normal people suddenly became rage-fueled killers, tearing and slicing their way across the city. Within hours, Chicago was a battlefield, the dead strewn in the streets like trash.

Stacy, Chad and a few others are just a few of the immune, unaffected by the virus but not to the violence surrounding them. The *changed* are ravenous, sweeping across Chicago and perhaps the world, destroying any *normals* they come across. Fire, slaughter, and blood rule the land, and the few survivors are now an endangered species.

This is the story of the first days of the Dead Rage virus and the brave souls who struggle to live just one more day.

When the smoke clears, and the *changed* have maimed and killed all who stand in their way, only the strong will remain.

The rest will be left to rot in the sun.

# The Zombie in the Basement
by Anthony Giangregorio
Illustrated by Andrew Dawe-Collins

The spooky house at the end of the street was the one all the kids avoided. With its overgrown shrubs and weeds, the place was a modern day haunted house. Especially at night. So when Ricky sneaks into the yard to retrieve his favorite ball, he comes across something he'd only seen in movies and bad dreams. He sees a zombie in the basement window of the old house, but when he tells his friends, no one believes him. Ricky knows what he saw, that something lurks in the old house, something that isn't supposed to exist.

With his best friend Eric by his side, Ricky will find out the truth and prove to everyone that zombies are real. And when the night is done, everyone will know about the zombie in the basement.

Note: This book is for young adults and for those who are young at heart.

# DEADFREEZE
by Anthony Giangregorio

**THIS IS WHAT HELL WOULD BE LIKE IF IT FROZE OVER!**

When an experimental serum for hypothermia goes horribly wrong, a small research station in the middle of Antarctica becomes overrun with an army of the frozen dead.

Now a small group of survivors must battle the arctic weather and a horde of frozen zombies as they make their way across the frozen plains of Antarctica to a neighboring research station.

What they don't realize is that they are being hunted by an entity whose sole reason for existing is vengeance; and it will find them wherever they run.

# VISIONS OF THE DEAD
### A ZOMBIE STORY
by Anthony & Joseph Giangregorio

Jake Roberts felt like he was the luckiest man alive.

He had a great family, a beautiful girlfriend, who was soon to be his wife, and a job, that might not have been the best, but it paid the bills.

At least until the dead began to walk.

Now Jake is fighting to survive in a dead world while searching for his lost love, Melissa, knowing she's out there somewhere.

But the past isn't dead, and as he struggles for an uncertain future, the past threatens to consume him. With the present a constant battle between the living and the dead, Jake finds himself slipping in and out of the past, the visions of how it all happened haunting him. But Jake knows Melissa is out there somewhere and he'll find her or die trying.

In a world of the living dead, you can never escape your past.

## DEAD MOURNING: A ZOMBIE HORROR STORY
### by Anthony Giangregorio

Carl Jenkins was having a run of bad luck. Fresh out of jail, his probation tenuous, he'd lost every job he'd taken since being released. So now was his last chance, only one more job to prevent him from going back to prison. Assigned to work in a funeral home, he accidentally loses a shipment of embalming fluid. With nothing to lose, he substitutes it with a batch of chemicals from a nearby factory.

The results don't go as planned, though. While his screw-up goes unnoticed, his machinations revive the cadavers in the funeral home, unleashing an evil on the world that it has not seen before. Not wanting to become a snack for the rampaging dead, he flees the city, joining up with other survivors. An old, dilapidated zoo becomes their haven, while the dead wait outside the walls, hungry and patient.

But Carl is optimistic, after all, he's still alive, right? Perhaps his luck has changed and help will arrive to save them all?

Unfortunately, unknown to him and the other survivors, a serial killer has fallen into their group, trapped inside the zoo with them.

With the undead army clamoring outside the walls and a murderer within, it'll be a miracle if any of them live to see the next sunrise.

On second thought, maybe Carl would've been better off if he'd just gone back to jail.

## ROAD KILL: A ZOMBIE TALE
### by Anthony Giangregorio
### ORDER UP!

In the summer of 2008, a rogue comet entered earth's orbit for 72 hours. During this time, a strange amber glow suffused the sky.

But something else happened; something in the comet's tail had an adverse affect on dead tissue and the result was the reanimation of every dead animal carcass on the planet.

A handful of survivors hole up in a diner in the backwoods of New Hampshire while the undead creatures of the night hunt for human prey.

There's a new blue plate special at DJ's Diner and Truck Stop, and it's you!

## DEAD THINGS
### by Anthony Giangregorio

Beneath the veil of reality we all know as truth, there is another world, one where creatures only seen in nightmares exist.

But what if these creatures do actually exist, and it is us that are only fleeting images, mere visions conjured up by some unknown being.

Werewolves, zombies, vampires, and other lost things that go bump in the night, inhabit the world of imagination and myth, but all will be found in this collection of tales.

But in this world, fiction becomes fact, and what lurks in the shadows is real. Beware the next time you sense you are being watched or catch movement in the corner of your eye, for though it may be nothing, it might just be your doom.

# THE DARK
### by Anthony Giangregorio
### DARKNESS FALLS

The darkness came without warning.

First New York, then the rest of United States, and then the world became enveloped in a perpetual night without end.

With no sunlight, eventually the planet will wither and die, bringing on a new Ice Age. But that isn't problem for the human race, for humanity will be dead long before that happens.

There is something in the dark, creatures only seen in nightmares, and they are on the prowl. Evolution has changed and man is no longer the dominant species. When we are children, we're told not to fear the dark, that what we believe to exist in the shadows is false.

Unfortunately, that is no longer true.

# SOULEATER
### by Anthony Giangregorio

Twenty years ago, Jason Lawson witnessed the brutal death of his father by something only seen in nightmares, something so horrible he'd blocked it from his mind.

Now twenty years later the creature is back, this time for his son.

Jason won't let that happen.

He'll travel to the demon's world, struggling every second to rescue his son from its clutches.

But what he doesn't know is that the portal will only be open for a finite time and if he doesn't return with his son before it closes, then he'll be trapped in the demon's dimension forever.

### SEE HOW IT ALL BEGAN IN THE NEW DOUBLE-SIZED 460 PAGE SPECIAL EDITION!
# DEADWATER: EXPANDED EDITION
### by Anthony Giangregorio

Through a series of tragic mishaps, a small town's water supply is contaminated with a deadly bacterium that transforms the town's population into flesh eating ghouls.

Without warning, Henry Watson finds himself thrown into a living hell where the living dead walk and want nothing more than to feed on the living.

Now Henry's trying to escape the undead town before he becomes the next victim.

With the military on one side, shooting civilians on sight, and a horde of bloodthirsty zombies on the other, Henry must try to battle his way to freedom.

With a small group of survivors, including a beautiful secretary and a wise-cracking janitor to aid him, the ragtag group will do their best to stay alive and escape the city codenamed: **Deadwater**.

## DEAD END: A ZOMBIE NOVEL
by Anthony Giangregorio
### THE DEAD WALK!

Newspapers everywhere proclaim the dead have returned to feast on the living!

A small group of survivors hole up in a cellar, afraid to brave the masses of animated corpses, but when food runs out, they have no choice but to venture out into a world gone mad.

What they will discover, however, is that the fall of civilization has brought out the worst in their fellow man.

Cannibals, psychotic preachers and rapists are just some of the atrocities they must face.

In a world turned upside down, it is life that has hit a Dead End.

## BOOK OF THE DEAD 2: NOT DEAD YET
### A ZOMBIE ANTHOLOGY
Edited by Anthony Giangregorio

Out of the ashes of death and decay, comes the second volume filled with the walking dead.

In this tomb, there are only slow, shambling monstrosities that were once human.

No one knows why the dead walk; only that they do, and that they are hungry for human flesh.

But these aren't your neighbors, your co-workers, or your family.
Now they are the living dead, and they will tear your throat out at a moment's notice.

So be warned as you delve into the pages of this book; the dead will find you, no matter where you hide.

**ANOTHER EXCITING ADVENTURE IN THE DEADWATER SERIES!**
## DEAD SALVATION
### BOOK 9
by Anthony Giangregorio
### HANGMAN'S NOOSE!

After one of the group is hurt, the need for transportation is solved by a roving cannie convoy. Attacking the camp, the companions save a man who invites them back to his home.

Cement City it's called and at first the group is welcomed with thanks for saving one of their own. But when a bar fight goes wrong, the companions find themselves awaiting the hangman's noose.

Their only salvation is a suicide mission into a raider camp to save captured townspeople.

Though the odds are long, it's a chance, and Henry knows in the land of the walking dead, sometimes a chance is all you can hope for.

In the world of the dead, life is a struggle, where the only victor is death.

# The Lazarus Culture
### by Pasquale J. Morrone

Secret Service Agent Christopher Kearns had no idea what he was up against. Assigned on a temporary basis to the Center for Disease Control, he only knew that somehow it was connected to the lives of those the agency protected...namely, the President of the United States. If there were possible terrorist activities in the making, he could only guess it was at a red alert basis.

When Kearns meets and befriends Doctor Marlene Peterson of the Breezy Point Medical Center in Maryland, he soon finds that science fiction can indeed become a reality. In a solitary room walked a man with no vital signs: dead. The explanation he received came from Doctor Lee Fret, a man assigned to the case from the CDC. Something was attached to the brain stem. Something alive that was quickly spreading rapidly through Maryland and other states.

Kearns and his ragtag army of agents and medical personnel soon find themselves in a world of meaningless slaughter and mayhem. The armies of the walking dead were far more than mere zombies. Some began to change into whatever it was they ate. The government had found a way to reanimate the dead by implanting a parasite found on the tongue of the Red Snapper to the human brain.

It looked good on paper, but it was a project straight from Hell.

The dead now walked, but it wasn't a mystery.

It was The Lazarus Culture.

# DEADFALL
### by Anthony Giangregorio

It's Halloween in the small suburban town of Wakefield, Mass.

While parents take their children trick or treating and others throw costume parties, a swarm of meteorites enter the earth's atmosphere and crash to earth.

Inside are small parasitic worms, no larger than maggots.

The worms quickly infect the corpses at a local cemetery and so begins the rise of the undead.

The walking dead soon get the upper hand, with no one believing the truth.

That the dead now walk.

Will a small group of survivors live through the zombie apocalypse?

Or will they, too, succumb to the Deadfall.

## LOVE IS DEAD: A ZOMBIE ANTHOLOGY
### Edited by Anthony Giangregorio
### THE DEATH OF LOVE

Valentine's Day is a day when young love is fulfilled.

Where hopeful young men bring candy and flowers to their sweethearts, in hopes of a kiss...or perhaps more. But not in this anthology.

For you see, LOVE IS DEAD, and in this tome, the dead walk, wanting to feed on those same hearts that once pumped in chests, bursting with love.

So toss aside that heart-shaped box of candy and throw away those red roses, you won't need them any longer. Instead, strap on a handgun, or pick up a shotgun and defend yourself from the ravenous undead.

Because in a world where the dead walk, even love isn't safe.

# ETERNAL NIGHT: A VAMPIRE ANTHOLOGY
### Edited by Anthony Giangregorio

Blood, fangs, darkness and terror...these are the calling cards of the vampire mythos.

Inside this tome are stories that embrace vampire history but seek to introduce a new literary spin on this longstanding fictional monster. Follow a dark journey through cigarette-smoking creatures hunted by rogue angels, vampires that feed off of thoughts instead of blood, immortals presenting the fantastic in a local rock band, to a legendary monster on the far reaches of town.

Forget what you know about vampires; this anthology will destroy historical mythos and embrace incredible new twists on this celebrated, fictional character.

Welcome to a world of the undead, welcome to the world of Eternal Night.

# BOOK OF THE DEAD
## A ZOMBIE ANTHOLOGY VOL 1
### ISBN 978-1-935458-25-8
### Edited by Anthony Giangregorio

This is the most faithful, truest zombie anthology ever written, and we invite you along for the ride. Every single story in this book is filled with slack-jawed, eyes glazed, slow moving, shambling zombies set in a world where the dead have risen and only want to eat the flesh of the living. In these pages, the rules are sacrosanct. There is no deviation from what a zombie should be or how they came about. The Dead Walk.

There is no reason, though rumors and suppositions fill the radio and television stations. But the only thing that is fact is that the walking dead are here and they will not go away. So prepare yourself for the ultimate homage to the master of zombie legend. And remember... Aim for the head!

## REVOLUTION OF THE DEAD
### by Anthony Giangregorio
### THE DEAD SHALL RISE AGAIN!

Five years ago, a deadly plague wiped out 97% of the world's population, America suffering tragically. Bodies were everywhere, far too many to bury or burn. But then, through a miracle of medical science, a way is found to reanimate the dead.

With the manpower of the United States depleted, and the remaining survivors not wanting to give up their internet and fast food restaurants, the undead are conscripted as slave labor.

Now they cut the grass, pick up the trash, and walk the dogs of the surviving humans.

But whether alive or dead, no race wants to be controlled, and sooner or later the dead will fight back, wanting the freedom they enjoyed in life.

The revolution has begun!

And when it's over, the dead will rule the land, and the remaining humans will become the slaves...or worse.

## KINGDOM OF THE DEAD
by Anthony Giangregorio
## THE DEAD HAVE RISEN!

In the dead city of Pittsburgh, two small enclaves struggle to survive, eking out an existence of hand to mouth.

But instead of working together, both groups battle for the last remaining fuel and supplies of a city filled with the living dead.

Six months after the initial outbreak, a lone helicopter arrives bearing two more survivors and a newborn baby. One enclave welcomes them, while the other schemes to steal their helicopter and escape the decaying city.

With no police, fire, or social services existing, the two will battle for dominance in the steel city of the walking dead. But when the dust settles, the question is: will the remaining humans be the winners, or the losers?

When the dead walk, the line between Heaven and Hell is so twisted and bent there is no line at all.

## RISE OF THE DEAD
by Anthony Giangregorio
## DEATH IS ONLY THE BEGINNING!

In less than forty-eight hours, more than half the globe was infected.

In another forty-eight, the rest would be enveloped.

The reason?

A science experiment gone horribly wrong which enabled the dead to walk, their flesh rotting on their bones even as they seek human prey.

Jeremy was an ordinary nineteen year old slacker. He partied too much and had done poorly in high school. After a night of drinking and drugs, he awoke to find the world a very different place from the one he'd left the night before.

The dead were walking and feeding on the living, and as Jeremy stepped out into a world gone mad, the dead spotting him alone and unarmed in the middle of the street, he had to wonder if he would live long enough to see his twentieth birthday.

## THE CHRONICLES OF JACK PRIMUS
### BOOK ONE
by Michael D. Griffiths

Beneath the world of normalcy we all live in lies another world, one where supernatural beings exist.

These creatures of the night hunt us; want to feed on our very souls, though only a few know of their existence.

One such man is Jack Primus, who accidentally pierces the veil between this world and the next. With no other choice if he wants to live, he finds himself on the run, hunted by beings called the Xemmoni, an ancient race that sees humans as nothing but cattle.   They want his soul, to feed on his very essence, and they will kill all who stand in their way.   But if they thought Jack would just lie down and accept his fate, they were sorely mistaken.

He didn't ask for this battle, but he knew he would fight them with everything at his disposal, for to lose is a fate worse than death.

He would win this war, and he would take down anyone who got in his way.

## THE WAR AGAINST THEM: A ZOMBIE NOVEL
### by Jose Alfredo Vazquez

Mankind wasn't prepared for the onslaught.

An ancient organism is reanimating the dead bodies of its victims, creating worldwide chaos and panic as the disease spreads to every corner of the globe. As governments struggle to contain the disease, courageous individuals across the planet learn what it truly means to make choices as they struggle to survive.

Geopolitics meet technology in a race to save mankind from the worst threat it has ever faced. Doctors, military and soldiers from all walks of life battle to find a cure. For the dead walk, and if not stopped, they will wipe out all life on Earth. Humanity is fighting a war they cannot win, for who can overcome Death itself? Man versus the walking dead with the winner ruling the planet. Welcome to *The War Against Them*.

## DEADTOWN: A DEADWATER STORY
### BOOK 8
### by Anthony Giangregorio

The world is a very different place now. The dead walk the land and humans hide in small towns with walls of stone and debris for protection, constantly keeping the living dead at bay.

Social law is gone and right and wrong is defined by the size of your gun.

### UNWELCOME VISITORS

Henry Watson and his band of warrior survivalists become guests in a fortified town in Michigan. But when the kidnapping of one of the companions goes bad and men die, the group finds themselves on the wrong side of the law, and a town out for blood.

Trapped in a hotel, surrounded on all sides, it will be up to Henry to save the day with a gamble that may not only take his life, but that of his friends as well.

In a dead world, when justice is not enough, there is always vengeance.

## END OF DAYS: AN APOCALYPTIC ANTHOLOGY
### VOLUMES 1 & 2

Our world is a fragile place.

Meteors, famine, floods, nuclear war, solar flares, and hundreds of other calamities can plunge our small blue planet into turmoil in an instant.

What would you do if tomorrow the sun went super nova or the world was swallowed by water, submerging the world into the cold darkness of the ocean? This anthology explores some of those scenarios and plunges you into total annihilation.

But remember, it's only a book, and tomorrow will come as it always does.

Or will it?

**THE PLACE TO GO FOR ZOMBIE AND APOCALYPTIC FICTION**

# LIVING DEAD PRESS
### WHERE THE DEAD WALK
#### www.livingdeadpress.com

## COSCOM ENTERTAINMENT
### Where Imagination is Truth
www.coscomentertainment.com

**Blood of the Dead**
A.P. Fuchs

**Bits of the Dead**
edited by
Keith Gouveia

**Axiom-man
The Dead Land**
A.P. Fuchs

**Dead Science**
edited by
A.P. Fuchs

**Zombifrieze**
W. Bill Czolgosz
Sean Simmans

**Don of the Dead**
Nick Cato

**Snarl**
Lorne Dixon

**World War of the Dead**
Eric S. Brown

**The Lifeless**
Lorne Dixon